A GENTLEMAN FALLEN ON HARD TIMES

THE LORD JULIAN MYSTERIES—BOOK ONE

GRACE BURROWES

GRACE BURROWES PUBLISHING

DEDICATION

To those returning from the wars

CHAPTER ONE

Society addresses me as Lord Julian Caldicott, though as that aristocratic curiosity, a legitimate bastard, I bear no blood relation to Claudius, the late Duke of Waltham. Toward the end of His Grace's life, when he and I were both using canes as more than fashionable accessories, we got on tolerably well.

Not so in earlier years, though let it be said both parties as well as my mother had a hand in instigating skirmishes.

I survived those battles and even weathered Waterloo in better shape than many. The worst blows to my body and spirit were dealt long before Wellington's great victory, when I'd been held as a prisoner of war by the French.

The guns have gone silent, the ghosts have not. The best medicine for me of late is solitude and quiet. I was thus starting my day with an ancient Sumerian text involving agrarian metaphors and procreation when Lady Ophelia Oliphant sailed into my study like a seventy-four gunner bearing down on the French line.

"Julian, do instruct your butler that his harrumphing and stodging are pointless. I call only when you are on the premises, and his posturing will not serve."

"I am at home because you pounce at an indecently early hour, Godmama. Good morning to you." I drew a blank page over my translation—Godmama could read upside down and, I am convinced, with her eyes closed—and came around the desk to kiss her ladyship's proffered cheek. She smelled of bourbon roses and mischief, and in my youth, she'd been one of my favorite people.

Her ladyship had known considerable sorrow, burying two husbands, a son, and a daughter, the latter two in their early child-hoods. She banished life's woes with a determination I envied, except when she aimed her schemes at me. Since I'd returned from the battlefields, she'd left me mostly in peace, though the look in her gimlet blue eyes said my reprieve was at an end.

"How can it be a good morning," she began, "when you look like a death's head on a mop stick and your hair needs a trim? Young men today might as well be die-away schoolgirls for all they primp, lisp, and sigh. Back in my day, men could wear the most elegant fashions and still comport themselves like men. You lot, with your scientific pugilism and Hungary water, make me bilious."

"The only pugilism I engage in of late is verbal, dear lady, and never a drop of Hungary water has touched my manly person. Shall I ring for a tray, or will you swan out the door before my poor, stodging Harris can heed my summons?"

"You wish." She settled onto the sofa, her presence a contrast to the masculine appointments and closed curtains of my study. Godmama had been a beauty, to hear her tell it, and my mother—who would argue with the Almighty over the ideal order of the Commandments—did not contradict her. The former beauty still indulged in every fashionable whim her heart desired or her modistes suggested.

She donned pale silk when sprigged muslin would have done nicely, and she wore jewels during daylight hours. Her slippers, gloves, and reticules were exquisitely embroidered and usually all of a piece—today's theme was roses and gold. No grand diva ever assembled her stage appearance as carefully as Godmama put herself together simply to disturb my peace on a Tuesday morning.

My mother muttered about Lady Ophelia's flamboyant style, but I was nobody to begrudge Godmama her crotchets. One coped with grief as best one could, as I, half of England, and much of the Continent had occasion to know.

"Cease pacing about, dear boy." Her ladyship patted the place beside her. "I come to you in my hour of need, and you must not disappoint me."

I settled a good two feet away from her ladyship. I wasn't keen on anybody making free with my person, and Godmama was extravagantly affectionate. I had a valet. Sterling tended to my clothing, and I tended to... me. I was working up to allowing him to trim my hair, but until that day, an old-fashioned queue served well enough.

Though I have yet to obtain the thirtieth year of my age, my hair is snow white, a gift from my French captors. I owe the French army for my weak eyes, as well. My vision is adequate, but strong sunlight, London's relentless coal smoke, or simple fatigue can cause my eyes to sting and water. Tinted spectacles help, though they add to the eccentricity of my appearance.

To my dismay, my looks render me far too appealing to frisky dowagers. Lady Ophelia likely finds my situation hilarious.

"I have disappointed you any number of times, my lady. I'm sure you'll weather another blow if need be, stalwart that you are."

Before I'd gone for a soldier, she would have countered with a witty retort about her fortitude being the result of the thankless job of godparenting me, but now she frowned, glanced at the clock, and held her silence.

"What brings you to my door, my lady?"

For all her imperiousness, Godmama could be bashful. On behalf of others, she blew at gale force on the least provocation. When it came to her own needs, she was the veriest zephyr, though I suspected the contrast was calculated.

"The Season is ending."

I refrained from appending a heartfelt *thank God* to her observation. "Will you join Mama for a respite by the sea?"

"Her Grace might find a respite by the sea. I find a lot of aging gossips. I'm off to Betty Longacre's house party. Her oldest girl failed to snag a husband, so Betty is compelled to take extraordinary measures. The chit goes on well enough, but she's overshadowed by all those diamonds and heiresses and originals."

Betty Longacre—Viscountess Longacre, in point of fact—was about ten years my senior. That she had a daughter old enough to be presented came as an unpleasant shock.

"What has any of this to do with me?" I asked. "I am firmly indifferent to the concept of matrimony, and even my mother has accepted that I will not be moved from that opinion."

"You are an idiot. Your mother has other children to manage, and thus it falls to me to chide you for the error of your ways."

I rose, a spike of disproportionate annoyance threatening to rob me of my manners. "Chide away, but your efforts will be in vain. We both know that I am not fit for matrimony, much less fatherhood, and there's an end to it."

I expected Lady Ophelia to fly at me, wielding eternal verities, settled law, and scriptural quotation at my preference for bachelorhood. Godmama remained brooding on my favorite napping sofa, confirming that even she conceded my unfitness for family life.

Her relative meekness came as a disappointment and a relief.

"I ask nothing so tedious as matrimony of you," she said.

"Perhaps you ask me to make up the numbers at this house party, to lend whatever cachet a ducal heir has to the gathering. Thank you, no."

I managed to make the refusal diffident rather than rude, and now Lady Ophelia did rise, though she paced before the hearth in a manner calculated to make my heart sink. This, too, was evidence of the damage done to me during the war, and of Lady Ophelia's shrewdness. She'd noted my reluctance to sit near her, and I wished she hadn't.

I was improving in many regards, though the pace of my recuperation was glacial.

"One does not wish to be insulting," she said, "but I assisted Betty with the house-party guest list. The numbers match quite well, thank you, and if we allowed a ducal spare to lurk among the bachelors, the other fellows would all hang back, assuming you had the post position in hand. All I ask is that you escort me down to Makepeace. Maria Cleary will be among the guests, and we were bosom bows once upon a naughty time. I have not seen Maria for eons."

As best I recalled, the Longacre family seat was a reasonable day's travel from Town in the direction of the Kentish coast.

"Since when do you need an escort, Godmama? Any highwayman who accosts your coach would get the worst of the encounter. You'd scold him into submission and demand his horse for your troubles." Or she'd brandish her peashooter at his baubles.

"You don't get out much," Lady Ophelia said, "so I forgive you for ignoring the fact that former soldiers are swarming the countryside. They can't find honest work, many of them have come home to families incapable of supporting them in the shires, and the dratted Corn Laws have driven the cost of bread to the heavens. We all thought we wanted peace, but we didn't plan for the reality. Thanks to the great and greedy men charged with ordering the nation's fate, English highways are unsafe these days."

During the Season, I did not get out socially *at all* if I could manage it, but I read the papers. I corresponded with some of my fellow former officers and a few who still held their commissions. I paid courtesy calls on the widows of my late comrades and the families of fallen subordinates—those who would admit me.

I had a platoon of sisters, cousins, and in-laws who were very active in Society and who made their duty visits to me.

Godmama had a point. The peace following Waterloo was creating violent upheaval in Merry Olde England, for the reasons she'd alluded to. Napoleon had claimed to rule by conquest, and the British economy had thrived on war as well. Without the French threatening our southern coast, the great military appetite for everything—from canvas to cooking pots, wool to weapons, chickens to chaplains—had dried up in the course of a year.

Britain had emerged victorious from two decades of war appended to a century of war, only to find herself fantastically in debt and ruled by a buffoon. The populace that had made endless sacrifices in the name of patriotism was now deeply discontent for many of the same reasons that had fueled revolution in France.

The rich had grown very rich, while the poor had grown very numerous. The government's response was to counter potential upheaval with real oppression, which, of course, contributed to greater unrest.

The Corsican was doubtless enjoying a good laugh over the whole business, while I... I did not bother my pretty head with national affairs, though I did bear an inconvenient fondness for my godmother.

"I shall see you safely to Makepeace," I said, "then take my leave of you. You can travel back to Town in company with some of the other guests who will doubtless return this direction."

She pushed aside a curtain to let in a shaft of morning sun. Had she taken a knife to my eyes, the result would have been less painful.

"Your staff is remiss, Julian. These windows require a thorough scrubbing. If your windows are this filthy as summer approaches, I shudder to contemplate their condition in winter."

I rooted about in my desk drawer for my blue-tinted spectacles while all manner of profanity begged for expression.

"I shall pass your insult along to my housekeeper. She will delight to know that you, she, Harris, Sterling, and my neighbors on all sides are in agreement."

"The light hurts your eyes," Lady Ophelia said. "That's why you lurk like a prisoner in an oubliette, isn't it? Your mother hasn't said anything about you having vision problems."

Because Mama did not know my eyesight was in any way impaired. Only my older brother knew, and as the ducal heir, Arthur had been consuming discretion before he'd first thrust a spoon into runny porridge. Arthur was the family strategist, also our patriarch, though he was barely six years my senior.

"The physicians assure me the impairment to my eyes is temporary. I see well enough. Bright light is painful, though, hence the tinted spectacles."

She bustled toward me, and I steeled myself to endure a hug, but her ladyship merely patted my cheek with a gloved hand.

"Your secrets have always been safe with me, Julian. That hasn't changed, and it never will. We leave on Thursday, and I will hope for cloudy weather. We can keep the shades down, though you shall not smoke in my traveling coach."

"I don't smoke anywhere."

She collected her reticule, scowled at my window, and scowled at me. "You used to smoke. All young men do."

"I used to do a lot of things. I'll be on your doorstep by eight of the clock."

Thus did I embark on a journey that would involve far more than a jaunt to the Kentish countryside and test much besides my ability to endure bright sunshine.

∼

In Lady Ophelia's company, reasonable people were frequently tempted to expostulate, "But that's not so!" Or, "There is no such word!" Or, most frequently of all, "My lady, have you taken leave of your senses?"

My godmother enjoyed the purity of conviction known to seven-year-old girls expounding on the topic of unicorns. No force of logic, theology, or science could prevail against such confidence, nor—in many cases—should it. Ophelia managed to be happy from what I could see, or to give that appearance anyway.

In defense of my wits, I chose to accompany her coach on horseback. My steed was an agreeable old campaigner by the name of

Atlas. He was a seventeen-hand bay who dealt as calmly with the vagaries of Town as he did the temptations of the countryside. I'd bought Atlas off a lieutenant colonel lordling who'd been drummed from the regiment for conduct unbecoming with the general's wife.

The poor sod, like most officers, had lived beyond his means and lacked funds for buying passage home. He'd told me that Atlas was steady, keen, and nimble in battle. A prince among horses. He'd clearly miss the horse, but would the general's wife miss her randy lieutenant colonel?

Masculine dignity avoided the obvious answer.

I amused myself with these ponderings as we navigated the hideous tangles of the London toll booths and eventually made our way to the Kentish countryside. The morning was overcast, which suited me quite well, though being the end of the social Season, the roads were thronged.

"We'll not change in Dorville," I called to the coachman. "The Laughing Dog in Frederick will do."

John Coachman nodded and called for the team to trot on. I cantered forth rather than eat the coach's dust. Not having ventured this far from Town in many a month, I had anticipated some hesitance of the spirit about the journey. To my surprise, I wasn't exactly relieved to get out of London, but neither was I unnerved.

We pulled into the yard of The Laughing Dog a quarter hour later, and the footman had no sooner let down the steps than Ophelia sprang forth in full cry.

"For God's sake, Julian, what are you thinking? The Dorville Arms is fashionable, while this establishment..." She glanced pointedly at a pile of horse droppings. "Quaint is not my style, nor will I allow it to become yours."

"*Quiet* is not your style," I countered, offering my arm while a groom took Atlas to the water trough. "And when the Dorville Arms passed off four high-stepping chestnuts on you, two of which would come up lame before the first crossing, you'd become very loud indeed. Half of Mayfair wants to see and be seen at The Dorville

Arms because Wellington is said to favor it as a trysting place. The teams are more reliable here, and the food is good."

The Dog was also *quiet*, which my nerves much preferred.

Godmama peered at me owlishly. I could hear her deciding not to ask the rude question: *How does a recluse know which coaching inn is a la mode, why, and where to change teams in the alternative?*

Once a reconnaissance officer, always a reconnaissance officer— that's how. "Are you hungry, my lady?"

"Always. Sometimes for food, sometimes for excellent champagne, sometimes for the company of an agreeable gentleman. Hunger is a blessing in this life. Be glad of your hungers, Julian."

House parties put Ophelia on her mettle, while they now terrified me. Not all hungers were cause for rejoicing. Rather than engage in a game of philosophical battledore with her, I shepherded her toward the steps.

"Let's be glad of the inn's kitchen, shall we?"

When I handed Ophelia back into the coach an hour later, the sun was attempting to break through the clouds. I directed our coachman to make all possible haste to our destination, though my imperative was for naught. By the time we cantered up the lime alley that formed Makepeace's formal driveway, my head was throbbing and my eyes burned.

"What imp of ambition prompted me to attempt this journey?" I asked my horse as we waited our turn behind another coach debouching its occupants.

Atlas sniffed at the toe of my dusty boot. I patted his sweaty neck. "You are too polite to reply." The imp had not been an ambition, but rather, hope. Maybe now, I hoped, after weeks spent pacing behind heavy curtains, after declining invitation after invitation, worrying my family, and going out on only the dreariest of days, my eyes would be better enough to meet the challenge of a day of travel.

"More fool I."

"May I assist with your horse, my lord?" A young groom had

taken the initiative to move up the queue while the coach ahead of us appeared stuck fast at the foot of Makepeace's front steps.

"Please. I am Lord Julian Caldicott," I said, swinging down carefully. My balance had improved enough that I would not fall on my arse before half of polite society and their horses, though bodily caution had become second nature.

"This good fellow is Atlas," I went on. "He's come all the way from Town and will benefit from close association with a bucket of oats and a grassy paddock in which to roll. He and I will start back for Town before nightfall."

We'd get as far as the first decent inn—The Fool's Paradise, several miles to the west—and bed down there, possibly for a day or two if the place was clean, quiet, and possessed of heavy curtains.

"Very good, my lord. Welcome to Makepeace."

A former cavalry officer always made an adjustment upon quitting the saddle. Atop his charger, he was a lesser god, capable of wreaking death with his saber or galloping across battlefields on the wings of his equine eagle.

On the ground, aching from his toes to his temples, he was a mere mortal, his locomotion a humble and achy business relying on two sore feet. I had forgotten about this transition. I had forgotten much. I *excelled* at forgetting.

I collected my saddlebags lest they become lost amid a confusion of baggage and directed my feet to the door of Ophelia's coach, prepared to hand her down as a proper escort should. She'd traveled alone, her lady's maid keeping company with an extra groom in the baggage coach. What had Ophelia got up to while I'd been cursing the sunshine?

She descended with a gracious smile, suggesting she'd enjoyed a nap, light refreshment, a humorous French novel, and the latest newspapers.

"Well, my boy, you got us here. My thanks for that. Now see me up to the terrace where, if I'm not mistaken, our host awaits."

What followed was a sort of *Via Crucis*, though instead of

contemplating the sorrows of Jesus station by station, as Ophelia and I passed from host, to hostess, to butler, to housekeeper, I meditated intensely on a cold glass of lemonade, a washstand, and a change of linen. My objective was to find someplace to bide until the light waned—some dark place that lent itself to a nap—and then slip away without further socializing.

Ophelia was among the first guests to arrive, and thus I managed with a few nods, a bow, and a passing greeting or two. The talk would soon start. *Was that Lord Julian? Here? Is he staying? What was Ophelia thinking?*

I had become inured to whispers months ago. Let them talk, while I rested in the darkest available corner. I saw Godmama to the door of her guest room and then accosted a footman and explained my situation.

"You'll want the conservatory, my lord. Plenty gloomy, lots of padded benches and such. The fellows like to congregate there to smoke in the evening. His lordship says the smoke keeps the aphids off the roses. I'll have a tray sent in, and the gents' retiring room is just around the corner from the conservatory. Towels, soap, wash water, all on hand."

"My thanks." I passed him a coin, which earned me a smile and a wink.

"Sweet dreams, my lord."

"What's your name?" The fellow brought pleasant associations to mind, as if I'd known him or somebody very like him in a happier time. His looks were unremarkable and, for that very reason, struck me as also having a familiar quality. Blond hair and blue eyes were ubiquitous among the footmen's ranks, though his friendly air set him apart.

"I'm Canning, my lord. They call me Canny Canning." He jaunted off, and I envied him both his energy and his apparent aptitude for his post. He exuded that combination of dignity and graciousness unique to a competent domestic or junior officer.

Sterling, by contrast, lacked polish, but he could starch a cravat and had a good ear for servant gossip. More significantly, he was loath to share my personal business with my family's retainers or with my siblings and my mother. For loyalty and discretion, I was happy to pay handsomely.

I found the men's retiring room, washed the dust of the road from my person as best I could, changed my shirt and neckcloth, and felt marginally less grubby. My head still pounded, but with a dull thunder of agony rather than the full symphonic fortissimo.

Darkness was the best medicine, and thus I sank onto a cushioned sofa in the conservatory with the same rejoicing as a man greeted his long-lost beloved. A gentle breeze bore the fragrance of rich earth and ferns, and a pillow placed just so at my nape brought further relief of my suffering.

Two hours of quiet rest and darkness, and I'd be restored enough to hole up at The Fool's Paradise. After a day or two of respite at that commodious establishment, I'd begin my London-bound travels as dawn approached, the better to ensure the sun would be at my back.

I drifted off to sleep, pleased with myself for having ventured from London with nothing worse than a headache to show as punishment for my boldness.

I was in the nether regions of consciousness, dreamily flirting with tavern nymphs while Atlas slurped summer ale from my upturned top hat, when a female voice cut through my musings.

"What the hell are you doing here, and why didn't you at least do me the courtesy of warning me that I'd have to put up with you?"

CHAPTER TWO

I tried, oh, I tried to remain in the land of the friendly nymphs, but I knew that voice and knew the hurt lurking behind the temper. I opened my eyes and sat up carefully. When I'd managed that much without incident, I rose, as a gentleman must.

"Hyperia, greetings. I wasn't aware that you'd be here. I am not a guest. In fact, I am planning to leave within the hour. I won't trouble you in the least, and my apologies on Ophelia's behalf for failing to warn you that I'd escort her to Makepeace."

Miss Hyperia West had lost weight. She'd always been a lovely armful, and she doubtless was still, but her face was thinner, her green eyes sharper. She'd known humiliation and loss, and I was to blame for most of it. Like any self-respecting woman, she'd been enraged at my perfidy.

Though she seemed rather too enthusiastically attached to her temper. It's not as if she'd been in love with me. Her mama had been in love with the notion of having a daughter leg-shackled to a ducal spare, and Hyperia was loyal to her family.

"You are still gaunt, my lord."

Was she pleased or dismayed that my clothing was a bit loose? A year ago, I could have read her expression. Now, her composure defeated my attempt at analysis.

"I am tired and dusty as well," I said, offering a belated bow. "If you trot back the way you've come, nobody need know you were burdened with the sight of me. I'll be gone at sunset, Hyperia, I promise."

She began to pace, and the tattoo of her heeled slippers on the stone floor reminded me that I had a grand headache.

"This is Ophelia's doing," she said. "She dragooned you into escorting her, didn't she?"

"She also assisted with the guest list, so she well knew you'd be here. Given that your family seat is less than ten miles distant, she probably knew you'd be among the early arrivals too."

Hyperia was dark-haired, shortish, and restless. She was the opposite of the cool, pale beauty Society favored, and I liked that about her. She was real. She was smart, and she deserved a better partner in life than I would have made.

"You came in the front door," she said, scowling at my cravat. "Greeted by host, hostess, butler, and so forth. Society knows you're here, even if I did not. I came in the front door as well."

"One hopes the guests at Makepeace are not consigned to climbing in windows."

She tossed herself onto the sofa. "We must think, Julian. This looks like a bad joke, but it could be an opportunity. Stop looming over me."

I was, to the horror of my older brother, the tallest of the siblings. I had Arthur by half an inch, six foot two to his six foot one and a half. He styled his hair a la Brutus to gain that extra half inch back, because duke or not, he was still my only surviving brother.

I took a seat on the sofa about a foot from Hyperia—a proper distance, thank you very much. "What possible opportunity could this house party present? I don't want to be here, you don't want me here, and what we both especially do not want is to inspire gossip."

"You did that handily enough when you threw me over last autumn, my lord."

We'd had an understanding, not an engagement. I'd explained to Hyperia that soldiers did not become engaged in a time of war, lest a young lady find herself yoked to a missing person or invalid when a better opportunity came along.

Hyperia, ever sensible and ever stubborn, had conceded the point and remained steadfastly loyal for the whole of my military years. I had wasted her best Seasons, while the thought of her waiting patiently for my return had saved my sanity, or what remained of it.

Jilting her was the least consideration I owed her.

"If we caused gossip during the Little Season," I said, "our parting was a nine days' wonder. Nobody questioned the decision for long once they got a look at my hair."

She glanced at my white locks. "People used to spend a small fortune on rice powder to get hair that color."

"My altered appearance was not purchased with pounds and pence, Hyperia." Rather than expound on that detail, I stated the obvious. "We are better off apart."

I'd wanted to preserve my bachelorhood as long as possible in any case, and after the war, the thing I'd wanted and the right thing to do had converged like a planetary conjunction. I'd seized the moment, had the difficult discussion with Hyperia, and had not laid eyes on her since.

"You never talk of your captivity," she said, slanting a look at me. "Was it awful?"

Damn my sisters for their endless concern. "To be taken captive is to fail as a soldier and an officer. That alone is mortifying."

"Mortification doesn't turn a man's hair white, my lord. I refuse to be mortified by Ophelia's nonsense."

The pounding in my temples had resumed and now took on the ominous reverberation of war drums.

"I'll sidle out the garden door," I said, "and nobody need know you've clapped eyes on me. I'll saddle Atlas myself or slip out the damned postern gate. The last thing I want is to inconvenience you."

"To inconvenience me *again?* How good of you." Hyperia flopped back against the cushions. "Ophelia will merely retreat and regroup for another ambush. She will push us together, all but compromise us, and then smile sweetly and protest her innocence. The invitations went out weeks ago, Julian. This is deliberate."

No point in arguing the obvious. "What brought you to the conservatory?"

"I ran into Ophelia in the library, where she was ostensibly searching for a book. I allowed as how I craved solitude and quiet, and she suggested... Who knew you were here?"

"A footman, though if Ophelia lurked at her parlor door, she would have heard him direct me here. You are right. She has schemed, and our encounter is her doing. I'd best leave now, before we are compromised when she swans through that door with three of her closest, most gossipy friends. She mentioned some old crony who'd be among the guests, though Godmama enjoys a wealth of old cronies."

I rose, prepared to exit stage left in quick time, but Hyperia was on her feet in the next instant and blocking my path.

She did not attempt to touch me, curiously enough. "Don't go."

"I beg your pardon? You loathe the sight of me, and well you should, and I want only to return to Town." I did not, in fact, want to return to Town, but I did want to return to dark rooms, quiet, and safety, which Town represented.

"Stay one night," she said. "Walk with me in the garden before supper, fix me a plate at breakfast. Show the whole dratted world that we are cordial and that Ophelia's machinations are of no moment. Plead a tired horse or a tired arse, Julian, but face down the jackals with me for the space of a few hours."

So much of war was strategy. Show the enemy your massed guns, and he learned your strength at the same time that his infantry gained a reason to fear you on the battlefield. Direct your mortar at his powder wagons—as Napoleon had learned to do in Italy—and cinder his resources and his confidence with one hellish explosion.

Hyperia's suggestion had tactical merit. Ophelia would continue to scheme, manipulate, and interfere, all the while claiming the best of intentions. I was already at the blasted house party, and my presence had doubtless been remarked.

"Very well," I said, doing my best to glower down at her. "One night. A tired horse. I can manage informal attire for the evening buffet, but I'm leaving after breakfast."

She patted my cravat. "I will be the first to wish you a safe journey in the morning, my lord. See you at supper."

Then she was gone, and I was wondering what the hell I'd got myself into. I resumed my supine posture on the sofa and tried to mentally summon Morpheus's nymphs.

My efforts were in vain. My mind was fixed on two thoughts.

First, Ophelia had betrayed me. She'd deceived me and treated me like a small boy who had no idea where his own best interests lay. She thus moved from the short column of people whom I liked but did not trust to the longer list of people in whom I could repose neither confidence nor liking.

A loss, but in matters of human nature, one always profited from an honest assessment of the realities.

The second thought was equally unsettling in a different way: Hyperia, who had reason to dislike me intensely, had patted my cravat, and I hadn't minded her presumption much at all.

~

Life on campaign taught an officer many lessons, not the least of which was to be prepared for the unexpected. As a consequence, I'd brought with me a few personal necessities and stashed a small valise among Lady Ophelia's luggage. The valise had gone astray, apparently, but when the first bell sounded, I was presentable for an informal gathering.

I'd notified the stable that Atlas was to have a night of rest, but other than that... I had no need to send an express back to my London household informing them of my change of plans. My family knew I'd taken escort duty for Ophelia, and I had no senior officer expecting a report of my whereabouts.

As I ran a brush through my hair, it occurred to me that nobody much cared whether I tarried indefinitely in Kent, hared back to Town, or jumped into the sea.

"And that is precisely how I want it," I muttered. I'd spent my childhood in the shadow of handsome, witty, accomplished, older brothers, and then had been overshadowed by more enthusiastic scholars at university and more seasoned officers at war.

To be free of scrutiny was my heart's fondest desire. White hair rather foiled my ambitions. I peered at my reflection in the vain hope that I'd find a few russet hairs among the snowy locks. A French physician who'd seen much of war and read widely in medical literature had given me hope that my hair might one day regain its youthful color, "with rest and quiet."

I'd been resting quietly, pacing quietly, cursing quietly, and having nightmares as quietly as I could for months, and still, my hair would have been the envy of Father Christmas.

My hostess greeted me graciously when I joined the other guests at the buffet laid out in the orangery. The space was warm, and the glass walls turned the chatter of greetings and gossip into ricocheting volleys of noise. My objective was to locate Hyperia and exhibit conspicuous geniality when walking with her in the garden. I would exude gracious indifference toward all who stared, whispered, and goggled like spectators at a carriage accident.

Hyperia was not yet among those gathered, so I accepted a glass of champagne from a footman—Canny Canning, as it happened— and out of long habit distracted myself with surveillance of the environs.

In the corner by the overwatered ferns, Godmama flirted with Lord Longacre, who had to be a dozen years her junior. His lordship was giving as good as he got, which spoke well for his gallantry, if not for his judgment. By a pair of camellias potted in half barrels, William Ormstead, with whom I'd served for a few months in winter quarters, was in earnest conversation with Miss Longacre, on whose behalf this gathering had been organized.

Though, of course, one did not *say* that.

A bevy of other young ladies who'd also had a less than stellar Season wandered about on the arms of younger sons, wealthy gentry scions, and a few former officers. I watched the company as I'd watch an amateur stage play, with a blend of boredom and polite tolerance. Nobody was tipsy yet. Nobody's heels were unfashionably worn. Nobody was showing too much cleavage.

For *this*, I'd risked my life? For this, I'd watched countless comrades die agonizing deaths? Old anger began to well and, with it, a resurgence of my headache. I suffered merely a headache—no nausea, no vertigo, no strange distortions of sounds, vision, or scents, yet—so I remained at my post by the potted lemon trees.

Was Hyperia deliberately making me pay for my many transgressions against her?

William Ormstead chose that bleak moment to catch my eye, nod, lift his glass in my direction, and then resume his conversation with Miss Longacre. He need not have acknowledged me, but his small courtesy fortified me, and I resolved to wait for Hyperia until Domesday if she required it of me.

"You are lurking," she said, appearing at my elbow two interminable minutes later and helping herself to my drink. "This is a social gathering, not an opportunity for espionage."

"Reconnaissance, please, not espionage. As an intelligence officer, I gathered information. Spies disseminate falsehoods, and I am not temperamentally suited to subterfuge." Alas, for me. If I'd succeeded in lying to the French, men dear to me might well still be walking the earth.

"You are actually very good at ruses," Hyperia retorted. "Right now, you'd rather be anywhere but here, and yet, you're doing a credible impersonation of a genial bachelor. Let's circulate, shall we?"

"I agreed to a walk in the garden, Hyperia, not a parade inspection." She shouldn't have used the word *espionage*, and neither should I. Some words—*treason, betrayal, dishonor*—tainted a conversation no matter how innocuously they'd been meant.

"The garden," Hyperia said with exaggerated patience, "is *out there*, while we are *in here*. To get from *here* to *there*, we must pass at least twelve other guests. We will greet them cordially lest somebody think I'm about to heave my champagne into the lavender border."

Hyperia would have made an excellent cavalry officer, which was about the highest praise I had to offer anybody. "Nobody would think that of you."

"Shall we spat for a few more rounds to put the roses in your cheeks, or shall we get some air?" Her smile was subdued gaiety incarnate, and I entertained the possibility that Hyperia was enjoying herself.

"I am as pale as a recovering invalid is expected to be. That's a pretty frock." The same mossy green as her eyes, gracefully draped and modest, but hinting at curves and wonders a gentleman pretended not to notice.

"Such flattery, my lord, will gain you nothing. Come along." She did not take my arm—a mercy, that—and did keep hold of my champagne. This prevented me from courteously offering to fetch her a drink and consigned me to tagging along as she dragged me through a gauntlet of feigned cordiality and hastily averted stares.

Ormstead alone seemed genuinely pleased to see me. "Glad to find an ally among the bachelors," he said. "And glad to see you've left Town, my lord. London in summer leaves much to be desired, and the company Lady Longacre has assembled is not to be missed."

He winked at Hyperia, who rolled her eyes when another woman would have simpered. "The company here is given to inanities," she said. "Come, my lord, we have roses to admire—or something."

I wanted to tarry with Ormstead, though what did I have to say to him? He was the quintessential charming officer—tall, blond, slightly weathered. Even his swept-back hair conveyed a dashing air.

He had acknowledged me, gently scolded me, and been nearly friendly. Hyperia swanned off, so I followed in her wake when I wanted to resume my post by the lemon trees and contemplate Ormstead's kindness.

The journey through the crowd to the door might have been twenty feet, though it felt as if navigating that distance required twenty years. Sir Pericles Renner, a crony of my late father's, did not seem to recognize me even when Hyperia marched us through the introductions.

Mrs. Pickton-Thyme used her lorgnette to peer at my hair. She was prevented from attempting to touch it by Hyperia batting at a presuming—and imaginary—fly.

Mr. Mendel Cleary—landed gentry with bloodlines back to the Conqueror, nephew to Lady Ophelia's erstwhile bosom bow—fell prey to a pressing need to decamp for the punchbowl when I came within six feet of him.

And so it went until we gained the garden, a ruthlessly patterned work of horticultural domination that nonetheless strived to exude nature's early summer exuberance. I had occasion to know that true nature was glorious, impartial, and dangerous. The rectangular pattern of walks comforted me, while the thorny roses reaching, always reaching, to snag a sleeve or a child's finger told the real story.

"That went well," Hyperia said, bending to snap off a stalk of lavender and bring it to her nose. "If you'd once bothered to smile, it would have gone better."

"Rome wasn't built in a century, Hyperia. I could use a sip of that champagne." She passed over the glass, and I resisted the urge to bolt what was left of my libation. I knew better than to succumb to the lure of spirits, the poppy, or the patent remedies that blended the two.

I did not deserve oblivion, and my family did not deserve one more reason to fret over me.

"Many soldiers came home from war the worse for their service." Hyperia plucked more lavender, making herself a little nosegay. "Healy said I was to leave you in peace, not that I invited fraternal advice. I wanted to call, but..."

But what? "To regard you at a loss for words unnerves me, Hyperia. I would have received you." I hoped I would have.

"One dreads to appear desperate after a jilting. We had an understanding, until you decided we would not suit. I respect your decision, but, Jules, if one is not changed by war, then one is not human. I wanted to say that to you, and now I have."

Was she forgiving me for coming home in disgrace? For coming home at all? Or was she offering me a friend's acceptance of what could not be ignored?

In any case, she meant well. "Thank you, Hyperia. I am changed, and I do not refer to my hair. I keep thinking I've reached the end of the list of adjustments—don't care for thunder when I used to love a good storm, fife and drums give me the collywobbles, cannot abide rum, have nightmares in French—but then I round a corner and find another slippery mental ditch."

She rearranged the sprigs in her bouquet. "Are we still friends, Jules?"

Jules. Hyperia alone used that familiar address. "I dread the prospect of becoming your enemy." I tried for a smile and got a glower in response.

"Are we still friends?"

The evening light was sweetly oblique, no threat to my eyes, and the garden was all but deserted. I was assailed by a wave of melancholy, the certain knowledge that I would never have back the ebullient, trusting, *confident* manhood I'd taken with me to Spain. I could not be friends with Hyperia as she doubtless grasped the concept—congenial, considerate, humorous, affectionate, all the things I had been—but I could make some effort.

"We are friends," I said, gesturing to a bench that faced the tiered fountain in the center of the garden, "if that's what you want."

She sat, and a few more couples wandered out of the orangery into the slanting evening light.

"You protected me," she said. "From my first Season and my second. You were my escort of choice and conscientious in that role. You went off to war, but by then, the fortune hunters and widowers knew not to bother with me. I did not have to *take*, did not have to be witty or pretty, because Lord Julian had stood up with me enough times and waltzed the good-night waltzes with me. I was spoken for, and I wanted it that way."

"If any of those loitering Lotharios have troubled you recently, please tell me." Healy West was well equipped to deal with slights to his sister's honor, but Healy was a hothead, and his family needed him whole and alive.

"They would not dare, Jules. I am no longer fresh from the schoolroom, wet behind the ears, and eager to waltz. I wanted you to know that I missed you and that I do not regret our understanding."

Inside the orangery, with polite acknowledgments and friendly smiles, Hyperia had confirmed to any with eyes to see that she and I remained cordial. Disappointing the gossips was always a worthy objective.

As laughter drifted out over the garden, and crickets began to sing, I wondered if this conversation hadn't been her real objective. To tell me she'd missed me, that I'd had value in her eyes without even knowing it, that my goodwill still meant something to her, as hers did to me.

"You are being beyond decent, Hyperia. How much has Healy told you of my situation in France?"

"That you survived every officer's nightmare, and none of your former comrades know how to face you now. I am not some decorated war hero to be troubled by niceties of protocol. I'm the girl who beat you on her pony most every time we raced. You didn't let me win, Jules. You lost to me fair and square. You can't know what that means to a female forbidden to so much as blow out a candle because it's unladylike."

Most times, Hyperia had defeated me fair and square, but when a girl enjoyed winning that much, a fellow defined victory as that term best suited the occasion.

Hyperia was not proposing that we become engaged, of course. Always sensible, that was Hyperia, but she was marching headlong through a bog of memories and regrets to seize me by the figurative ears.

I might have lost my soul in France, but Hyperia was still Hyperia.

If we could not be married, she seemed to be saying, we could be cordial. Truly cordial. The strangest impulse came over me—to take her hand. We had eschewed gloves because a buffet was in the offing, and I had not clasped hands with another living soul for several eternities.

The impulse was there in my heart, benign and perhaps even normal. "We should go in," I said, rising.

Hyperia stood as well, her bouquet of lavender in her hand. "I wish you could stay, Jules. I'll wave you off with great good cheer tomorrow after breakfast, but I wish you could stay."

What she wished was that I *had* stayed—in England, rather than buying my colors and jaunting off to Spain. That particular wish was not among my regrets. An officer's commission was one of few alternatives for a ducal spare, and I'd been happy to do my duty.

My duty now was to appreciate Hyperia's overture for the undeserved boon it was. "I am glad you came upon me in the conservatory. We are not granting Ophelia the result she doubtless wishes for, but I am very pleased to see you."

I stopped short of the next step: *Shall I call on you when you're in Town for the Little Season?* If the past year had taught me anything, it was that the state of my health was unpredictable. I'd been taken captive in the autumn—or let myself be taken prisoner—and last autumn had not gone well at all.

Before Hyperia turned onto the walkway that led back to the orangery, she laid her bouquet on the edge of the fountain so the stems trailed in the water. I tarried to steal a few sprigs from her posey and slipped them into my pocket. I would have caught up to her easily, except that a fellow was striding toward me from the direction of the stables.

Red hair, broad shoulders, confident walk. Before my mind could label him with a name, my gut was churning uneasily.

"Hyperia."

She returned to my side. "Shall I make your excuses? I'd rather not."

"Who is that man?" Even as I asked the question, my memory delivered an answer: Lieutenant Colonel Sir Thomas Pearlman had joined the gathering, and that was just bad news all around.

~

I managed to avoid Sir Thomas for the duration of the meal. As luck would have it, Miss Maybelle Longacre chose me for her supper companion, while Hyperia favored William Ormstead with her company. We dined *à quatre* beneath the lemon trees. After the meal, our hostess, with all the hospitality of a drill sergeant exhorting his recruits to form squares, invited the company to *enjoy the garden.*

A gentleman and a lady perambulated on such occasions arm in arm. I was capable of offering Miss Longacre that courtesy, but I did not want to. We were all but strangers, though I'd seen her riding in the park amid a bevy of fashionable sprigs. She was an heiress of sorts, quietly attractive in a pocket Venus sort of way, and had debated the merits of Shakespeare's tragedies with Ormstead.

Not a featherbrain and thus something of a puzzle: Why had nobody offered for her? Why had she chosen me, eligible only in theory, for her companion? Why not Ormstead or even Sir Thomas, an exponent of old-and-respected bloodlines?

"Lady Longacre has given us our orders," Ormstead said when we'd done justice to the tray of strawberries and cheeses that Canning had brought to our table.

He'd tossed me a wink, the blighter. "A constitutional beneath the moon sounds appealing," I said. "Ladies, shall you join us directly, or do we await you on the terrace?"

"You await us," Hyperia replied before Miss Longacre could opine on the matter. "I'm sure half a dozen of my hairpins are about to abandon their posts. Come, Maybelle, and we will effect what repairs we can."

"We need go only as far as the summer cottage," Miss Longacre replied, getting to her feet without my assistance. "The ladies' retiring room has been kitted out there. We won't be but a quarter hour at the most."

The distaff decamped arm in arm, while I stifled the urge to call after Hyperia, *Don't leave me!*

Foolishness. A traitor I might be, but a coward, I was not.

"He's coming this way," Ormstead muttered, taking a slice of cheese from the tray. "I'll happily serve as your second."

I barely had time to register the significance of Ormstead's offer before Lieutenant Colonel Sir Thomas Pearlman, with murder in his eyes, marched up to our table.

"Put one foot wrong, my lord," he hissed, "one word amiss, and I will have satisfaction of you."

Another day, another ambush. I ought not to have been surprised, and yet, my supper was threatening to reappear all over Sir Thomas's large and spotless boots.

Lord Julian Collywobbles, at your service. "If and when you demand satisfaction," I replied, "you must agree that we settle our difference in semidarkness. Otherwise, the contest would be unfair."

Sir Thomas was of a height with Ormstead and me, and his complement of muscle exceeded my own. He had enjoyed bullying the enlisted soldiers, who, being from the lesser ranks of society, had seldom matched him for brawn.

Though his horse had likely matched him for brains. Still, he'd lost a brother, as I had, and his rage at me was justified.

"One doesn't fence in the dark, you idiot," Sir Thomas sneered.

"I no longer see well in bright sunshine," I countered. "If you'd like to commit murder, feel free. The Continent is quite cheap these days, and regardless of the circumstances of my passing, His Grace would doubtless prefer discretion to scandal." Invoking Arthur's consequence was badly done of me, but Sir Thomas really did not deserve to have my demise on his soul.

Then too, I didn't know Arthur all that well. My oldest brother had been raised in expectation of the title, and that burden had set him apart. He'd welcomed me home with ducal politesse after Waterloo and allowed as how I was to be permitted some time to recover before Mama found me a bride.

Arthur acknowledged me, in other words, but little more than that. He'd consider my death regrettable, but he was still quite young enough to marry and be fruitful, so the succession would hardly be imperiled by my passing.

"You won't fight?" Sir Thomas treated me to the sort of look a lady aimed at a smear of dog shit on her favorite pair of slippers.

"I am happy to fight," I said, "provided the battle conditions will not reflect poorly on my opponent's honor, honor being rather the point of such violence."

"You want a fair fight, when my brother and half his unit never stood a chance thanks to you."

Sir Thomas was merely voicing a version of what many others thought. I was a traitor, though nobody could prove that. I couldn't even prove it myself, and yet, it had to be true.

"I lost a brother too," I said quietly. "That was war, and *this is a house party*, Sir Thomas."

Lady Ophelia chose that moment to go off into whoops over something her swain of the moment had said. She smacked his arm, then opened her fan with an expert flick of the wrist and fluttered the air.

She was providing a distraction, and probably on purpose, bless her.

"I'm leaving in the morning," I said, keeping my voice down. "I had not expected to do more than escort my godmother to Make-peace's door. I truly do not want to trouble you, Sir Thomas, and if I could apologize adequately for the sorrow you've suffered, I would."

I meant those words. Nothing I could do, say, wish, or pray could change what had happened in France. Arthur had coolly informed me that any act of self-harm on my part would reflect poorly on the family, else I might have spared Sir Thomas his righteous display.

"I'll be watching you. Put one foot wrong, and I will make certain you regret it." Sir Thomas executed an about-face that went a little unsteady toward the end and stalked off.

"As if he'd have held up under torture," Ormstead muttered. "Let's find the ladies, shall we?"

I wanted nothing so much as to saddle Atlas and ride off into the gathering darkness. "They'll be another ten minutes at least. If you want to part company with me and enjoy a smoke, I will idle about on my own."

"You don't care for the occasional cheroot?"

I started for the nearest exit rather than wend my way around tables, smirks, and curious stares. "The smoke bothers my eyes. London in winter nearly sent me to Rome, but salt-sea air isn't any improvement. Provided the day isn't sunny, I do best in the countryside."

Ormstead joined me on a side terrace to the orangery. "And yet, you wintered in London. Were you trying to wreck your sight?"

"I was trying to stay out of my family's way, and I own the town house."

"I called on you."

Ormstead was brave, and he had all but run Sir Thomas off simply by staying at my side through the exchange.

"Ormstead, while I appreciate your... your decency, I do not want, deserve, or seek your pity. I erred badly in France, men died, my brother died, and I am apparently to blame. Sir Thomas, whatever his other failings, is in the right on those points."

"Is he?"

A glow on the eastern horizon promised imminent moonrise. Moonlight was my friend. Gentle, silvery illumination that yet allowed a man plenty of comforting shadows. Ormstead was not my friend, but neither was he my enemy.

"I honestly cannot remember much of what happened in France," I said. "Whatever I told my captors, I yielded unwillingly, and I fell into their hands because I was trying to keep Harry safe. In that regard, I failed both my brother and my command badly. That is as much as I can recall."

"What was Lord Harry doing outside of camp on his own?"

I wanted to swat the question away as Hyperia had swatted at the imaginary fly. "We were reconnaissance officers. Ergo, we left camp."

"In the middle of the night? With the French less than ten miles off?"

"Of course in the middle of the night, and often out of uniform, and sometimes on mules or behind donkey carts. I am too tall to pass for a woman, but impersonating a French officer was within my abilities. One could hardly slip through the countryside discreetly in scarlet regimentals, could one?"

I had mentally scouted every culvert and ditch encompassed by this arid mental terrain—Harry's mission, about which he'd been uncharacteristically tight-lipped with me; my violation of protocol when I'd followed him; the perfidious French who had well known when they'd got hold of an officer and who had yet treated him as a common spy; the nightmares and the nightmares and the nightmares...

"I'm sorry," Ormstead said, looking damnably noble and contrite by the light of flickering torches. "One doesn't want to kick old ghosts, and the ghosts don't leave me in peace either. We all whispered drunken regrets to the whores. Some of us put too many details in our letters home. Others failed to notice the enemy skulking around our very mess tent. The damned war haunts us all."

I was reminded of Hyperia's words about war and change. "War is supposed to haunt us, lest we send our sons careering into a similar hellscape in the name of some king or despot."

The moon was inching up over the horizon, a great golden orb illuminating the splendor of the Makepeace manor house and the Capability Brown landscaping intended to glorify it. The leaves of the lime trees twittered gently in the evening breeze, and from the direction of the home wood, a nightingale began its silvery song.

I wanted to be alone with the peace of the night, but knew that somehow, this outing Lady Ophelia had goaded me into making was good for me. To face Hyperia's honesty, Sir Thomas's rage, and even Ormstead's kindness was all part of finding a life in England I could tolerate.

"Britain has been sending her sons careering into hellscapes for centuries, my lord," Ormstead replied. "We seem incapable of doing otherwise."

I could not read Ormstead's expression because he'd moved to the shadows of the nearest torch, but the bitterness in his tone comforted me as even moonlight could not. I was not the only casualty, not the only one haunted. Hyperia was right about that.

"Well, cheer up," I said. "The war is over, and the only ordeal you face now is escorting Miss Hyperia West around the garden. If you don't regard that prospect as pleasing, there's something wrong with you."

"So why did you toss her over?" Ormstead asked quietly.

I never had to answer him, because at that moment, a shrill, feminine scream cut through the night air.

I took off down the steps and across the garden, Ormstead on my heels. The cry had come from the direction of the summer cottage, precisely where Hyperia and Miss Longacre had been bound.

CHAPTER THREE

The thought of Hyperia screaming inspired me to fleetness. Then too, I hadn't had much to eat or drink, and I had a natural gift of foot speed. I was thus first on the scene at a bend in the path that connected the summer cottage and the orangery.

"Hyperia, are you injured?" I panted.

"I nearly *did* somebody an injury," she retorted, gathering a pale silk shawl about her shoulders. "I can't imagine what he thought to do, but a hard stomp to his foot, and he desisted."

He? A *he* had inspired Hyperia West, the personification of good sense and dignity, to scream? My first instinct was to demand a description and an accounting of the incident, but investigation would have to wait.

Miss Longacre stood a few yards off, scowling mightily. She, too, had collected a pale shawl, and the moonlight gave her the appearance of a shade.

"He went that way," she said, gesturing with her chin toward the stable. "Or, rather, I heard footsteps that way."

I was a decent tracker. If the miscreant had bolted for the stable,

I'd soon know it. "Hyperia, did something startle you?" I spoke as calmly as I could, which wasn't very calmly at all.

"He didn't bolt for the stable. He went for the home wood," Hyperia said, sounding as if she was willing to put up her fives to settle the question.

"Miss West," I said, lowering my voice to that of a senior officer losing his patience, "*did something startle you?*"

Ormstead came crashing up the path behind me. "Everybody accounted for?"

Hyperia stared at me as if I'd spoken in ancient Etruscan, then comprehension dawned in her eyes.

"Miss Longacre and I are unharmed," she said slowly. "A stray dog or loose pig brushed by me on the path. We don't have wolves in Britain any more, do we?"

"We killed the last of them in my grandfather's day," Ormstead said, looking puzzled. "You came upon a stray dog?"

"They do roam the countryside," Miss Longacre said, taking the place at Hyperia's side. "Such a nuisance. As for a loose pig, that happens, and the home farm is less than half a mile off. I'll tell Papa to have a word with the steward. I am certain the beast made for the stable. A cat perhaps or a large rat."

A few other guests had straggled up the path, though the undergrowth meant they could not all crowd around Hyperia and Miss Longacre, and instead had to essentially form a queue.

"No reason for upset," Ormstead called. "One of the ladies was taken aback by some creature dashing across the path. The full moon doubtless makes the wildlife more active."

That little detail showed a capacity for quick thinking on Ormstead's part. Wildlife cavorting in the moonshine lent a patina of credibility to Hyperia's explanation—to the explanation I'd suggested she offer.

"Let's return to the garden, shall we?" I offered her my arm, and Ormstead did the pretty for Miss Longacre.

The gawkers dissipated in pairs, and my heart eventually slowed from a gallop to a restless trot.

"What happened?" I asked when Hyperia and I were some distance from the other guests.

"I was certainly not accosted by a dog," she muttered.

"Not of the canine variety. You and Miss Longacre agree that your assailant was a man. Was he wearing supper attire? Livery? A stable boy's garb? Can you recall the texture of the fabric of his coat? Was he tall, short, stout, slender? Anything you recollect might be of use."

We passed the fountain, the sound of the water trickling in the darkness soothing to my nerves. Though what of Hyperia's nerves? Some scoundrel had *accosted* her.

She slipped her hand free of my arm. "I was on the porch, waiting for Maybelle to finish in the retiring room. The moonrise was lovely, and I was wishing I did not have to return to the other guests. The next thing I knew, some fellow had me about the middle and was hauling me into the bushes."

"You resisted?"

"Of course I struggled, and I hoped he'd realize I was not whichever merry widow or obliging chaperone he thought I was. No such insight befell him, and thus I screamed. I also tromped hard on his instep, and he cursed."

"Good for you. Did he say anything?"

"'Bloody hell.'" Hyperia settled onto a shadowed bench, her prim tone making the vulgar expostulation all the more shocking. "Not a mean 'bloody hell.' More of a surprised, annoyed 'bloody hell.' Like when your saddle horse comes up lame, and you're already running late for an engagement."

I paced before the bench, sorting through a few *bloody hells* of my own. "His tone is why you conclude he mistook you for a trysting partner. I suppose that's possible." In which case, no threat to Hyperia remained.

Some randy bachelor had had too many glasses of champagne

and not enough light to see by. Miss Longacre would support the feral dog/frisky wildlife story, and by morning, half the company would believe a fox or a badger had caused Hyperia's fright. The other half would keep their unkind thoughts to themselves.

"Thank you," Hyperia said, watching me pace.

"For what?"

"For your quick wits. I'm sure Lady Longacre would rather not have her house party become grist for the gossip mill. I would dislike becoming an object of talk, for that matter."

Polite society had a relentlessly dirty mind. If it became known that a male with nefarious intent had put his hands on Hyperia's person, speculation would ensue: Had she enticed him? Had he done more than maul her? What was she *doing*, standing all alone on the moonlit porch, if not waiting for a lover?

Did Hyperia have a lover? Half of me hoped so. The other half of me kicked my curiosity in the arse for even presuming to speculate.

"Stop pacing, Jules. You'll draw attention, and right now I wish I were invisible."

I settled on the bench. "One sympathizes. Tell me more about this fellow. Colorful waistcoat? Gloves? Watch chain glinting in the moonlight? Was there any accent to his 'bloody hell,' or did he sound Etonian? Was it 'bluddy 'ell' or 'bluidy hell'?"

"He didn't drop his aitch, if that's what you mean, but Kentish lads don't, so that doesn't tell us much. Not Scottish either. He was good-sized, though shorter than you. Strong."

And he had used that strength to disrespect Hyperia. I gained new sympathy for Sir Thomas's seething rage. "Clothing?"

"Good wool. He wasn't a stable lad or drunken gardener, though his breath bore the scent of wine."

"Any other scent? Pomade? Horse? Tobacco? *Hungary water?*"

The moon was well up now, appearing smaller as it rose. That I was discussing a criminal assault with my former almost-intended rather than reciting poetry or whispering of half-acknowledged dreams struck me as symbolic of the man I'd become.

I'd never really sought a *romantic* attachment with Hyperia. I liked her and respected her. Now I could never have that sentimental attachment, though I could contribute in some minor way to her continued safety.

"He mashed me against his chest," she said, "and his coat smelled of... a roast in the kitchen, gravy, ham and potatoes."

"Of a supper buffet in a rather overheated orangery?"

"Yes. Exactly like that. By design, the company has a full complement of strutting bachelors, Jules. One of them mistook me for some other woman, and there's an end to it."

Hyperia articulated the simplest theory that explained all the facts, and yet, I was unconvinced. The bachelors were strutting, but they weren't blind or blind drunk—not yet. Hyperia was notably petite, and the summer cottage had likely been abuzz with ladies directly after the meal. To mistake her for another woman was possible, but quite the foolish error.

Then too, the footmen had been moving around in the orangery and would have frequented the kitchen. They might well smell of roast, have proper diction, and wear good wool.

"Jules?"

"I'll walk you to the house, Hyperia. You don't have to ask me." I'd walk her to the door of her room and loiter in the corridor until I heard her lady's maid greet her and the lock click into place.

"I do have to ask. Might you linger another day or two here at Makepeace? Healy was supposed to come with me, but he was delayed and isn't expected until the day after tomorrow. Until he arrives, you won't upset the numbers, and you will be a source of... reassurance for me."

From Lady Ophelia, such a request would have been blatant manipulation. Her style would be to turn an ankle or come down with a mysterious ague, then bid me to wait for her imminent death before I returned to Town. Hyperia eschewed intrigue, and she was as proud as any of my sisters.

"You are asking me to stay?"

"Only until Healy arrives. A day or two at most."

I could not refuse, and yet I hesitated to oblige. The other guests wanted me anywhere but underfoot. They'd had their gawk at Lord Julian the Traitor and would doubtless prefer I gave them a clear field in which to gossip about me.

"You haven't a chaperone here?" I asked.

"Lady Longacre is my sister's godmother, so I'm nominally chaperoned. Lady Ophelia could also serve. Healy would not have allowed me to come otherwise, and he will be upset if he learns that I was..."

"Frightened by a badger." I hated the hesitance in Hyperia's voice, the way her fingers plucked at the tassels of her shawl. I knew how it felt to realize that the world I'd grown up in had become unsafe for me.

"Ormstead will keep an eye on you if I ask it of him."

Hyperia sat up straighter. "Ormstead will not see me to my room, take up a lantern, and search the undergrowth for tracks until cock-crow. Ormstead will not think to ask about aitches when all I heard was two words. Ormstead will not expect me to recall the quality of wool I felt for only a moment."

"You are a woman of fashionable tastes. Of course you can evaluate wool at a touch."

"I am little, notably reserved, and past my prime, Jules. Why any man would *do* that..."

The scoundrel had had his hands on her for less than ten seconds, but that had been plenty long enough to shake her confidence.

As my matrimonial desertion had doubtless shaken her confidence. "Let's get you inside, Perry, dear." I rose and offered her my hand. "I do want to have a look around the summer cottage." I also needed to have a word with Miss Longacre, but I'd have to find a way to chat with her discreetly.

"You'll stay, then?" Hyperia asked, rising unassisted. "For a day or two?"

"I'll stay until Healy arrives, but I also want to have a quiet word with our host. If women aren't safe on his property, he needs to know that and to take appropriate measures to address the problem."

"I wish I hadn't come," Hyperia muttered as we traversed the length of the garden. "I'm too old for this nonsense, and it is nonsense. Maybelle will find a swain when she's good and ready to. A lady ought to have a few years to enjoy herself between the schoolroom, the altar, and childbed. Two of the girls I went to school with are dead, you know."

I hadn't known. "Child birth?"

"Of course child birth. One of them had been married less than a year. What woman seeks to risk her life for the sake of some fellow's elegant knee or witty repartee?"

I thought of my friends from university, so eager to buy their colors, knowing that if they gave their lives in uniform, they'd die a hero's death.

"I'm glad you are alive, Hyperia. Very glad." I couldn't think of anything more gallant to say than that. "Where is your room?"

"East wing, with the other hens and untitled makeweights. Second floor, facing the orangery."

"I'm in the east wing as well, third floor. My door has no carving. Third on the left after the light well if you come up the main staircase. A portrait of Good Queen Bess hangs opposite my accommodations." My room was probably intended for an upper servant—first footman, underbutler, under-steward—or a visiting solicitor or merchant from Town. Plain, though more than adequate to a soldier on bivouac.

If my billet was intended to insult the son of a duke, the ploy failed. I didn't want to be here, and the more obscure my quarters, the better I could hide.

"Collect me on the way to breakfast, will you?" Hyperia asked. "I want to know what your examination of the woods reveals."

I bowed good-night to her at her door, waited until I heard the murmur of female voices and the snick of a lock, then retraced my steps to the garden. I helped myself to a torch and returned to the scene of the crime—because it had been a crime, and I intended to get to the bottom of it.

~

"I don't want you here," Lord Longacre said as we strolled a dewy bridle path on the perimeter of the yearling paddock. On the other side of the fence, young horses started their day engaging in mock battles, napping, swishing flies, grazing, and embarking on what would doubtless be the most enjoyable summer of their equine lives.

If they only knew... But as far as they were concerned, life would always be high grass and herd politics.

"I don't want to be here," I replied, "though I appreciate your hospitality insofar that it has been extended to me." My room smelled of mildew and dust, and the mattress was an abomination, but I would not have slept any better in the staterooms. I was no better at sleeping than I was at remembering.

"Her ladyship said we must be mindful of Lady Ophelia's situation," Longacre replied, "and thus you were given a bed for the night. My fondest wish is that you make your farewell in the next hour, before we have any further upheaval in your vicinity."

Lord Longacre was of an age to be taking his first hard look at approaching middle age. Gray dusted his temples. He carried some extra provisions about his middle. He had a daughter to launch now, and his wife's concerns had abruptly become his concerns. Socializing for Longacre had acquired a tactical aspect, and he was in the uncomfortable position of having to rely on his spouse's skills to advance their shared agenda. I recalled the same heightening of awareness in my father when the time came to launch my sister Ginny.

Papa had shifted the ducal artillery, switching his aim from Parliament to the family my mother had been managing handily for decades. Such rows they'd had, and not over me for once.

"The upheaval," I said, catching a hint of innuendo in Longacre's last comment, "was in the vicinity of your daughter. I was at the orangery in Ormstead's company when Miss West nearly stepped on that badger."

"Maybelle says it wasn't a badger."

Good for Maybelle, getting her oar in before the paternal mind had been closed by breakfast gossip.

"Both Miss West and Miss Longacre agree that Miss West was accosted by a grown man. Miss West further informs me that her attacker was wearing good wool clothing, and he spoke at least somewhat proper English. He was tallish and strong and put his hands on Miss West in a most familiar and forcible manner."

Longacre ceased his perambulations and rested his elbows on the topmost fence board. "I realize I am being unfair, my lord, but I associate this unfortunate incident with your unplanned addition to my guest list."

Unfair was human, but I drew the line at irrational. "Apply a little logic, Longacre. I am the last man who'd seek to bring attention to himself at a social gathering. I have no wish to be here, but Ophelia importuned me and promised me I could simply drop her at the gate, so to speak. I planned to get a room at The Fool's Paradise and trot for London this morning."

He slanted a puzzled look at me. "What's stopping you?"

"Miss West is unnerved by last night's assault."

He had the grace to flinch at my word choice. "A presuming footman thinking to dally with a willing maid. It happens, particularly at house parties. You'd know that if you'd been to more of them."

Polite society longed to forget that, until I'd come home from the war in disgrace, I'd been one of their number. I'd attended countless house parties hosted by my father and brothers-in-law. I'd ridden to hounds, gone up to university, racketed about Town, and acquainted myself with all the gentlemanly vices.

But that part of me—the *normal* part—had become invisible, leaving only the traitor on view.

I was also a former officer who'd mostly done my duty, regardless of the cost. "Do your willing maids wear pale silk shawls? Do they style their hair in coronets and loiter on moonlit porches where any guest might pass by? Those features were obvious even in the limited light, though Miss West's specific identity was not."

"Then one of the horde of bachelors her ladyship has assembled was bent on a little mischief and got his paws on the wrong female. No harm done."

I yearned to strike the smug dismissal from his eyes. "Hyperia West was frightened and mauled while she was a guest in your house. What have you done to address the situation?"

"I'm asking you to leave, that's what. For all I know, the incident was intended to cast aspersion on you and inspire your departure."

"I was with a witness of impeccable integrity and in view of other guests. Sir Thomas was likely keeping an eye on my whereabouts, so ask him if I could have caused that scream."

In the paddock, a chestnut colt and a bay were rearing and pawing at each other, squealing and trotting around like subalterns arguing battle tactics. The bay was bigger and meaner, though the chestnut was more nimble.

"Sir Thomas told me as much," Longacre replied. "Volunteered the information, as did Ormstead. I still say it was a footman getting above himself."

And just when did Sir Thomas *volunteer* the information, and in response to whose questions? "Then your male domestic staff is out of control, my lord, and you cannot guarantee the safety of your garrison. Miss West has asked me to stay until her brother arrives, and unless you tell me to leave, I plan to accede to her wishes."

He muttered something that sounded suspiciously like *bloody hell*. In the pasture, the bay aimed a kick at the chestnut's head, which the chestnut narrowly avoided. The smaller horse trotted off, but the bay wasn't content with mere victory. More squealing and rearing followed.

Longacre looked not at his young horses and not at me, but at the soaring edifice that was his home, visible through the trees of the park.

"Stay if you must," he said, "until Healy West can join us, but behave yourself. You are a blot on your family's escutcheon, and I don't want anybody to think you're welcome here."

As if I'd needed reminding of my perpetual blot-ship. "I apologize for inconveniencing you, Lord Longacre, but hasn't it occurred to you that the intended victim of this assault was your own daughter?"

He straightened, and for the first time, he looked at me not as if I'd just toasted the Corsican monster, but as if I'd said something that merited consideration.

"*Maybelle* was at risk? How do you figure that?"

"The ladies dined at the same table. They went to the summer cottage together. They are of a height, they are both dark-haired and petite, and they both wore pale shawls and dark evening gowns. Given the shadows, Miss West could easily have been mistaken for Miss Longacre."

"You are making too much of this." Lord Longacre pushed away from the fence and marched in the direction of the stable. "A full moon, pretty females, champagne flowing like the Thames at spring tide—good champagne, at that—and somebody had a weak moment."

"The somebody wore Hoby boots," I said, falling in step beside mine host. "I inspected the scene last night and that evidence was plain to see. Miss Longacre heard footsteps moving off in the direction of the stable. Miss West said her attacker decamped for the garden proper. You might well have two somebodies intent on accosting your daughter."

We reached the corner of the yearling pasture just as the bay landed a stout kick on the quarters of the chestnut.

"That bay will harm your other colts and enjoy the exercise," I said. "You had best castrate him as soon as may be. The chestnut tried to cede the field, and your bully boy wasn't content with a clear offer of surrender."

"The bay is too fast to geld," Longacre said, pride in his tone. "Mean, but fast."

"Then for God's sake put him in with the draft mares until he learns his place."

Longacre appeared to consider the notion. "They might hurt him."

Somebody long, long ago should have planted his lordship a facer or two. "Then get him away from the others and tell the grooms to put some manners on him. You might well have left it too late as it is."

Lecturing a peer on the management of his horseflesh probably ranked above treason in terms of bad form, but Longacre's bay was going to kill somebody. One of his lordship's guests might well rape somebody, and the viscount appeared more concerned about protecting his colt than protecting his own daughter.

"You're an expert on young horses now, Caldicott?"

I was properly addressed as Lord Julian, but I'd offended the man —for the sake of a horse—so I let the slight pass.

"I am a former cavalry officer decorated for bravery and raised by a duke who owned one of the finest racing stables in the country. I merely offer a friendly, cautionary word between horsemen."

Longacre's pace slowed, while I felt an increasing compulsion to get indoors. The sun was spreading painfully bright beams over the land, and I had been ordered to accompany Hyperia to breakfast.

"I want to hate you," Longacre said. "Not very Christian of me, but you betrayed your country, or so Sir Thomas claims. He served loyally and well, and he won't say more than that, but he speaks with conviction. You can call me out for it, my lord, but I'd be much more comfortable extending my hospitality to you if I simply knew what happened in France."

What I took from that recitation was that Lord Longacre did not hate me, for which I ought to be grateful, but wasn't.

"All I can tell you is that I followed my brother Harry into the night, concerned for his welfare. He had not discussed his mission with me, which was unusual, and the French were camped less than ten miles away. They got him—my worst fears come to life—and all I could think to do was let them get me so I could spring him.”

Harry had gone peaceably into the company of his executors. In hindsight, I'd wondered if he had known I was trailing him and had been attempting to save me with his passivity. Harry had been that strategic in his thinking, though not always as observant as he ought to have been.

“By the time the commandant got around to questioning me,” I went on, “it was apparently too late for Harry. The guards said he'd died honorably. If his captors could have said otherwise, they would have simply for the joy of tormenting me with the news.”

Oddly enough, I had not recounted these memories to anybody previously, save one grizzled brevet general, who'd listened as if enduring the recital of a bad amateur soprano. He'd asked me numerous questions about what I'd observed while in captivity, then informed me that a court-martial was in nobody's interest. Harry and I had both doubtless meant well. I was to return to my regiment and say no more on the matter.

“I managed to escape,” I went on, “but by the time I found my way back to British forces, the French had had their bloody moment with me. I assume I told them where to look for our advance party as we prepared to cross the mountains, but I have no memory of doing so.”

I could recall other details, but not that moment.

Longacre studied me much as my superior officer had: *That's the best you can come up with? You cannot recall betraying your country? You cannot admit you are a traitor and bear responsibility for dozens of deaths?*

“One pities your mother,” Longacre said at length. “One son dead, another disgraced and mentally defective. You may stay until Miss West's brother arrives, but then please take yourself back to London. You are further informed that we will avoid inviting Lady Ophelia to another gathering for some time.”

Oh, right. Lady Ophelia's consequence was such that he could not punish her directly for imposing me upon his household, so he would punish me with guilt. Very tactical of him.

And tiresomely small-minded. "I will decamp at the first opportunity. I have agreed to escort Miss West to breakfast, so you will please excuse me." I bowed and left the path to cut across the park. "And please," I called over my shoulder, "do something about that bay. He's a nasty piece of goods now, and if you don't intercede, he'll soon be dangerous."

I intended to escort Hyperia to breakfast, but the more pressing objective was a quiet conversation with Miss Longacre. She'd claimed the attacker had run off in the direction of the stable, but he hadn't. He'd run parallel to the gravel walkway toward the orangery, then stepped onto the path, where I'd lost him.

Before I tucked tail and left the house party in disgrace—yet more disgrace—I would determine for myself whether Miss Longacre had been confused or had purposely lied about what she'd heard.

CHAPTER FOUR

"Miss West." I bowed over Hyperia's hand for the benefit of the lady's maid hovering in the doorway. "Would you do me the honor of accompanying me down to breakfast?"

"I would. I'm famished, and Crumpet can't get rid of me fast enough. She has designs on the remains of my tea tray."

Crumpet, a well-rounded, red-haired soul who looked to be of an age with Hyperia, tried to appear affronted. "Miss, I would never."

The twinkle in her eye said she did, regularly. Crumpet and I would get on famously, should the need ever arise.

"Good food shouldn't go to waste," Hyperia said, joining me in the corridor. "I'll probably have a lie-down after lunch, Crumpy, but the morning is your own. Get off your feet, flirt with the footmen, commiserate with the maids."

Hyperia moved off down the corridor, and I caught up with her where the east wing joined the central façade.

"Crumpy heard some interesting gossip in the servants' hall."

"All the best gossip is belowstairs, according to my mother. You look none the worse for your ordeal." Hyperia looked a little pale, but composed. Her dark chestnut hair was in a plain bun, and her dress was chocolate brown and hemmed for walking.

"I had nightmares," she muttered, peering in all directions. "But then, Lord Longacre's dairyman apparently chose this week to separate the calves from their mamas. I doubt anybody got much rest for all the bovine bawling coming from the home farm."

"I was more distracted by all the banging bedroom doors." The house party was off to a lively start in that regard. "I did go back to the summer cottage last night and have a look around. From what I could see, your assailant was one man, good-sized, as you said. He moved off at a steady sprint, suggesting he wasn't too far into his cups, and he knew exactly where he was going. He had sense enough to dart onto a gravel walkway at the first opportunity, and that put paid to my tracking skills."

"He wasn't trying to compromise me," Hyperia said, starting down the corridor. "That's something."

I remained where I was. "Perry, you're going the wrong direction. The main staircase is the other way."

She stopped but didn't rejoin me. "Maybe I want the maids' stairs."

Oh, no, she did not. "Repeat after me," I said, approaching her until she was close enough to grasp by the shoulders if need be. "You were startled by wildlife darting past you on the path, probably a fox out hunting to feed her pups. You felt something brush against your skirts. A stray dog is possible, or a barn cat on the lookout for mice and squirrels. The path is shaded, so even under a full moon you could not see anything but waving foliage."

She waited for my lecture to end. "I remembered something else."

"Don't keep me in suspense."

"A whiff of honey, Jules. It makes no sense."

I thought back to the previous night's menu. "Was honey available at the buffet? A honey glaze on the ham or a honey garnish on a fruit compote?"

"I can't recall, but Crumpy mentioned that Cook set out honey in the servants' hall along with butter for the morning porridge, and that sparked my recollection."

I offered my arm, and Hyperia took it, in her tentative, barely touching fashion.

"You don't have to be so careful with me," I said. "I can manage an escort's duties, provided you don't titter."

Her touch remained as light as a wish. "I correspond with your sisters, Jules. I know what your gallantry costs you. I wanted to take a breakfast tray in my room, but that would have been more work for the staff and cowardly."

Ouch. "That would have been understandable. Remember, though, that your attacker wants to take a tray in his room this morning as well. He bungled badly, grabbed the wrong woman, or grabbed a woman he should never have touched. He'll be nervous, wondering how much you saw clearly, how much you've told anybody. He might brace you on the topic himself, all the while oozing concern on your behalf. Keep your eyes and ears open, and you might catch him out."

"You'll speak to Maybelle? If he mistook me for her, she might know something relevant."

"I cannot approach Maybelle directly," I said as we reached the top of the main staircase. "Her father caught me looking in on Atlas this morning and all but told me to gather up my effects. I am here on sufferance until your dear brother shows up. But for my ducal connection, I'd be sent packing with a flea in my ear. I agreed to slink away to be a disgrace anywhere else as soon as Healy arrives."

I did not blame Lord Longacre for repelling boarders, but being an outcast was tiresome. No insult society could deal me compared with the burden of shame and bewilderment I dragged with me everywhere.

What had I told the French? I had no recollection of telling them anything. The memories I did have made less sense the longer I considered them. The French *capitaine* pouring me a glass of wine and consoling me on the loss of my so-brave brother. The postern gate ever so casually left unlocked... An opportunity intended to justify shooting me as I escaped, surely, but then, why not simply execute me for the fool I was? None of it made any sense.

"How do you stand it?" Hyperia murmured as we rounded the landing. "Everybody staring, everybody thinking they *know* something about you."

"All they know, Hyperia, is that you were startled, and that much is certainly true. Tell me about the other guests."

"Lady Ophelia is the better source for that information. She knows all of polite society and is related to half the peerage. She's great friends with Mrs. Pickton-Thyme and the third of their trio— Miss Maria Cleary—is also among the guests, though I've yet to see her."

Lady Ophelia was related to me, as it happened, a cousin at several removes on the wrong side of the blanket, a variety of cavorting that had apparently been all the rage in her day.

"I am angry with Ophelia," I said. "She did not warn me you'd be here."

We reached the bottom of the steps and were in the soaring front foyer. Ancestors variously scowled or smiled down at us from life-size portraits, potted ferns bobbed gently in an unseen breeze, and even a whisper would echo off the marble and plaster surfaces.

Hyperia leaned close. "Ophelia did not warn me either, but perhaps she did us a favor. It's good to see you, Jules."

What was I to say to that? To be confronted with Hyperia in person confused me. The sight of her was pleasing—she looked well, I was fond of her, I wished her every happiness—but also disconcerting. She was of my past, a happier past that I should have appreciated when it had been my present.

What came out of my mouth? "Let's find the breakfast parlor, and if you can invite Miss Longacre for a stroll in the kitchen garden, I will contrive to join you." I walked off in the opposite direction from where I knew the library to be.

Hyperia fell in step beside me. "The kitchen garden?"

I'd scouted the terrain in the misty dawn, old instincts prompting my reconnaissance. "Behind and attached to the orangery. I'd put it at about four acres enclosed by eight-foot walls. Out of sight of the house, free of guests. You can get to it from a door in the orangery as well as through several doors in the garden walls. Please contrive to stroll the orangery about ten of the clock with Miss Longacre and duck into the kitchen garden when nobody's watching. Stick to the east wall if possible, where there will still be shade."

A burst of laughter from down the corridor and the scent of bacon and toast suggested our destination lay just ahead.

"You were very good at reconnaissance, weren't you, Jules?"

"I was born to observe and report. One develops the skills of necessity as a younger sibling." A younger sibling who'd known from a tender age that he was different from his brothers and sisters, and not in a good way. I still did not know who my father was, though I had my suspicions.

"Do you miss it?"

We were just outside the door of the breakfast parlor, and like Hyperia, I wasn't looking forward to the meal. *Everybody staring, everybody thinking they know something about you.* Because I was focused on girding my mental loins for another gauntlet of stares and whispers, Hyperia's question took me unaware.

"Miss the military?" I asked slowly.

"The military, and the task—gather intelligence on the enemy without him knowing you're about it. Give the generals any edge you can find, be alert to every opportunity. I abhor all the risks you took, but it must have been exciting."

With her, I could be honest. "I have never felt so alive, Hyperia. I suspect the same is true for most soldiers. Many of us were destined for quiet, ordinary lives, but for a few years, we made a difference. Because I could ride like hell, and because Harry had chosen recon-naissance, I slipped into a role where I could make a substantial contribution. To have failed in that role... To say I am ashamed is the monarch of all understatements."

And just beneath the shame was incredulity. I had *loved* the whole business, the danger and daring, the disguises and details, and the hard riding and the hope. How could I, who'd excelled for the first time in my life, have made such a hash of the one job I was born to do?

"Come in, you two!" Lady Ophelia called. "Stop lurking in the corridor, or the locusts will consume all the chocolate."

Hyperia took me by the arm quite firmly. "I do not care for chocolate, my lady," she said, politely hauling me through the doorway. "And the last I heard, when it comes to chocolate, you will go to any lengths for first crack at the pot. My lord, I am in the mood for eggs, if you'd fix me a plate?"

She beamed gracious good cheer at the guests seated at the table, bobbed a curtsey at Lady Longacre sitting at the end, and parted from me at the groaning sideboard. The footman Canny had drawn guard duty, and while he did not exactly smile at me, he gave me the barest nod in greeting.

A breach of protocol, that, and I liked him for it.

Ever one to follow orders, I bowed to my hostess, took up a plate, and heaped it with fluffy eggs redolent of cheese and chives. I added a fat slice of bacon and two croissants before setting those offerings before Hyperia.

"Perfect. Fetch the same for yourself," she said, whisking a table napkin across her lap. "And a fresh pot of tea as well. Fine weather always puts an appetite on me. Somebody remind me—when is the archery tournament?"

Though I felt all eyes upon me as I filled my own plate, I knew that impression to be my overactive imagination at work. Yes, I was a curiosity, but less so with each passing hour, and Hyperia's brush with a fox—it must have been a fox, Lady Longacre opined, such sly creatures, foxes—had diverted attention from me. I collected a full teapot from those swaddled in linen on the sideboard and bent low to place it before Hyperia's plate.

"Thank you, my lord. Do have a seat. Your eggs will get cold."

I obeyed, but first I lingered a moment to whisper in her ear, "I've missed you too." Then I took my assigned seat at her side and set to work on breakfast.

~

After Hyperia demolished a breakfast that would have done a gunnery sergeant proud, she prevailed upon Miss Longacre to serve as her guide on an exploration of the grounds. Miss Longacre acquiesced graciously and declared a need to change into boots the better to fulfill her assigned office.

I finished my tea and wrestled with the realization that Mayfair could effect as great a change on a person as the military could. When had darling little Perry grown devious? Why had she learned the same deceptive arts that I had relied upon in Spain?

She had chatted up Miss Ellison on her right and the notably vague and elderly Miss Cleary on her left. Miss Cleary, a contemporary of Ophelia's, might have been twenty years Godmama's senior. Her face was that lined, her voice that whispery.

Hyperia had coaxed a smile from the old dear, and that had clearly pleased Ophelia as well.

"You up for a stroll?" Ormstead asked as I took my leave of the breakfast parlor. "I don't suggest we impose ourselves on the ladies, but I always like to have a look at the particulars of a well-run estate."

"I appreciate the invitation, but the day is proving fantastically bright. I'd best limit my outdoor activities to shady places admired from behind my tinted spectacles." I took said specs out of my pocket and affixed them to my nose.

"So wear your eyeglasses, and we'll find a bridle path to wander." Ormstead's pace down the corridor was leisurely, while I needed to march quick time. "If I don't move about, I will fall asleep. Summer nights are too short by half when a fellow is up playing cards until all hours. I don't suppose you box."

"I have—had—two older brothers. Of course I learned a few basics, but I don't fancy appearing at lunch with a shiner. I'm for the kitchen."

Ormstead pretended to admire a gilt-framed landscape that was probably Makepeace before Capability Brown had hacked down ancient hedgerows and diverted the stream so it flowed through the park and brought the deer along with it.

"We just had breakfast," Ormstead said. "Why the kitchen?"

"Because I want to know if honey was on last night's menu."

Ormstead scowled at me. "Word is you left a few of your wits in France. Whyever this interest in honey?"

That was the second slight to my mental faculties in the space of two hours. Those barbs bit deeper than either Longacre or Ormstead could know.

"I left a brother in France," I said, "but my wits remain generally accounted for. Miss West recalled the scent of honey about her attacker."

Ormstead turned in the direction of the conservatory. "Honey? Are there fragrances blended to evoke the aroma of honey?"

"Honey evokes the aroma of honey. If there was a fruit compote swimming in honey, a honey glaze on the ham, I want to know who consumed those items, who might have ended up with a smear of honey on his cuff." Besides any and every footman.

"The grilled fowl was marinaded in honey," Ormstead said, opening the door to the conservatory and letting out a humid, earthy breeze. "Very good it was too. Honey tenderizes meat, apparently, and keeps it moist. A camp cook told me that."

"Do you recall any other honey on the buffet?"

"No, but I wouldn't. I made a flying pass before Lady Ophelia could dragoon me into playing her cicisbeo, or Lady Longacre could match me up with her spinster cousin. I snatched what looked good and ducked behind the potted lemons, where I found you."

"Lady Ophelia can be good company." Self-absorbed, but good company. Sometimes.

"Lady Ophelia can be very *friendly*," Ormstead retorted. "One doesn't know whether to admire such stamina at her age or light out for Bristol before she imposes on one's gallant nature. A footman told me this is the best place to nap during the day. I was up a bit too late losing my shirt at whist."

"I noticed that Mendel Cleary is among the guests. Try not to oppose him at cards." I'd crossed paths in Spain with his younger brother, a jolly, stout fellow, who had held a poor opinion of the oldest sibling kicking his heels back in Merry Olde.

Ormstead bounced onto the sofa and promptly stretched out. "Mr. Mendel Cleary? Funny you should mention his name. I'm down two pounds six to him. Remind me to go easy on the brandy when the hour grows late. I deserve to lose if I'm trying to play cards when sozzled."

And Cleary had no doubt refilled Ormstead's glass generously and often. "Set yourself a budget and stick to it," I said. "Once you've lost your limit, *get up*, plead a headache, fatigue, a pressing need to water the hydrangeas, but do not sit down at the table again. Once you sit and the cards are dealt, it's nearly impossible to get free, and then you are kicking your heels in Rome with the rest of the remittance men."

Harry had delivered that sermon to me upon the occasion of my going up to university, and he'd been right.

"Yes, Auntie Julian. Good luck with your honey inquiry. That fowl was delicious. You will be hard-pressed to find a guest who didn't enjoy a few bites of it. Now that I've spared you a trip belowstairs, where are you off to?"

To fetch my hat, because I wasn't about to venture forth with merely my spectacles for protection.

"I need to send a note to Town. If I'm to tarry here for a day or two, I'll want some fresh clothes." I'd brought sufficient clothing with me for a few days, but Ormstead didn't need to know that. I had yet to see my luggage, and was managing on what I'd stashed in my saddlebags.

"Borrow from me if needs must," Ormstead said, cramming a pillow behind his head and crossing his arms. "We're of a height, though you could use more meat on your bones. Any particular reason I should avoid Cleary?"

"Instinct and experience. I'm none too fond of Lord Brimstock either."

"Fucking popinjay, that one, and I do mean fucking." Ormstead sat up and pulled off his boots, then resumed his supine posture. "Maybe Lady Ophelia should sort *him* out."

"Don't be distasteful. Lady Ophelia has standards." Though what they were, I could never be too sure. Her ladyship had assisted with the guest list, after all, and there sat Cleary and Brimstock among the bachelors, and rather near the top of the list as eligible fellows went. Both were comely enough and of adequate pedigree and means. So was Sir Thomas, come to that.

And popular opinion hadn't convicted any of them of treason, always a point in a fellow's favor. "I'll leave you to your beauty sleep."

"Mmph."

I hadn't gone two yards from the conservatory door when Lady Ophelia sang out from the direction of the breakfast parlor.

"Halloo! Julian, my boy! Help an old lady up the steps, if you please."

"I happen to be going that direction myself. My lady, good morning." I did not offer my arm, but instead gestured toward the stairs. "I trust you slept well?"

"With all those poor calves calling for their mamas the livelong night? Lady Longacre was tempted to send his lordship to sleep in the hayloft for that bit of folly. It's even odds whether the under-steward or farmer will be sacked for terrible timing."

"Tonight might not be much quieter, and tomorrow night only a marginal improvement. If Longacre bred some fall calves, he would not have to be as precipitous about weaning his spring heifers."

"You should tell him that," Ophelia said, pausing on the landing to pat my lapel. "Or perhaps not."

"I vote not. Why are Cleary and Brimstock here, Godmama? They both have tiresome bad habits."

"Now, now. Mustn't be jealous. They are easy on the eye, solvent, and from good family. Cleary just needs a wife to settle him down. Then too, I so wanted Maria to have a little outing. She was least in sight during the Season, and she does not look well to me. Not well at all. Breakfast exhausted her, and she hardly ate a thing. Brimstock is mostly flirtation."

Aunt preferred Saxon coloring, and Brimstock—Broomstick to his familiars, for exceedingly vulgar reasons—and Cleary were both about six feet tall, blond, and muscular. In another life and with less social standing, they'd have been in demand as footmen.

"Cleary cheats at cards," I said. "Brimstock will cheat on his wife and his mistress both."

"One cannot cheat on a mistress, Julian. Don't be absurd."

The fair courtesans of Mayfair likely saw the matter differently. "So you added Brimstock and Cleary to the guest list for aesthetic reasons?"

"I added Cleary because I could not expect Maria to get here without her nephew's assistance. She never did marry, and of her three nephews, Mendel is devoted to her."

Ophelia stopped at the top of the steps, hand on the newel post in a posture that was to evoke my concern for a frail, aging woman struggling valiantly to guard her dignity.

Hah. "Mendel would do well to marry a viscount's daughter," I said. "The ancient gentry like to pretend that theirs is the bluest blood, but I'd bet Mendel covets a title as desperately as any cit ever did."

"Maybelle Longacre did not acquit herself well in Town," Ophelia said, moving off down the corridor. "She didn't exert herself to be charming. She's a bit too headstrong, too... plainspoken. Not in words, but she'd fail to smile at a gentleman's *on dit* and forget to thank him for standing up with her. I don't judge the girl for being unimpressed with the Town whirl, but her unwillingness to play the game limits her options."

There was the godmother who'd told me to apply myself to my Latin studies, but to leave expertise in Greek to Harry. The godmother who'd explained to me that even if I didn't care for strong drink, I had to learn how to appear as if I did. Her gems of wisdom had been hidden among much prattle and self-indulgence, but she'd been an asset to my younger self.

"Then you are looking for a crooked lid to fit Miss Longacre's crooked pot?"

"Dreadful boy." She continued briskly along the corridor. "No wonder your mother chose me to take a hand in your upbringing. You have the old duke's ability to deliver the truth in its least appealing guise, but yes. The more dubious characters on the guest list are my attempt to either dangle semi-forbidden fruit before dear Maybelle, or to show her where marriage to some scoundrel will lead. Mendel Cleary is a paragon, if somewhat inclined to pinch pennies. Sir Thomas would be easy to manage. They aren't all that dubious by today's standards."

Of course not, when measured by a woman who decried the modern emphasis on marital fidelity and referred to London's most dedicated rakes as a lot of overly fragrant, hymn-singing peacocks.

"If Maybelle is bent on rebellion," I observed, "she can simply run off with a footman. It's been done."

"Footmen cannot pay the milliner's bills. Maybelle is headstrong, she's not stupid, somewhat like you. Lady Longacre does have good taste in footmen, though. All very well trained too."

"You are attempting to corrupt my morals again, Godmama. I am still angry with you for ambushing me and Hyperia. Shame upon you."

Ophelia paused outside a carved door, Zeus and Leda cavorting eternally in a single panel of oak. "I noticed how wroth Hyperia was at breakfast, Julian. Towering with rage to find herself thrust into your company again. Fuming, fit to be tied. Do come in."

I was aware of time fleeing—I had to secret myself in the kitchen garden in the next twenty-five minutes, and I'd spend fifteen of those minutes making a discreet progress around the park's perimeter to keep to the shade and avoid being seen.

"I really cannot tarry," I said, stepping into her parlor.

"Right. You are in demand to captain the soon-to-be-winning team at bowls, no doubt. Who accosted Hyperia, Jules?"

The comment about captaining a bowls team was nearly mean. Longacre had been mean to me, and Ormstead's remarks—leaving my wits in France, et cetera—had been inconsiderate. Not yet ten of the clock, and I was tired of being disrespected.

The sooner I returned to London, the safer I would be. Much more casual insult and sneering condescension, and my temper might slip its leash.

"I don't know who accosted Hyperia," I said, "and neither does she. She didn't get a good look at his face, but he wore good-quality wool and Hoby boots, he spoke as if somewhat educated, and he was tallish and strong."

"To Hyperia, every man would seem tallish. The Hoby boots don't tell you much. Lady Longacre uses the London agencies when hiring, and they have mostly London fellows on offer. A used pair of Hoby boots probably graces the feet of half her indoor male staff."

"I doubt the underbutler has designs on Miss Longacre's person. I'm more tempted to think Cleary and Brimstock got up to some sort of bet, though that would be fast work even for them."

And that bet might well have related to Hyperia, who approached old-maid status, rather than to Miss Longacre or one of the other tender beauties. Hyperia had noted herself that the objective had not been to compromise her.

Which left... what? A stupid bet, a half-blind guest intent on bothering a maid. Neither explanation satisfied me.

"Leave it, Julian," Lady Ophelia said, passing me a shawl, which I obligingly draped around her shoulders. "In my day, mauling young ladies wasn't considered a prank, but young people today have no taste. If it was foolishness, then it's best ignored."

Her sitting room was ten times more commodious than the bedchamber I'd been assigned. Another insult.

"And if it wasn't foolishness?"

"Then nobody will appreciate you pointing fingers. Young ladies know to be cautious, and I am on hand to deal with the randy bachelors."

She'd been no use at all when Hyperia had been in the clutches of a bounder. "You all but hoodwinked me into coming here, and now you are trying to run me off. What do you know that you are trying to keep from me?"

She arranged her shawl so it came just under her chin, obscuring the effects of age obvious about her neck. She really did have extraordinary eyes.

"I know Sir Thomas tried to call you out, and I hadn't counted on him being such an ass. A miscalculation on my part, I admit it. You and Hyperia have been seen in a public rapprochement, and that's sufficient progress for the nonce. I will understand if you remove to London later today."

Perhaps she was telling the truth, and perhaps she was again trying to hoodwink me.

"At Hyperia's request," I said, "I will not leave until Healy West is on the premises. I'm off to have a discreet chat with Miss Longacre."

"Be careful, Julian. These people hold themselves in very high esteem." She didn't say the rest of it, but then, she didn't have to: They held me, by contrast, in contempt.

I bowed and withdrew and made my slow, quiet way to the kitchen garden's shaded east wall. Five minutes into my conversation with Miss Longacre, it became clear I didn't have much standing in her eyes either.

And thus, my grasp on my temper became yet more tenuous.

CHAPTER FIVE

Near the sunny west wall of the garden, a fellow in a cap and leather apron was picking peas. Other than that good soul, no staff was on hand. They had doubtless harvested most of the day's vegetables in the cool of earliest morning and were hard at work turning green beans, butter, and shallots into *haricots verts avec beurre et échalotes*.

Strips of grassy turf ran between cultivated plots, and the south wall had been modified with a glass-pane abutment that formed a long, low version of a conservatory. Even in winter, Makepeace's residents would eat well.

"My lord, you must be in error," Miss Longacre said as we passed a bed of partially harvested asparagus. The hacked-off stems seemed to reproach their thriving brethren, and I was reminded that asparagus had been on last night's menu as well.

"I searched most thoroughly, Miss Longacre. No tracks, human or otherwise, ran from the summer cottage through the undergrowth to the stable. I did find tracks that led more or less back to the orangery, suggesting Miss West's attacker was a guest."

Hyperia pretended to admire the orderly expanse of the garden, though cucumber vines and potted aubergines hardly made for a compelling vista. Her sturdy brown walking dress and serviceable straw hat were a contrast to Miss Longacre's more extravagant plumage.

For a stroll about the grounds, Maybelle had chosen a fluttery gold muslin walking dress embellished with lacy cuffs, floral embroidery, and a green and blue peacock shawl. Miss Longacre might not be trying to attract the notice of a husband, but neither was she hiding her light under any bushel baskets.

"You had best look again, my lord," she said. "With sunshine to aid you, I'm sure you will find what you missed by dark of night. I know what I heard, and I trust my hearing more than I do your ability to search the bracken for tracks. The fellow dashed away in the direction of the stable. Tell me, when exactly are you returning to Town?"

Hyperia turned a placid eye on Miss Longacre. "I have asked Lord Julian to remain until Healy can join me. The situation last night has left me somewhat shaken. The presence of an old and dear friend is a comfort."

Miss Longacre blinked at Hyperia. She tried looking down her nose, and when that tactic yielded no results, she fiddled with her green silk bonnet ribbons.

"I see. Well. In that case, please excuse me. I will entrust you to the company of that dear friend and ask if Mama has any use for me. I believe the schedule calls for battledore this afternoon, and I can help make up the teams. My lord, I saw those tracks myself this very morning. A trail through the trees cuts over to the stable not twenty yards from the summer cottage. Our prankster was doubtless making straight for it."

Meaning Maybelle had tramped all over the scene and probably taken her own tracks for those of the perpetrator. *Prankster indeed.*

"What prompted you to go looking for tracks?" I asked as pleasantly as I could.

"I wanted to jog any latent recollections I might have had of the incident. My inspection served only to reinforce the fact that our miscreant bolted hotfoot for the stable."

She tossed off half a curtsey, which Hyperia returned with casual grace. I bowed, and we were soon shut of dear Maybelle.

"I want to like her," Hyperia said, "but she has a restless, sulking quality that suggests she was overindulged in childhood. Gracious, I sound like Lady Ophelia. Let's get you out of the sun."

"We are in shade, I have my specs, and my hat brim protects my eyes as well. You need not cosset me."

Hyperia strolled toward the door that led to the orangery. I had no choice but to stalk along beside her, old and dear friend that I was.

"You weren't this cross before breakfast, Jules."

"Since last we met, Godmama has ordered me off the property, and Ormstead has cast aspersion on my sanity. Before that, our host gave me my congé. Now Miss Longacre tells me that I can't read the obvious signs of another man's hurried progress through dense undergrowth. What does she think I did in Spain and France? Compose odes to my horse?"

"Atlas is a splendid horse." Hyperia said this with the deadpan earnestness my sisters resorted to when twitting our eldest brother.

"Cut line, Perry. Ophelia shares your opinion of Miss Longacre. Nobody has used the word 'spoiled,' but clearly, the young lady did not *take* in Town and regards that as Society's loss. Godmama has recruited the likes of Mendel Cleary and Lord Brimstock to take Maybelle off her parents' hands if the young lady seeks to marry a prig or bounder. In the alternative, those two might inspire Maybelle to sober reflection on the lifelong consequences of youthful folly."

"Both fellows are pretty enough," Hyperia said, stepping back so I could hold the door to the orangery for her. "Cleary isn't all that bad, though he has an exaggerated sense of his own appeal. He's devoted to his auntie, which speaks well of him. Crumpy says his name came up in the servants' hall."

"The maids and footmen will wait until kingdom come for any vails from that one," I said. "His wealth is almost exclusively agricultural, and his tastes exceed his means. He's perpetually pockets to let and apparently cheats at cards to make up the shortfall." Or so his youngest brother had opined. Spendy-Mendy had not endeared himself to his junior siblings.

Hyperia stopped amid rows of potted orange trees. "Mr. Cleary *cheats*? That's a serious accusation, Jules. A deadly serious accusation."

"I had it from his youngest brother, whose path I crossed on the Peninsula. Cleary is prodigiously lucky at cards, too lucky. When I was on winter leave in Town, I confirmed the younger brother's allegations.

"Ormstead probably fell into Cleary's clutches last night," I went on, "or into an overly handy decanter. The question is, where does Mendel spend all that money? His family has some means, and the youngest brother was honorably lamed at Talavera and given desk work thereafter. Nobody seems to know much about the middle brother other than that he's a spendthrift too. Two sisters have already made their come outs and married suitable *partis*."

I had Lady Ophelia to thank for the annotated version of Debrett's that I carried in my head, that, and a tendency to recall what did not matter while forgetting what did.

"Younger brothers are always getting up to nonsense," Hyperia said, plucking a ripe orange and rolling it between her hands. "If Mendel Cleary were my older sibling, I'd yield to a pressing need to study Viking runes on Orkney. He's very full of himself. I do love the smell of oranges."

She sniffed her prize. "If Brimstock and Cleary are the visual delights of the gathering," she went on, "then Rupert Westmere and Osgood Banter win top honors for coin of the realm."

"Both of those bachelors bear the taint of the shop," I said, which puzzled me. Ophelia was closely connected to any number of titled, wealthy, and powerful families on both sides of the blanket. She truly must not care for Miss Longacre, because the eligibles on hand were all, like Miss Longacre herself, not quite *quite*.

Not in the first stare. Flawed goods. Crooked lids for crooked pots.

Banter was received everywhere, quite the gentleman. He was gentry on his mother's side, with an estate not ten miles from the Caldicott family seat, but the paternal branch of the family tree had been in trade in German George's Day.

Westmere, while even wealthier, bore the same taint a mere two generations back.

"Do you suppose Ophelia wanted Miss Longacre to look favorably on *you* as a potential suitor?" Hyperia asked, settling on a white wrought-iron bench. "Ophelia can play a deep game, and she cares for you."

Hyperia's idle question had the ring of dread possibility. I came down beside her. "I'll peel that orange for you. Godmama wouldn't be so stupid. I'll be leaving tomorrow or the day after at the latest, and Miss Longacre is not... I will never let it be said that I tossed you over for the likes of her."

Hyperia pitched the orange straight up, and I caught it on the descent. "One is moved by your loyalty, Jules. Truly moved."

"Sorry." A change of topic was in order. "What did Crumpy have to say about Cleary?"

Hyperia huffed out the sort of sigh that said further castigation of me, while tempting, was a waste of her time, which it was. I hadn't truly tossed her over—had I?

"The handsome Mr. Cleary was overheard rowing with a footman."

"Berating a footman, I can believe, but arguing?" I tore open the skin of the orange, juice spraying over my fingers and the scent reminding me of Spain. "The footman must not need his post."

"The footman is quite popular belowstairs. Canning, by name. Cleary wanted his services as a makeshift valet, and Canning said something to the effect that if a ducal heir can fend for himself and sleep in a broom closet, then a mere mister could manage to tie his own cravat. The other footmen are taking bets whether Canning will be sacked or promoted."

"Neither." *How odd.* I had a champion of sorts in Canning,

while my social equals felt comfortable insulting me. "Lady Longacre cannot afford to sack anybody for the duration of this gathering, and two weeks from now, she won't give a wilted rose for Cleary's lopsided cravats. If Cleary offers for Miss Longacre, Canning might have to endure a scold or two, but he's too well suited to his job to be cut loose for one outburst. The other footmen would pout, and Lady Longacre knows better than to foment domestic discord when she has a daughter who isn't launching successfully."

Though the aging Miss Cleary—Maria—had brought staff with her. Why couldn't Mendel make do by borrowing one of his aunt's footmen if he was too tight-fisted to bring along his own valet? Perhaps he was too proud to impose on such an elderly relative?

Hyperia passed me a handkerchief that was more embroidery than linen. All bright flowers and foliage and a light lavender scent. "You think like an officer."

"I am... I was an officer." Properly addressed, I was Lieutenant Lord Julian Caldicott, though I preferred to be spared the military rank.

I tossed the peels into the camellias, and Hyperia and I shared the orange. She had given me a few things to think about. What was Godmama truly, truly up to? Sabotaging Maybelle's chances, ensuring Maybelle had a second Season to choose from a wider field? Presenting Hyperia to me in a field where my former not-quite-intended was the clear standout?

Why did I feel a nagging unwillingness to return to Town when I wasn't in demand to captain a bowls team, or any other team?

Not that I cared for bowls.

"Let's have a look at the summer cottage path," Hyperia said when we emerged from the orangery. "Miss Longacre was all but insistent that you study it again."

"Then study it, we shall, though bright sunlight has disadvantages when it comes to tracking."

"How can that be?" Hyperia trundled at my side as we crunched along the gravel path. "I can barely do close work unless I'm sitting in bright sunshine."

Then her handkerchief represented many sunny hours spent squinting at her embroidery hoop.

"I don't know why, but tracks are often more clearly visible if the light is minimal and you set a lantern on the ground. The low angle of the illumination makes the tracks show up more easily, which is part of the reason I had a look last night."

"What's the rest of the reason?"

"Sightseers will obscure the signs, just as Miss Longacre doubtless did this morning." Then too, I'd been upset for Hyperia's sake last night and eager—even desperate—to put what skills I had to use.

We did, indeed, find indications that Miss Longacre had tramped this way and that. Just as she'd said, somebody else wearing larger footwear had marched off through the undergrowth to the path that led to the stable.

"What?" Hyperia asked, coming up on my elbow as I stared at tracks I'd apparently missed the night before.

"Either I am losing my powers, or something is very wrong."

"I doubt you are losing your powers, but I suppose both could be true, couldn't they? Somebody is out to do mischief, and you aren't feeling quite the thing? This house party has to be a strain on your nerves."

I resented her understanding bitterly, which was ridiculous of me. "Let's proceed with the out-to-do-mischief hypothesis. I'll need my sketchbook, and you can sit along the walkway, distracting anybody who thinks to take a spontaneous ramble through this undergrowth."

Hyperia scuffed her toe through the leaves at her feet. "Must we? I'm fine, Jules. I see no need to stick our noses any further into this situation. If you think it's not safe for me here, then I can come down with influenza and take my leave."

Her departure would be blamed on me, but more to the point, Hyperia should not have to retreat from the gathering. She deserved to look over the eligibles, dubious though some of them were. She ought to have her turn twirling down the room in a pretty frock, and God knew she did Society a favor by putting Miss Longacre in her place.

"I'll explain why the tracks bother me," I said, "because they do. Very much so."

~

"The degree of wilting tells us a lot," I said, holding up two little branches of rhododendron. "This one,"—I twirled the specimen in my left hand—"was broken off last night and left dangling in the breeze. I saw it, and it helped confirm that your attacker returned to the orangery."

Hyperia scowled at the twig. "Must we call him my 'attacker'? Can't he be the 'culprit'? The 'scoundrel'? The 'malefactor'?"

She was doing what every soldier did after a hard battle, mentally distancing herself from the experience. The near misses, the fallen comrades, the stink and gore and sorrow. Some used humor, some used drink, some memorized Bible verses, but we all tried to shove those days to the back of our mental catalogs until we'd revised them into occasions memorable for bravery, luck, and skill.

"Very well," I said. "The culprit. Compare last night's twig with a broken branch I found this morning." I held up the specimen in my right hand.

"Not as wilted," Hyperia said. "Might the second bush simply have been in wetter soil?"

"Neither bush shows any curled or drooped leaves, and they are less than twenty feet apart. Both have had adequate rain, though you raise precisely the sort of question a competent tracker would. This bit in my right hand was clearly broken off hours after the one in my left, and there's more."

Hyperia looked unconvinced. "More what?"

"More indications that somebody with mischievous intent came around after I'd looked the scene over last night. They sought to create evidence to support Miss Longacre's version of events."

"The ran-off-to-the-stable version," Hyperia said. "Sound can play tricks, especially as the dew is falling. Miss Longacre doubtless had a few glasses of wine with her meal."

"I trust your hearing," I said. "I trust that you would note where your... where the wretch went, lest he turn and attempt to make off with you again." I put the twigs on a nearby rock. "He was already pelting through the trees for the nearest crowd when Miss Longacre insisted he'd lit out for the stable."

Hyperia studied the two wilting exhibits from the prosecution. "You are saying that my... the culprit had an accomplice. Somebody who wanted to cast suspicion on the stable lads, or somebody who offered that suggestion to the real scoundrel so he could come back and arrange matters for his convenience."

"Possibly, or over cards last night, somebody—without any nefarious intent—recounted Maybelle's words about the stable, and the miscreant himself got ideas. In any case, we have further indications that the man who put his hands on you was a guest. We still don't know why."

"Because he thought I was somebody else. Nearly every woman used the retiring room after supper, Jules."

Hyperia clearly wanted that explanation to suffice. I wanted to get to the truth.

"Before we tackle that part," I said, "let's finish with the evidence. This morning's footprints are not the same size as last night's, though they are fairly close, and the ones leading to the stable were made at a more deliberate pace than those leading to the orangery."

"How can you tell?"

"Most of us amble about, landing on the heel first and pushing off with the toe as we prepare for the next step. If you're running, your weight lands with greater force, and your stride lengthens. The fellow bolting for the orangery took long strides—nearly as long as my own running stride—and his heels made fairly deep depressions in the soft ground. This morning's intruder was shuffling about by comparison. He had a short stride and left nowhere near as deep an impression. Either the second person was considerably lighter despite having roughly the same size feet, or he was merely toddling."

Hyperia scowled at the undergrowth. "Or both."

"Or both."

She struck out for the summer cottage. "You are sure these other tracks weren't here last night? Sure you didn't miss them?"

"Almost. I am a thorough tracker, Hyperia. I was good at it, and one doesn't lose the knack any more than one loses the knack of forming letters into words."

She plunked down on the steps leading up to the summer cottage, a two-story whitewashed stone structure with a wide porch encircling three sides. The cottage had been built to nestle against the shade of the home wood and catch a prevailing southerly breeze. Had not Makepeace been sitting seventy-five yards away on its majestic rise, I would have enjoyed biding in such a place.

"How do you learn to track?" she asked. "It's not as if the squirrels will tell you, 'I passed this way on Thursday at noon, and that's where the cat came along to sniff my trail on Saturday.'"

"You pay attention," I said. "You listen to anybody with tracking knowledge, and you set up little studies for yourself. Tramp through a muddy patch one day, come back the next and look at how the footprint has changed. Look closely enough to sketch it. Break off a twig and note how quickly that variety of shrub wilts on a hot day versus a cold day, a windy day, a foggy day. Expert trackers have a nearly mystical ability to read signs, but they tend to do best in their own locality. They become intimately familiar with the weather, the behavior of the soils, and the flora and fauna of their home territory."

Hyperia plucked a sprig from the bed of lemon balm growing on either side of the steps. "I don't believe I've heard you string together that many words since you last came home on winter leave."

Hyperia paid attention too. I'd do well to remember that.

"This tracking business, Jules, the deducing and peering beneath rocks, you like it."

"I was valued for my reconnaissance skills in Spain. Tracking is one way to add to the store of facts at an officer's command and to reduce the degree to which his decisions are based on conjecture. Tracking skills come down on the side of reason and logic. If they can be of use bringing a criminal to justice, I will offer what I have to give."

"And if he wasn't a criminal?" Hyperia asked, crushing the lemon balm in her fist and releasing its characteristic tangy fragrance. "If he was a trysting partner who simply got hold of the wrong woman? That is the most likely explanation, and we do nobody any favors by ferreting out his identity."

The scent of the herb was pleasant and soothing. Hyperia's company was pleasant and not soothing. Her questions reminded me that though we'd known each other forever and been almost engaged, we'd also spent little informal time together in adulthood.

And no time at all lounging on shady porch steps, actually conversing about something other than the latest risqué wager at White's or a younger son gone for a tourist one step ahead of his creditors.

"Two factors weigh against your hypothesis of a bungled assignation, Hyperia. First, if you were embraced in error, why go to all the trouble to manipulate the evidence? House parties are nothing if not occasions for frolic, and a mere kiss by moonlight hardly signifies, no matter who the parties were, provided both are willing."

She sniffed at her fingers. "If Lord Longacre was expressing his affection for Lady Ophelia, I doubt Lady Longacre would view the situation benignly." Hyperia clearly took a dim view of marital infidelity, which was nearly quaint of her, given the circles she traveled in.

"If Lord Longacre or Mendel Cleary, for example, took liberties with you in error, they would apologize, beg your pardon, and hope nobody saw anything. They would claim to have stumbled in the dark, to have meant nothing by their clumsiness. They would not steal away like an inept thief."

Hyperia turned her face up to the sun, exposing her graceful profile. "If those gentlemen were thinking clearly, they'd smooth the moment over. If they were very ashamed or facing grave consequences for erring, they might panic."

She had a point. A man didn't panic over stealing a kiss at a house party. He laughed it off, expressed contrition, and wiggled away from responsibility for his actions—unless others could construe the situation as compromising the lady's good name, which this batch of guests would be only too happy to do.

Who was the most profligate bachelor among those assembled? Would the prospect of matrimony to Hyperia have sent him into a panic?

That same possibility had sent *me* into a panic, though I'd had my reasons.

Hyperia tossed the mangled lemon balm into the bed from whence she'd plucked it. "You said two factors weighed against dismissing the whole thing as a bungled overture. The first is all the fussing about in the bracken, though I take leave to debate your conclusion. What's the second?"

"You are distinctive."

She glowered at me. "You mean I am short."

"You are petite, dark-haired, and you've set aside the insipid pastels the sweet young things are adorned in, despite pale colors suiting few of them. I suspect Miss Longacre's bolder wardrobe is an attempt to emulate you." Though both ladies had worn pale shawls the previous night, a factor that supported Hyperia's mistaken-identity hypothesis.

Hyperia wrinkled her nose. "Lady Longacre should have made Maybelle wait a few years to leave the pastels behind. I'm on the shelf now, or as good as, and I have my own funds. Maybelle is barely out of the schoolroom, and her money is all tied up in trusts and competences until she turns one-and-twenty."

"How do you know that, Hyperia?"

"Healy came across the information."

"Why do I have the sense you came across the information and passed it along to Healy?" As any good reconnaissance officer would.

"Damn you, Jules. Lady Ophelia let it slip, or pretended to let it slip. Healy has no need to marry for money, but some man will come into significant means if he can talk Miss Maybelle around."

Actually, the talking-round would be aimed at Maybelle's father. She was not of age in the marital sense, and a match undertaken without parental approval could be set aside by the bishops.

"Who else among the ladies here is petite, dark-haired, and no longer wearing vestal robes?" I asked.

Hyperia rose. "I'd have to think about that. One or two of the chaperones. I wish you'd let this drop."

I was on my feet as well, though the shady steps and the lazy droning of honeybees tempted me to linger. I hadn't spent much time in the country since coming back from France, and rural life had its charms.

"That's what you want?" I asked, peering down at her. "Put it aside, a minor mystery of no consequence?"

"That's what I want. Further inquiries into a passing incident can only inflame tempers and fuel gossip. Healy ought to be here tomorrow, and then you can return to Town."

She wanted me to drop the matter, and yet, she also wanted me to remain on hand until her brother arrived. I concluded that the *passing incident* had upset her more than she cared to admit, while for me the notion that some other fellow could hold top honors in the scoundrel department, albeit temporarily, appealed too strongly.

Explaining the evidence to Hyperia had also reminded me that I'd had some skills—once upon a time in a land far away—and I had enjoyed using those skills again, however modestly.

I returned Hyperia to the manor house, where she joined a group of ladies intent on practicing their battledore. I then shut myself into the conservatory, where Ormstead yet communed with Morpheus, found a comfy reading chair, and mentally began reviewing the guest list.

Despite Hyperia's request, I would keep an eye out for any petite, dark-haired chaperones and the bachelors who either pointedly ignored them or made too much of them. I was looking for a man nearly my height, based on his length of stride, and—this came to me as I was halfway asleep—a gait rendered slightly uneven by the application of Hyperia's heel to his foot.

I hadn't asked her which foot had been her target, more's the pity, but I could watch carefully and wait, at least until Healy arrived.

~

Battledore was intended to be an amiable diversion, the shuttlecock genteelly lobbed back and forth among the players while laughter filled the air. The nitwit bachelors Lady Longacre had assembled were determined to turn a boring game into successive displays of single combat.

A lady and a gentleman were paired on each side, making up two teams of two each, but after the third quartet of contestants had quit the court, the nature of play had been set. The ladies stood by, rackets nominally at the ready, while the idiots—I could not refer to them as gentlemen—whacked at the shuttlecock as if they'd ram it down one another's throats.

This was all supposed to be great good fun until Osgood Banter miscalculated in his attempt to break Cleary's nose and gave Miss Henrietta Ellison a shiner instead. I expected Lord Longacre to put a stop to the nonsense, but he was deep in conversation with one of the local squires and gesturing frequently in the direction of the yearling paddock. Lady Ophelia wasn't on hand to speak peace unto the heathen, and Lady Longacre was pretending grown men typically tried to commit murder with a bunch of cork and feathers.

"Champagne, my lord?" Canning kept his voice down, but I gathered he'd been hovering at my elbow for some moments.

"Thank you." I took a glass, but did not drink. "Did somebody lose more than he should have at cards last night?"

"Several somebodies," Canning said softly, his gaze straying to Miss Ellison, who was protesting that her eye would be fine, really, even as redness became redness-and-swelling. "Mr. Cleary enjoyed extraordinary luck."

Canning's tone discreetly conveyed that he disapproved of such *luck*. Another slight breach of decorum.

"He asked you to valet him?"

"He assumed I'd be delighted. He had no clue how impressing me into his personal service would have burdened the rest of the staff. I've no wish to stay up until all hours waiting for the dashing swain to stumble into bed, just so I can untie the cravat he's too drunk to remove himself."

Canning's speech was educated, and yet, his sentiments were pure infantry. "Did you take the king's shilling, Canning?"

Now he adopted the impassive, middle-distance gaze of the well-trained footman—or soldier at attention. "Three years. I was a sharp-shooter for most of that."

One out of every sixth British male had worn a uniform in recent years, and one out of ten had carried arms in battle. We were no longer the nation of shopkeepers various Frenchmen had labeled us, if we ever had been.

"God bless the Rifles," I said, lifting my glass and reciting a prayer common to many an officer. With modern weapons and eagle eyes, the sharpshooters of the 95th Regiment of Foot had become legendary, and deservedly so. They were often the first into battle, and unlike the usual infantry unit that formed squares and fired a general volley at an advancing enemy, the sharpshooters *aimed* their weapons with deadly accuracy from strategically chosen cover.

"God bless the Rifles," Canning said, "but wearing livery is much safer than wearing a uniform, my lord. Ye gods, her ladyship will allow play to resume. I'd best fetch Miss Ellison some ice, if you'll excuse me."

He marched off toward the refreshment tent, while Miss Longacre stepped in to take Miss Ellison's place. Cleary was apparently as stupid as he was lucky, because not two minutes later, his shot whizzed by Miss Longacre's ear, close enough that the feathers of the shuttlecock caught her earbob, and the whole business became tangled in her hair.

My sisters would expect me to intervene before one of the ladies was maimed. I was already persona non grata and planning to leave on the morrow, so what could speaking up possibly cost me? I set my champagne aside, brandished my plain linen handkerchief, and approached the latest victim of Cleary's bad sportsmanship.

"You are bleeding," I said, passing Miss Longacre my handkerchief. "Hold still, and I'll get the blasted thing free of your hair."

Lady Longacre chose now to get to her feet and bustle over, all maternal concern. "I'll see to my daughter, my lord. Maybelle, one can use the racket to deflect a shot, you know."

"Mama, I'm not a child. Did he ruin my earbob? Why did I have to wear my pearls today?"

I was halfway succeeding at freeing Miss Longacre from the shuttlecock, so I pressed on despite Lady Longacre's clear wish that I remove myself from the vicinity of her daughter's person.

"My lord," Lady Longacre said, all but cramming her elbow into my ribs, "I can manage quite well if you'll—"

"There." I held out Miss Longacre's pearl earbob and stuffed the shuttlecock into my pocket. "Your bauble appears undamaged, though we can't say the same for your ear. You'll want to repair your coiffure as well, I'm sure."

The men appeared to find the whole situation amusing, with Sir Thomas cuffing Cleary playfully on the shoulder and some other fellow pantomiming a hit to the earlobe.

"Thank you," Miss Longacre said, snatching her earbob from my grasp and shoving her racket at me. "If you'll excuse us, my lord."

She sent her father—still oblivious in the shade of the refreshment tent—a glower, then stalked off, her mother fussing and fretting beside her, while I... I considered the racket Miss Longacre had passed into my keeping.

In my head, I heard my brother Arthur, sounding very much like our late papa, warning me to resist temptation. *Don't be an ass. Don't stoop to their level. Tantrums are for children.*

I hefted the racket and assayed my emotions. I was angry, though I was not having a tantrum. The other fellows, bringing their resentments from the card table to the battledore court, were behaving badly.

"Maybe you should play for the ladies," Sir Thomas sneered. "But then, you're the next thing to an invalid, from what I hear. Too mentally unsound to recall what most of us will never forget. Wouldn't be fair to the distaff to saddle them with the likes of you."

In point of fact, I had not been included on any team, though had Healy West been present—he for whom I temporarily stood in—he'd doubtless have been near the top of the roster.

"Right," I said, smiling at Sir Thomas. "Seeing as the ladies are down a few in numbers, I'll happily join their side. Cleary, I believe it's my serve."

Osgood Banter tossed his racket to a footman. "I'm for a glass of champagne. You're on your own, Caldicott."

That's Lord Julian to you. "No need to state the obvious, Banter. Cleary, shall we enjoy an exhibition match?"

CHAPTER SIX

Mendel Cleary, being the eldest son, had not served in the military. He'd inherited the entailed family seat from his father three years past and was still, apparently, in the strutting phase of having acquired his birthright.

He tossed his racket aloft with his right hand and caught it with his left. Weighing options, no doubt. Half the male assemblage badly wanted to see Cleary's luck turn, even if I was the instrument whereby the scales were evened. The other half would appreciate just as much seeing me publicly disgraced.

The ladies were likely relieved to be spared further nonsense. A few had already drifted in the direction of the refreshment tent. Hyperia remained in her wicker chair, gaze impassive.

"Let's make it interesting," Mendel said. "My horse against yours, best of three volleys."

Cleary was not known to abuse his cattle, and as interested as he seemed to be in amassing coin, I could doubtless buy Atlas back if I had to surrender him for honor's sake.

"My horse is a seasoned campaigner, veteran of the wars, not some pretty hack who couldn't jump a row of buckets," I said, bouncing the shuttlecock on my racket. "Choose another wager."

"Your spectacles for my horse," Cleary retorted. "Or will you protest that the care and feeding of a second mount is too great an imposition on your finances? I, alas, have no spectacles to wager. I will throw in the saddle and bridle to sweeten the pot."

Nasty sod. I bowed. "My spectacles, without which I cannot bear to venture forth on a sunny day, for your horse, whom I do not need and whom you can easily replace. Best of three volleys."

"Your serve," Cleary said, bowing in return and stepping off the required paces.

Among the spectators, a few murmured bets were placed. Hyperia looked bored—ominously bored—while Lord Longacre had left off singing the praises of his killer colt to aim a raised eyebrow in my direction.

Nearly rip his daughter's earlobe off and come close to blinding a lady guest, and his lordship couldn't be bothered to notice. A polite wager among the gents, and he turns up all sniffy.

Typical.

I let my myriad sources of irritation simmer while I removed my coat and turned back my cuffs. I was, in the opinion of the other guests, mentally unsound, socially undesirable, physically unimpressive, and morally deficient.

Very well. Guilty as charged.

I'd also grown up amid an army of older siblings who'd played battledore and every other sport nigh to the death, and I'd learned to hold my own against their larger, stronger, more powerful competition.

The situation merely wanted a little guile and fortitude. "Ready?" I asked as I resumed bouncing the shuttlecock on my racket.

"Any time before Michaelmas will do. Put off your comeuppance as long as you like."

A clumsy attempt at public school goading, but the dictates of protocol had been met. On the next bounce, I popped the shuttlecock aloft and slammed it at Cleary's face. His reflexes were sufficient to spare him the fate Miss Ellison had suffered, but I'd got the drop on him, and he and every onlooker knew it.

I let him find his feet and used a protracted volley to learn his style. Two polite bats, then he tried for a point, which I parried. I let him work in the same rhythm twice more—bounce, bounce, pounce— before I dispatched a stinger of my own on the second bounce. The shuttlecock glanced off my opponent's boot, at which he stared with gratifying annoyance.

"Lucky shot," I said. "Your serve." I tossed him the shuttlecock, ready for the real battle to begin. His opening maneuver was conservative—I'd got his attention, apparently—and when he tried for his next point, I contrived to miss by a whisker.

He really wasn't very nimble, though his confidence rose sufficiently that he bowed to a smattering of applause for having evened the score.

Don't get too cocky. The mental warning came from Lady Ophelia, my mother, and all my siblings. The fate of England did not ride on the outcome of the next volley, but what was left of my pride certainly did.

Though I was at my best in enemy territory. I'd forgotten that— that too. The French had captured me solely because I'd chosen to be taken prisoner.

I served politely, and Cleary volleyed with equal good manners, though on the next return, he tried to steal my strategy and spike the shuttlecock at my boots. I replied with an underhand lob, inviting him to try for another spike, but he failed to note the opportunity.

The spectators gave tongue as the shuttlecock flew back and forth. "You'll look a treat in those fancy glasses, Cleary!" and "Tire him out, Cleary, then finish him off!"

Nobody, not even Hyperia, spoke up on my behalf, but then, I didn't need her to. Cleary was flagging, his next attempt at a point going a good three feet wide. I parried and decided that the better part of honor required me to end the exhibition forthwith.

Cleary tried again for the aggressive coup de grace, and for his trouble, I drove the shuttlecock hard at my target, thus ending the match.

He dropped his racket and bent over, rubbing furiously at his thigh. "Good God, Caldicott, three inches to the left, and you'd have unmanned me."

"I beg your pardon?" I collected the shuttlecock and his discarded racket. "I did not hear you."

He stared up at me. "I said you damned near hit me in a very unsporting location."

And walloping Miss Ellison in the eye had been all in good fun? "I know. It's more of your legendary good luck that I aimed my shot where I did and not where you deserved to have it land. Miss Ellison might well have been blinded, and Miss Longacre left the court to tend to a bloody ear."

Lord Longacre appeared surprised at that last disclosure, but still he did not intervene.

Cleary straightened. "Bad business, I agree. The ladies are due an apology. I'll see to it, Caldicott."

Oh, how very noble of him. I examined my racket, which was of no particular interest to me save as a cudgel.

"I said, Caldicott, I will be only too happy—"

I held up the racket and studied its face, my temper driven by bad sleep, the beginnings of a reprise of my headache, and sheer stubbornness. "I heard what you said and how you said it."

Perfectly arched blond brows drew down. "Trafalgar's a good horse and quite sound. I'll introduce you to him after breakfast tomorrow. One wants to enjoy a farewell hack with an old friend. I'm sure you'll understand, Caldi—"

Somebody, possibly Hyperia, cleared her throat.

I cocked my head as if I hadn't quite heard aright. "You were saying?"

The nattering spectators had fallen silent, the better to hear our verbal combat. From the home farm, the occasional desolate heifer bawled for her calf. Battlefields had the same sort of quiet, before every hell-spawned demon cut loose.

Cleary apparently yet claimed a modicum of intelligence. "I'd like to show you my gelding's paces before you take possession. I'm sure you'll understand... *my lord.*"

"Of course I do, and you will need a mount to see you home at the end of the house party, while I am in no hurry to acquire another horse. Atlas will pout if he has to share my custom with a younger fellow. You may surrender the horse anytime that's convenient."

I dropped the equipment on the ground, collected my jacket, and bowed. "You will excuse me. Even with my trusty specs, the sunshine grows unbearably bright."

As I stopped by the refreshment tent for a glass of lemonade, the spectators began to dissipate in chatty twos and threes. Cleary headed for the house in the company of Lord Brimstock.

Had I not been observing Brimstock from the back, I would have failed to note that his gait was slightly uneven. He hadn't been among the athletes either, despite being a robust specimen and something of a show-off.

Not quite limping, but surely favoring one foot. Well, well, well.

～

By nightfall, I was truly tired. For a few minutes on the battledore court, I had exerted myself physically and mentally, and the effort had done me good. I'd whacked Cleary in the thigh with the shuttle-cock, after his open disregard for my standing had whacked me just as tellingly in the region of my self-respect.

As far as I was concerned, we were even. As for the rest of the guests...

Who were these people to judge me? Sir Thomas, as a fellow offi-cer, could view me with contempt if he pleased to, just as I'd viewed him with contempt for bullying his subordinates. William Ormstead, the other former officer among the guests, took a more compassionate view of my situation.

But as for the rest of them... My superior officers, after giving my actions considerable thought, had decided to let the matter of my captivity and escape rest in all its messy ambiguity. More to the point, those superior officers had sent me back to my regiment to recuperate and resume my duties after the fall of Paris. Had they judged me to be a traitor, the outcome would have been very different.

Whether I'd betrayed my brother was no concern of military justice or the prancing ninnyhammers assembled by Lady Longacre. And speaking of mine hostess, what gave her the right to treat me as if I were a cousin on remittance who had turned up drunk at the Christmas feast?

These thoughts accompanied me as I ambled around the garden's torchlit formal parterres, serenaded by the laughter of the other guests flirting and gossiping on the terrace. Hyperia seemed to be getting on well with Ormstead, so I'd left them to their diversions while I enjoyed the darkness.

"A message for you, my lord." Canning approached with a slip of paper on a silver tray.

Would Lady Longacre give me my marching orders by letter? I moved closer to the nearest torch, took the note, and unfolded it.

Cleary reiterated his invitation to join him for a dawn hack, the better to acquaint me with his mount's—now my second, unnecessary mount's—paces.

"Olive branch or ambush?" I murmured.

"Beg pardon, my lord?"

My lord. I'd taken the polite address for granted until nobody save a footman yielded it to me. "I'm invited to ride out with Mr. Cleary at the crack of doom. I don't suppose you need a horse, Canning?"

Canning's usual ebullience faltered. "Could not afford to feed him, sir. Mr. Cleary cuts a dash on his chestnut. The beast will fetch a pretty penny at Tatts if you have no use for him."

I admired pragmatism in anybody. "Not done, though, to win a fellow's personal mount in a wager and turn around and sell the beast at auction. An unfeeling thing to do."

Canning maintained his silence, and I wondered who had treated him unfeelingly. The Rifles were respected, but demand for sharp-shooters in Merry Olde was curiously lacking.

"Suppose I'd best accept the invitation." Atlas had had his day of rest and would benefit from the exercise. "Can you send somebody around to wake me at first light? I don't trust myself to keep country hours, and Cleary will be insulted if I accept his invitation and then stand him up."

"He would at that, sir. I'll have the boot-boy knock on your door, unless you'd like some assistance dressing?"

The moment became awkward. Was Canning extending me a courtesy, angling for a vail, or looking for a way to emphasize his earlier point to Cleary about protocol and rank?

"That is kind of you, Canning, but if a former cavalry officer can't get himself into riding attire, he's not fit for the saddle. Besides, you are run off your feet and need every quarter hour of rest you can steal. Much like being on campaign, isn't it?"

Canning grinned. "Hadn't thought of it like that, my lord. If you ever do need a hand, dressing for dinner and so forth, please ask for me. I prefer the footman's job—always plenty to do—but I'm a fair hand with the starch and iron when Lord Longacre's valet is under the weather." He studied the torch flame dancing in a night breeze. "I know what it is to find your tent moved to the edge of camp, no mates, nobody looking out for you. I don't fancy it and suspect you don't either."

He bowed and departed on that extraordinary speech.

"Please convey my acceptance to Mr. Cleary," I called after him, because I had no intention of seeking Cleary in the cardroom or billiard room or wherever he was trying his *luck* at such an hour.

Canning waved his acknowledgment with a gloved hand and trotted up the terrace steps.

"Cheeky fellow." Cheeky, presuming, but also a former soldier who was apparently experiencing his version of the difficult solo mission. "God bless the Rifles."

The Rifles had been oddly egalitarian for a military unit. They took a man who exhibited some native talent, gave him the best equipment, and turned him into an expert. A cobbler's apprentice in the Rifles could march alongside a gentry family's younger son, and they marched as equals.

They *had* marched as equals, but they were equals no longer, now that they'd marched home.

As I made my way up to my broom closet, I realized that Canning's situation had inspired a different sort of thought regarding the war than I usually entertained. My typical musings were about France—what *had* I told those blasted Frogs, and why couldn't I recall the telling?—or the horrors of battles and sieges.

The aftermath of a siege could make hell look like a garden party.

To reflect on the struggles of an infantryman upon returning to England was a different perspective on the whole campaign, a perspective that did not focus on me and my tribulations.

"Progress, I hope," I said as I went through the nightly ritual of searching for brown hairs among the white. The exercise was undertaken more efficiently in bright sunshine with a hand mirror, and my evening maneuvers before the vanity were more in the way of a nervous habit.

Why bother?

I tended to my ablutions, lay down on the lumpy cot made no less lumpy for being covered by a worn quilt, and closed my eyes. Within moments—or so it felt—a solid thumping disturbed my slumbers.

"Up and at 'em, guv!" called a boyish soprano. "Canny says ye wanted rousing, and Cook says only a fool tries to rouse the Quality without bringin' 'em a tray."

I cursed in my first language—French—then realized what I was doing and switched to English. The thumping continued, and with a soldier's ability to begin the day sleepwalking, I let the little wretch in.

"You don't got no fire," he said, strutting forth and setting the tray on the vanity. "I know how to make up a fire, guv. Won't be no trouble."

"Thank you, but no. Summer weather obviates the need for a fire." I smelled salvation in the form of coffee. An army might march on its belly, as *l'empereur* had famously said, but the cavalry had survived on coffee.

The boot-boy stared up at me from beneath a mop of dark brown hair that somebody had recently dragged a damp comb through, to no avail.

"Ob-vee-ates," he said, blue eyes narrowing. "'At's a new one on me. Ain't proper you don't got a fire and you a guest. Canny won't like it."

"Then we won't tell him, will we? What's your name?"

My polite inquiry got me a thoroughly skeptical assessment. Asking for a name could be a necessary prelude to making a complaint. Any recruit learned as much within three days of joining up.

"For God's sake, child, I already know you're the boot-boy. I ask because you brought me coffee rather than tea, and that was good thinking on your part."

"Canny said you'd prefer the coffee. I like chocolate meself, had it the once at Christmas, and I snitch from the breakfast pots whenever Cook ain't lookin'." He took himself back to the door and returned with my riding boots, polished to a gleaming shine.

"I don't use champagne," he said. "Waste of wine to polish boots with champagne, but I get 'em clean enough."

I poured myself a cup of the elixir of redemption and sat on the bed. "You've done a marvelous job with the boots and an equally impressive job of withholding your name."

The staff of a ducal residence took great pride in their posts and excelled at upholding the dignity of the family who employed them.

That same staff wasn't above swatting the arse of an uppish little lordling or dispensing homespun advice to a very young lady in the throes of her first romantic upheaval.

I had missed that sort of presumption, the kind that cared more for a family's wellbeing than for the appearance of unrelenting deference. My staff in Town, all hired since Waterloo, tiptoed around me as if I were on my last nerve and ready to sack them all without provocation.

Perhaps I had been, six months ago.

"Me name's Atticus," the boy said. "Not Atticus Smith or Atticus Miller. Just Atticus. I'm a hard worker, or Cook will know the reason why. You want I should polish your Sunday boots?"

"I didn't bring my Sunday boots, and with any luck, I won't need them." The coffee was strong, blessedly hot, and lacking the bitterness of the usual camp brew. "My thanks for a job well done. Snitch a croissant and be gone."

Surprisingly clean fingers swiped one of the three offerings on the tray. "You ain't so bad yourself, and I don't care what 'em fancy valets have to say about you."

"Maligning me as a traitor?" I asked, dunking a croissant into my coffee and trying not to sound interested.

"Something like that. Tattled to the Frenchies, but too highborn to pay the price. Canny took the king's shillin'. Told the lot of bleatin' old bounders to shut their gobs because they didn't know shite. They hated that, but they stopped their gabbling. Valets is worse than butlers for puttin' their noses in the air, but they wipe their arses same as the rest of us, I say. Can I have another croissant?"

My worst nightmare recited along with the imp's opinions on domestic hierarchy was somehow comforting.

"You may, and then leave me in peace, if you please."

Atticus speared me with a very adult look. "Mind you don't fall back asleep, guv. I'll hear about it, and it won't be my fault. Cook's temper has gone all raggedy with this house party, and she can swing a switch at my innocent rump like nobody's business."

"I am for the stable, and you had best make haste back to your post."

He sniffed his croissant. "What was the word you said? About summer weather?"

"Obviate, to render unnecessary." I took a coin from the night-stand and tossed it to the boy. "Best of luck, Just Atticus."

He missed my play on words, of course, but he caught the coin. "Thanks, guv." He slipped out the door and had the presence of mind to close it quietly in his wake.

I finished two cups of coffee and a croissant, dressed for riding, tucked my specs into a pocket, and made my way to the stable. A very dapper Cleary was waiting for me, tapping his riding crop against his field boot.

"Is this your idea of a joke, *my lord?*"

"Good morning, Cleary." I bowed in retaliation for his sneered use of my honorific. "Something has upset you enough to part you from your manners."

"Not upset me, by God, enraged me, and you know damned well what it is."

"Until twenty-five minutes ago, I was fast asleep on a minimally adequate bed. I am here at your invitation and prepared to ride out with you for purposes which I need not recite. What has you in such a lather?"

William Ormstead sidled out of the barn, his expression troubled. "His horse has been stolen, my lord. Stall is empty. Door closed, halter and bridle missing from the door. If this is a prank, somebody's sense of humor is sadly wanting."

Ormstead peered at me with a complete lack of warmth.

"And you two prodigies," I said, "have decided that *I* stole a horse which is already mine by rights, am I correct?"

"I hadn't handed him off to you," Cleary said. "Trafalgar was still in my possession, and somebody wanted to make me look like a fool."

"That somebody," I said as French curses piled up in my head, "is not I. I have no motive to steal from myself, and where exactly do you think I stashed this horse of mine, when I'm miles from my own mews and entirely without allies in present surrounds?"

"He has a point," Ormstead said. "A man can't steal what he already owns, and all manner of confusion can result at a house party. Somebody might be trotting about on the beast as we speak, thinking he took out a guest horse."

And nobody had thought to question the stable lads. A pair of bleating bounders who didn't know shite, to quote a wise fellow.

"Come on," I said, "let's have a look. Is the saddle missing?"

The bleating bounders exchanged a look. They'd been too busy labeling me a horse thief to even look that far, but I could remedy their oversight.

～

"Saddle's gone too," Ormstead said, surveying the gear filling a row of wooden racks in what might have been a feed room in bygone years. "Do we wait for the horse to come trotting over the rise, or do we organize a search?"

Cleary filled his sails with an audible inhale through his nose. "I'll not be made a fool of like this. If Caldi—Lord Julian didn't purloin Trafalgar to humiliate me, then who did?"

"I humiliated you yesterday," I said, returning to the airy barn aisle and the sound of horses munching a morning's ration of hay. "Rather, you humiliated yourself, and making off with the horse you no longer own is *your* attempt to humiliate *me*."

Ormstead followed me from the saddle room and rubbed his chin, which was yet shadowed with stubble. "Humiliate... you?"

Cleary came along as well. "Denying you the fruits of your puerile display does appeal."

I examined the stall's closed half door and refrained from indulging in a you-started-it volley. "Did you just incriminate yourself, Cleary? You are quite fond of this horse, aren't you?"

The mechanism was a simple, sturdy bolt. A bored and enterprising horse with nimble lips could wiggle the bolt free, but he could not close the door behind himself and put on his very own bridle and saddle.

Cleary commenced pacing. "I would ride only good-quality horseflesh, my lord. Trafalgar is sane, sound, and handsome. He's worth a pretty penny."

"He's easy to sell, you mean." And Cleary did so love his pounds and pence.

Cleary looked from me to Ormstead and resumed tapping his riding crop against his boot. "You're suggesting *I* sent him off to be sold rather than honor the terms of our wager?"

"Or you sent him home, or you hired a groom to get him to the nearest livery. You are the only person I can think of with a motive to move the horse." Cleary was also notably preoccupied with coin—winning it, even quasi-cheating to gain it. Parting with a valuable horse would not sit well with a miser.

His expression turned venomous. "I am the only person with a motive, other than *you*."

"How do I benefit from making it appear that *you* stole my horse?"

"You slap the label of blackguard on another guest. You shift the burden of gossip to another man's shoulders. I half suspect it was you who put your filthy hands on Miss West, and she's too loyal to your family to admit—"

I had the crop out of his hand with a simple twisting maneuver my sisters had shown me ages ago. I tossed it to Ormstead.

"You have insulted me for the last time, Cleary. You either apologize for your pointless conjectures or prepare to defend yourself."

I had not quite issued a challenge in the strictest sense. As a former officer, I knew exactly where that line lay, and I had not crossed it. I had merely warned the fellow I was in the mood to beat him bloody. I could not imagine a circumstance where I would willingly take another man's life in peacetime.

"Lord Julian was with me when Miss West was accosted,"

Ormstead said. "If you don't believe him, Cleary, then please believe me. Baiting each other serves no purpose, you two. Somebody made off with a horse, which is a hanging felony if the intent was to steal it. I am more interested in solving that puzzle than in refereeing a round of fisticuffs between grown men."

Cleary swiveled his glower to Ormstead. "He was with you? You're certain?"

"He was with me at the orangery's side terrace when Miss West cried out, and we were within view of the staff clearing the tables."

"Then I do apologize." Cleary bowed formally. "I was misinformed."

I retrieved the riding crop, a nondescript article going a bit frayed at the handle, and passed it to him. "Who lied to you regarding my whereabouts?"

"I can't..." He studied his crop as if even a moment in my hands might have somehow stolen its magical powers. "I heard idle talk around the decanter. Speculation made more confident for marinating in Longacre's brandy. I am sorry, my lord, but any excuse to disparage you is tempting."

"Tempting it might be, also ungentlemanly, ill-informed, and cruel. You did not serve in the military, Cleary, which makes your participation in these tactics doubly hard to stomach."

He took out a pocket watch with an ostentatiously long chain and noted the time. My father had done the same thing when struggling to curb his temper.

"My family," Cleary said, "sent two sons to Spain, and neither of my brothers returned unscathed. The one will never waltz as he once did. The other fell in with a bad crowd and sank himself into debt. I'll thank you to hold your tongue on the topic of sacrifices and duty."

"I've said all I have to say."

"About the horse?" Ormstead muttered. "Do we search? The decision is yours, my lord, because the horse was yours at the time it was... He's yours now."

Cleary declined to take issue with Ormstead's reasoning. Prudent of him.

"I search. Cleary, you may leave the matter in my hands, and I'd appreciate it if you'd exercise discretion."

"My aunt will expect me to look in on her before breakfast. I leave you to your *searching*." He sniffed, bowed, and withdrew.

If he and my brother Arthur ever met on the field of honor, they could have a sniffing duel. Except they wouldn't meet, because Arthur was a duke, and Mendel Cleary was a commoner. Arthur also wasn't a bleating ass, except on rare occasion.

The grooms, who'd been bustling up and down the barn aisle, taking this horse out to graze and bringing that one in from a night at grass, knew exactly what was afoot. They, however, were unlikely to talk to the guests about a horse going missing from their stable.

The grooms would, though, talk to the gardeners, who'd chat with the dairymaids, who'd flirt with the Makepeace footmen, who'd get to dicing with guests' footmen, who'd pass along an idle word to the valets, who'd drop a hint to the companions, and the news would eventually be all over the manor.

Somebody had stolen *my* horse.

"Well?" Ormstead said, gaze on the empty stall. "To fuss or not to fuss?"

"Precisely. On the one hand, I hear various family voices telling me to make nothing of it. I don't need the horse or the coin he'd bring. I have no wish to see another man hang on any account short of murder with malice aforethought, and the whole business will just stir up more talk of the sort I do not enjoy. Then too, I'm hungry."

A wiry young groom went by, leading a pair of geldings in from the water trough.

"On the other hand?" Ormstead asked.

"I'm supposed to leave today or tomorrow. Whoever did this is figuring that I am more interested in quitting the premises than in catching a thief."

"He might figure that selling that horse will keep his family fed for the summer."

"Poaching a few trout is easier. Stealing eggs is safer. Hiring on at Makepeace for a month or so to prepare for and manage the house party is easier still."

Ormstead ambled off toward the trough sitting outside the stable and to the left of the barn doors. I fell in step with him, though I'd have another look at the whole scene and chat up more than the head lad, who was bound by common sense to know nothing and say less than nothing.

"You think somebody wanted to make a point," Ormstead observed. "What will you do about it?" Clearly, Ormstead wished I'd saddle Atlas and trot off to Town.

"Somebody took the correct saddle, Ormstead."

"Noticed that, did you?"

A saddle had to fit the horse wearing it, or riding became more difficult. A poorly fitting saddle could also result in galls, a sore back, and even lameness for the horse. Some horses became fractious if the saddle impeded their movement or distributed the rider's weight incorrectly. Bridles and bits were similarly fitted specifically for each horse. No former cavalry officer could overlook that Trafalgar's saddle and bridle had been taken along with the horse himself.

"Which begs the question," I said quietly, "how many people knew which saddle belonged to that horse?"

"And answers another question," Ormstead replied. "You won't let this drop, will you?"

"Would you?"

The groom led two more thirsty geldings out of the barn and waited a few yards off.

"How could I," Ormstead replied, "how could *anybody*, possibly know what it is to stand in your boots, my lord? This might be another prank in exceedingly bad taste, or something more serious. Bruiting about a tale of horse thievery at the Makepeace house party will win you nobody's favor, though, so I'd let it drop."

I walked off to the shade of the nearest oak, a venerable specimen that had likely been guarding the stable yard since Good Queen Bess's day. Ormstead came with me, and the groom went about his task watering the stock.

"I don't intend to bruit anything about," I said, "but while I'm here, I'll see what I can learn." The part of me that had come alive reading signs by the summer cottage approved of that decision, as did the former reconnaissance officer who'd been able to predict the location of the French camp by watching a rain shower move across an otherwise parched valley.

"They won't like you for it." Ormstead's tone suggested he wouldn't like me for it.

"The other guests will delight in despising me no matter what I say, do, imply, insinuate, or fail to mention. I have become like a shuttlecock to them, an object to bat about for their amusement. The French commandant who took me prisoner had more regard for his captives than these people have for me."

A memory floated by, just out of reach. That French fiend Girard offering me wine and sympathy. Condolences on the loss of my brother... and something else. Something elusive and telling.

"I'm for breakfast, my lord. I'll wish you good hunting and Godspeed."

God speed you on your way. Ormstead was not my enemy, but he'd made it clear he wasn't an ally either. He'd also taken his sweet time speaking up on my behalf in the face of Cleary's aspersions.

A good officer learned to follow orders without question, to do as he was told and not step out of line. A smart officer learned to interpret his orders creatively on occasion, to set them aside for a prudent interval before reading them.

A brilliant officer defied orders and didn't get caught.

I'd never been a brilliant officer, but I certainly excelled at bending rules. On that thought, I took myself back into the stable and asked to speak not to the head lad, but rather, to whomever had been first on duty that morning.

The wiry groom presented himself before me at the watering trough. "You wanted to see me, my lord?"

"I do, but let's find some shade, shall we?"

He came along, his steps dragging. He apparently knew something pertinent to Trafalgar's disappearance and wished he did not.

CHAPTER SEVEN

The British military operated on the principle that enlisted men should be more terrified of their superiors than of the enemy, and all too many officers liked it that way. I had not, and thus I'd followed in Harry's footsteps and taken a job that freed me from ordering subordinates about.

I could not order this fellow about, so I adopted the sidewise approach common to most reconnaissance officers.

"I am in the awkward position of owning a horse I cannot describe," I said. "Can you tell me what this Trafalgar looks like?"

The groom's shoulders relaxed. "He's a big fella, my lord. Seventeen hands, maybe seventeen one. Well-sprung barrel. Clean legs, deep chest. Looked like a prime goer, but quiet to handle."

"He's a chestnut?"

"Aye, four white stockings and a white star on the forehead. Pretty piece of horseflesh and in good condition. He'd be up to your weight over fences."

"Any quirks?"

"My lord?"

We were enjoying the shade—and privacy—to be had under the

oak, which was slightly downwind of the stable yard. Another groom led Atlas out to the water trough. Judging from my horse's coat, he'd had a good roll somewhere pleasantly dusty and was enjoying house-party life.

At least one of us was having a fine time.

"That fellow," I said, nodding at Atlas, "is terrified of geese. He'll charge straight at enemy artillery, hold his own with a bossy mare, and swim the Channel, but a flock of geese sends him right 'round the bend. Always has."

The groom's lips quirked at one side. "Geese?"

"Parts with his dignity at the first honk, and him a warhorse."

"I've known some that can't stand sight nor sniff of the cows. Others take a fright at flapping laundry. There's no telling what goes on in a horse's mind."

"Did Trafalgar have any such quirks?"

"Nothing in partic—" The groom fell silent as Atlas slurped nois-ily. "Trafalgar loathes ponies. Mr. Cleary didn't bring a valet with him, but he has an older fellow along who's a kind of man-of-all-work. Not quite a footman, not quite a groom. He said to watch the chestnut around ponies—proper hates 'em—but nobody told Wicker-sham that. He went to turn out the gelding for a night at grass and led him around the pony paddock. You'd have thought the end times were a-coming for those ponies. There's Trafalgar, squealin' and kickin', ears flat to his head. You could have heard the ruckus clear to London. That horse despises ponies, or my name's not Jamie Chubb."

"I knew a mare like that once. She was gentle as a lamb most of the time, but a donkey wasn't safe around her."

Atlas finished drinking, water dripping from his hairy chin. He swung his head to peer at me.

"He knows your voice," Chubb said. "They have sharper ears than we do."

"And thank God for that. Wellington's camps were always protected by pickets, but the pickets were protected by the keen hearing and night vision of the horses."

"And who protected the horses?" Chubb murmured, revealing a true equestrian's priorities.

Atlas pulled gently on the lead rope as if he'd like to come over and have a word with me. The sun was above the horizon, but I still had an hour or so before the brightness would become painful.

"Can you direct me to a shaded bridle path, Chubb? I'm of a mind to take yonder steed for a hack."

"He'll like that. He's not a fellow given to idleness. Wick! Saddle that beast for his lordship."

Wick—a lanky, tow-headed lad—grinned and led Atlas back into the barn.

"If you want to avoid the sun, my lord, stay near the river. That path is in shade all day, and it's peaceful. You'll come to the village in a mile or so, but mind Potter's cider. Much more than a pint, you'll land on your arse if you down it too quick-like."

"My favorite kind of cider."

"Will you want a groom with you, my lord?"

Did Chubb hope to come with me—to escape the barn chores for an hour?—or dread spending time in the company of the official house-party outcast?

"I should be able to navigate to the village unaided."

Chubb eyed me in a manner a house servant never would have. He assessed me, not disrespectfully per se, but unapologetically. "You rode dispatch, my lord?"

"Some. Mostly, I was reconnaissance."

Chubb scuffed at the dirt with a toe of a dusty boot. "That chestnut, Trafalgar, has four white stockings."

"Very fashionable of him." Or vain of Cleary. One paid more for a horse with matching markings on all four legs. A plain trot became a trifle flashy on such a fortunate equine.

"Right hind stocking is a couple inches shorter than the other four. Somebody painted it or powdered it to match. This time of year, the grass is high and the dewfall heavy. When we brought the gelding in yesterday morning, we could see where the white was fading.

Cleary's man complained about it. Said his duties were never supposed to include painting and powdering horses, but that's the Quality for ya."

Stranger tricks were pulled at Tatts every week, which explained in part why horse trading had such a scurrilous reputation.

"And this morning, when you went out to fetch the gelding from his paddock, he simply wasn't there?"

"Not hide nor hair, and we looked all about, sir. We saw no trail through the wet grass, no scrapes along the top fence boards. The fairies snatched him."

A very different scenario than if the horse had been taken from his stall. In some ways, the shrewder approach was to liberate the animal from the field rather than risk waking whoever was on night watch in the barn.

If I compensated Chubb's honesty with coin, I risked offending a good man. If I did not, I risked offending a practical man.

"You have made it very easy for me to identify Trafalgar if I can find him in the next few days."

"But you'll be leaving soon, to hear Canny tell it."

I had been an object of gossip in the servants' hall, though perhaps not unkind gossip. "I'm reluctant to leave without my new horse. Which direction is the pony paddock?"

"Far side of the yearlings," Chubb said, gesturing with his chin. "Little blighters are worse than goats for taking the grass right down to the roots, so they get the scrubbiest patches and thrive on 'em."

"While the riding stock won't keep weight on without extra oats. When the end times come, my money's on the ponies and the mules."

Chubb smiled and cocked his head. "You're not a bad sort, my lord."

High praise, and sincerely meant. "Thank you. My fondest wish is that Atlas shares your opinion of me. You'll keep an eye on him until I take my leave?" That arrangement would allow me to pass along a vail on honorable terms.

"Aye, not that he needs much looking after."

"He's partial to apples and loves to have his shoulders scratched. Thank you for your time, Chubb."

He nodded and marched off.

Once I gained the saddle, I assessed the information Chubb had passed along. A brisk canter beside the river appealed to me, and—based on some silliness in the stable yard—to Atlas as well, but one must not exert one's mount too precipitously. I turned Atlas along the fence line to amble past the yearlings and on around to the pony paddock.

As I watched the bay yearling get up to his usual bad manners —he was bullying a sturdy gray today—I tried to picture what Chubb had described. Somebody had known which horse to steal, had known which saddle and bridle to carry out to the paddock, and had had the skill to catch the horse and get him bridled and under saddle by moonlight. That person had also been able to mount from the ground rather than with the aid of a raised mounting block—not so easy if the horse is tall and unsettled and the person short.

Had Trafalgar known his abductor? The facts suggested he had.

I was reminded that based on the tracks I'd found, whoever had accosted Hyperia had been about my height, perhaps a trifle shorter. Was I dealing with one culprit—an amorous horse thief?—or were the incidents unrelated? Miss Longacre had been adamant that Hyperia's attacker had run hotfoot to the stable, and somebody had been happy to support that fiction.

Atlas toddled along the pony paddock and past an enclosure apparently allowed to lie fallow for a few weeks, and then we came to the slightly overgrazed pasture where Trafalgar had been turned out.

Something was bothering the back of my mind like a persistent mosquito interrupting a picnic. Atlas stood patiently while I considered Chubb's recitation. A painted hind sock for vanity's sake, or was that measure intended to disguise the horse's true identity? But an adequate ruse would take more than adding a couple inches of white to the horse's markings.

That wasn't what bothered me. Something else, something to do with—

The bay brat began squealing and rearing at the gray, who wasn't giving ground. The smaller fellow instead got in close when the bay went up on his hind legs and delivered a solid double-barrel kick to the bay's belly.

"Serves you right."

The lord of mayhem stood for a good minute, head down, ribs heaving. He'd not go after the gray again today. The gray sidled up to the previous day's victim—a chestnut colt—and began companionably munching grass.

Pasture politics took all of five minutes to sort out, but the sorting was serious business.

"That's it," I said, urging Atlas forward. "Whoever stole Trafalgar knew not to make him pass the pony paddock again."

Of course, it was possible that avoiding the ponies had been purely coincidence, but not likely given how the bridle paths ran in the vicinity of the stable. To get to the trail along the river, I'd have to pass the ponies. To avoid the park with its exposure to the manor house, I'd have to pass the ponies.

Somebody who knew Trafalgar and knew the property had taken the horse. Mendel Cleary again came to mind as the most likely suspect, or Cleary's man had removed the horse from the premises at his employer's behest.

That struck me as the likelier scenario. In the event of discovery, Cleary could deny any involvement and see his employee tried as a horse thief. I knew many an officer built to the same self-serving specifications.

I was pondering the ramifications of my theory when I reached the river path. Atlas was ready for a run, but that was not to be. Hyperia, perched sidesaddle upon a dainty black mare, came to the path from the direction of the stable. A groom on a cob trailed a respectable dozen yards behind her.

"My lord." She nodded regally. "Good morning."

"Miss West. Shall we ride together?"

~

Hyperia arranged her skirts, which needed no arranging, and sent a glance to the groom. "Lord Julian will serve as my escort, Thurlow. You may return to the stable."

Thurlow touched a finger to his cap and reversed direction.

"Hyperia, I sense you are not in the best of spirits. Did you sleep poorly?"

"I am in fine spirits, but don't think to charm me. I am out of charity with you, Jules, and I plan to stay that way."

Part of me wilted at that scold. I had no idea what I'd done to fall from her good graces, and losing her approval hurt. Hyperia was fair to a fault, and even if we would not suit as spouses, I considered her a friend.

"Cleary has already branded me a horse thief, I take it? Fast work, but then, the best way for a culprit to deflect guilt is to loudly point fingers elsewhere."

"Somebody stole a horse?" Hyperia asked, nudging her mare forward.

"Somebody made off with Cleary's gelding, who is now my gelding, and Cleary attributed the crime to me. I'm that determined to make a fool of him, again, or so he'd have it."

Hyperia peered over at me. "That's not good, Jules. Stealing a horse is a serious accusation."

"If I stole from myself, it's merely malicious gossip. Cleary also tried to accuse me of mauling you."

"You did not and could not have accosted me."

Her spirited rejoinder was a minor comfort. "Ormstead set him straight, and he believed Ormstead."

She flipped a lock of her mare's mane so the whole lay smoothly on the right side of the horse's crest. "You're leaving today, aren't you?"

"If Healy arrives."

"I think, Jules, that you'd better go whether or not Healy shows up. I really do believe that would be for the best."

The hell it would. "You are assaulted in the dark, somebody tampers with evidence of that crime, and my new horse is stolen before I even clap eyes on him. This somehow adds up to I'm supposed to leave the premises. Your reasoning eludes me. Please do explain."

Hyperia galloped off rather than obey even a politely worded order, and Atlas gave chase, though being a sensible sort, his pursuit was undertaken a safe distance from the mare's heels. We thundered past the village and kept on for a good half mile, by which time the mare was flagging.

Atlas, by contrast, was in good form. He had that quality known on the Peninsula as *brío escondido*—hidden fire, hidden verve. He was all docile good manners around the stable, but point him at a challenge, and he leaped into the affray with courage and spirit, provided no geese were on hand.

We hadn't had a run like this in ages, and he gloried in pounding past the mare and then pulling away from her. I had to urge him to moderate his pace lest I fail in my duty as the lady's escort. By the time I trotted him back to Hyperia's mare, Atlas was passaging and snorting like a stud before his band of ladies.

"Don't let Brimstock see Atlas go like that," Hyperia said. "His lordship will try to wager the horse away from you."

"Atlas is family," I said, patting his sweaty neck. "And, for the present, my only riding mount. I would no more sell him than I'd leave this house party when there's serious mischief afoot and your brother is kicking his heels in Town."

We gave the horses a loose rein and turned them back in the direction of the village.

"Healy's not kicking his heels," Hyperia said. "I have the traveling coach and the baggage coach, and that left him only the Town coach, which has developed some problem with an axle or the single-tree or something. Summer means everybody needs their conveyances to get out of Town, so he can't borrow a vehicle. He doesn't want me here without my own carriage, else I'd send the traveling coach back for him."

"Then he can come by post."

"With his luggage? Two weeks of proper attire doesn't exactly fit in a satchel, Jules."

"Is he avoiding his duty?"

"Oh, perhaps."

Was Healy West avoiding *me*? Was he that angry at me for having backed away from an understanding with his sister? He and I had not crossed paths since I'd cried off, and perhaps that had been by design on his part.

"Hyperia, this business with the missing horse is serious, you are right about that." The business with somebody assaulting her was more serious. I'd raise that point later if need be. "Our horse thief knew the animal's particular habits—Trafalgar takes loud, violent exception to ponies—and knew exactly which saddle to put on his back. If we agree that the stable lads have no wish to be tried for horse thievery, Cleary appears in a very peculiar light."

"A suspicious light?"

The sun was making its inevitable ascent, but the bridle path remained shady. I had time and privacy to explain my reservations to Hyperia, so I gave her the benefit of my concerns.

"Why wager your horse if you aren't willing to part from him?" I asked in conclusion.

The *clip-clop* of shod hooves filled the bucolic quiet.

"Because you're mad keen for battledore and certain of victory?"

"Cleary wagered *his horse* for my specs, Hyperia, and that is an unsound bet, unless he was desperate to virtually blind me in bright sunshine. I have three spare pairs of tinted glasses. I'm carrying a spare set now, in fact."

"Your eyes are that bad?"

"They *were* that bad. Napoleon learned early in his military career that if he blew up his opponent's powder wagon, he created a hell of an intimidating explosion, threw the enemy into confusion, and seriously curtailed their fighting resources. Our artillery learned to retaliate, and I got too close to a bit of minor good luck for our side."

"But that was at least a year ago."

And what a fine year it had been. "My point is, Cleary wasn't thinking straight if he bet a horse he refuses to surrender against an opponent whose abilities he hadn't assessed."

"He probably did assess you. You are gaunt, white-haired, retiring to the point of eccentricity, have an unfortunate past, and you apparently cannot afford a valet."

I seized on the only charge I could refute. "I have a valet."

"I know that, and Ormstead might know that, but Cleary is not a former officer. He's rusticating gentry who doesn't travel in the same circles as your siblings. He judged you based on the available evidence, and you appeared eminently defeat-able."

Cleary had not brought a valet, but nobody considered that an eccentricity.

"But to bet his *horse*, Hyperia, when he's a pinchpenny miser in other regards, and Trafalgar is a handsome and well-trained specimen. Then Cleary tried to insinuate that I had attacked you. When I pressed him to reveal the basis for that accusation, he hedged."

The village came into view, a snug little gathering of houses and shops arranged around a glistening market green and punctuated with a low steeple adorning a whitewashed granite house of worship.

For this—for this peaceful, pleasant, sleepy little village and hundreds of others like it—I would risk my life again gladly.

"What's your point, Jules?"

"My point is that Cleary has behaved oddly. On the one hand, he's supposedly all solicitous devotion to his aging auntie, the brother left humbly tending the home fires when battle rages, an eligible and well-heeled bachelor. On the other hand, he more or less cheats at cards and shows more antipathy toward me than the men who by rights hate me. Cleary makes me uneasy."

"You make *everybody here* uneasy. What on earth was that battledore display supposed to prove?"

We had come at last to the reason for Hyperia's ire. "My display was supposed to prove that when grown men get to scrapping over stupid slights to their pride, they ought not to risk injuring innocent ladies in the process."

That seemed to spike her guns, albeit temporarily. "It wasn't your place, my lord. You are an uninvited guest."

What was she getting at? "Defending the defenseless is the place of every fellow of honorable character. I hope I didn't leave the entirety of my honor in France, Hyperia."

"Jules, you *punished* Cleary."

"Cleary damned near ripped Miss Longacre's earlobe off, and Lord Longacre refused to take a hand in matters."

"You were intimidating. You *frightened* these people. You nearly gelded Cleary over a stupid game."

Not nearly enough. "The shuttlecock went exactly where I aimed it. Is giving Miss Ellison a shiner within the rules of this stupid game? What of drawing Miss Longacre's blood? Nobody stepped forth, Hyperia. Nobody put a stop to the nonsense even when it turned ugly. Cleary got less than he deserved, and if you disagree, then we are at *point non plus*."

She gathered up her reins. "The men behaved badly, but your solution also put you in a bad light. Talk over breakfast is that you need a long repairing lease in the north to settle your nerves."

The north being a euphemism for walled estates where hysterical spinsters and inconvenient wives were sent to be forgotten, the less genteel version of putting a relative on remittance.

"And this is why you want me to leave? Because my behavior has become yet another inspiration for gossip?"

She nodded and did not meet my eyes. The part of me that was sick of being unwelcome, sick of causing talk, railed against her judgment. The part of me that could systematically search out the ideal location for slaughtering French farmboys and their uncles took a different view.

"At the usual house party," I said slowly, "my challenge to Cleary would have inspired him to wager his best sword stick against my pearl-handled peashooter. At worst, the loser would have had to swear off spirits for the duration of the house party or perform some aria for the amusement of the other guests. Cleary would have called me humorous names between points. I would have insulted his tailor. A winning shot that smacked his thigh would have inspired naughty innuendo from the onlookers. The same point would have been made, nobody the worse for the exercise."

"But this is apparently not a usual house party," Hyperia said. "I cannot put my finger on what exactly is amiss, but there's rancid butter in the recipe somewhere, and I want you away from it."

"You seek to keep me safe?"

She urged her mare forward at the trot. Atlas kept pace easily.

"You seek to keep me safe, but I'm not permitted to keep you safe?" I pressed.

"I am a spinster of no particular importance. You are... Lord Julian. You were a curiosity before you arrived, and now you have earned at least Cleary's ire. You are better off away from here."

Hyperia's mare had not yet recovered her wind from the earlier gallop. "Hyperia, slow down. For the sake of your horse, let us resume a more modest pace."

She acquiesced, while I entertained a riot of confusing emotion. Hyperia doubtless wanted smoother sailing for the house party and its guests going forward, but she was also protective of me.

Did I want her taking on that role? Did I need her to step into those shoes? Yesterday, she'd all but begged me to stay. Now, I was to decamp posthaste?

"Hyperia, is there something you aren't telling me?"

～

Hyperia let the reins go slack, and the mare resumed the plodding pace of the winded charger. "I overheard Lord and Lady Longacre on my way to bed last night. I looked for a shortcut to my room and ended up in the family wing."

"They want me gone too?"

"They were arguing with Miss Longacre, and, Jules, this was not a tiff. Miss Longacre was firing with both barrels, and her mother was returning insult for insult. They were furious."

"With a house full of guests. Interesting."

"Not interesting. Sad, wrong, completely uncalled for. Lord and Lady Longacre are going to great effort and expense to host this affair, and Miss Longacre was apparently against the whole notion. 'You did not listen to me. You never listen to me. Why did God afflict me with parents such as this?'"

The late duke had bellowed a similar litany about me. "We say things in anger that we don't truly mean."

"That platitude is generally served up when somebody has for once said exactly what they mean. I hurried away lest I be caught eavesdropping and also because the whole exchange was completely out of bounds. If Miss Longacre has no interest in any of the eligibles on hand, she can be merely polite to them for a fortnight, and they will move along to the next house party. I don't understand what fueled such a passionate disagreement."

"And those angry words upset you."

"Made me sick to my stomach, Jules. I might not adore my family at all times, but I'd never adopt such a scathing tone with them. If Miss Longacre seeks revenge on her parents for inflicting the house party on her, then you could become embroiled in an unfortunate situation."

"To what end?" I posed the question even as I heard the hoof-beats of an approaching mount from around the next bend in the path.

"I don't know to what end. I am worried, and I wish I had never accepted this invitation, except that I am glad to have spent some time with you. You truly are on the mend, aren't you?"

"Yes," I said with more confidence than I'd felt in ages. "I am."

William Ormstead slowed his horse to the walk and tipped his hat to Hyperia. "Miss West, my lord. Good morning. Beautiful time of day, isn't it?"

Hyperia bestowed on him a smile of quiet radiance. Had Atlas not been such a stalwart fellow, I might well have fallen from the saddle.

Miss Hyperia West was *lovely*. Not merely pretty, not just nicely curved or all the other things men said about women they couldn't admit they truly admired. She was *lovely*. The morning light found fire in her dark hair, her gaze was gracious and benevolent, and her features were a perfect assemblage of feminine pulchritude.

She dressed so as not to call attention to herself, spoke modestly, and behaved circumspectly, but my dear friend Perry had made a conquest, and damn Ormstead for being perceptive enough to see what a treasure she was.

"Ormstead, good morning," I said. "Atlas is ready for another run, while Miss West's mare has yet to recover from our last gallop. Miss West, would you be very wroth with me if I excused myself in the name of keeping my equine fit?" Atlas had no need to leave the scene, but I did.

Hyperia's smile dimmed but did not disappear, while Ormstead looked as if I'd gifted him with the Freedom of London's Pubs.

"Enjoy your gallop," Hyperia said, "but please consider what we discussed. Safe journey, my lord."

"I will consider your observations most carefully, Miss West."

Ormstead merely flicked a pleased glance at me and nudged his gelding alongside Hyperia's mare. I asked Atlas for a canter, and we parted company.

Safe journey *to London*. The prudent course, the course my ducal brother would doubtless advise me to take. Life had challenges enough, according to Arthur. One needn't use hornet's nests for target practice.

At the slightest urging, Atlas lifted into a gallop and added a little buck for good measure. My boy was happy to be in the country and letting me know it. We sailed past the turnoff to the Makepeace stable and continued along the river, which made a long, shallow curve at the foot of the park bordering the formal gardens.

Even Atlas, though, had his limits, and when I felt him begin to tire, I brought him to the trot and then the walk, aiming him on a shady track across the park.

"We can't work off the fidgets like that in London, can we?" As Atlas toddled along, I considered paying a call at the Caldicott family seat, a sprawling monstrosity over in Sussex. Arthur had not invited me to bide there this summer, and because I wasn't sure of my welcome, I had remained in Town.

"Stinking Town." Especially in summer, when the combination of higher temperatures and low water on the Thames turned the metropolitan jewel of the empire into an open sewer. I was toying with the notion that I did not truly want to return to Town—all house-party considerations aside—when a female voice joined the chorus of birds singing their greetings to the day.

The birdsong was lovely. The human contribution to the morning's melodies was, by contrast, one of the bawdiest to ever grace my no-longer-virgin ears.

～

I urged Atlas over to a faux ruin that boasted a sturdy belvedere. A good thirty feet up, Miss Longacre had propped a casual hip against the railing. As she sang, she gestured to me with a silver flask that glinted in the morning sun like a signal mirror.

"Lord Julian, good day. Fine horse you have there. *The Dey of Algiers, when afraid of his ears,*

A messenger sent to the Court, sir. As he knew in our state the women had weight, he chose one well hung for the sport, sir."

Great, roaring Jehovah. I knew not whether to burst out laughing or pretend I hadn't heard her. Instead, I joined in as I dismounted and started up the steps.

"He searched the Divan till he found out a man, whose balls were heavy and hairy. And he lately came o'er from the Barbary shore, as the great Plenipotentiary."

We were creating a racket sufficient to scare the game, but such was the morning breeze that I doubted we could be heard from the house. I gained the viewing platform, intent on coaxing the lady from her dangerous perch.

"I don't know the next verse," she said, waggling her flask at me. "Brimstone wouldn't tell me, the blighter."

Brimstone? An ironic nickname, and a tad less impolite than his *nom de boudoir*. I approached the balustrade cautiously and lowered my voice.

"When to England he came," I sang, *"with his prick in a flame, he showed it to his Hostess on landing, who spread its renown thro' all parts of the town, as a pintle past all understanding."*

Miss Longacre smiled devilishly. "The rest, please. I must have the rest, and what a fine singing voice you have."

"So much there was said of its snout and its head, that they called it the great Janissary: Not a lady could sleep till she got a sly peep, at the great Plenipotentiary."

The verses went on from there, each more ribald than the last. I held out my hand to Miss Longacre rather than further corrupt a delicate blossom of English maidenhood.

"Come meet my horse. He's a great fan of Captain Morris's songs."

She blinked at me owlishly, took my hand, got to her feet. "Morris wrote that verse?"

"And many others like it."

"Very naughty," she said with the exaggerated profundity of the inebriated. "A pintle past all understanding. They all baffle me. I haven't one myself, you know. A pintle, that is."

"No great loss, I assure you. Pintles have a tendency to lead one into foolishness. Atlas awaits us below. Shall we?"

I took my time on the dark, winding descent lest my singing companion lose her footing. She came along docilely, and we reached terra firma without incident.

"Miss Longacre, may I present to you Atlas, late of Iberia. Atlas, Miss Longacre, a fine soprano with very broad musical tastes." At a cue from me, Atlas bowed, and Miss Longacre went off into raptures about the darling horsey and why couldn't grown men be more like him—quiet and polite and ever so handsome? She did fancy his nose too. A grand nose, not a mere snout...

As she chattered on, I realized that Hyperia had been right: My continued presence at the house party had put me at risk to become embroiled in a *very* unpleasant situation. I had to discreetly return a sozzled Miss Longacre to the house and put her into the care of her trusted lady's maid.

Pray God she had one of those. Not all Gothic heroines did.

What's more, I had to accomplish this feat without appearing to have had any hand at all in bringing the young lady to her current state or location.

"How does the second verse go again?" Miss Longacre asked. "I can't recall it."

"*When to England he came, with his prick all aflame...*" I sang very quietly, Miss Longacre trundling beside me as I led Atlas around to the back of the belvedere. Trees and robust, blooming rhododendrons would obscure our presence from anybody at the house. I racked my brain for a solution to this peculiar contretemps—and for the rest of the verses to a most inappropriate song.

I sought a means of preserving both the lady's good name and my freedom, because she and I were in the mother of all compromising circumstances.

CHAPTER EIGHT

"I'm drunk," Miss Longacre observed, stroking Atlas's neck. "I've always wanted to be drunk. I do not want to be married."

"Strong spirits have a certain appeal." I assessed the belvedere, the rising sun, and the woods around us. "Though you shall pay for your excesses."

"Will I have a sore head?"

She might well have a husband in the person of my dubious self. "And you will ache and be so thirsty you could drink a Scottish loch dry. Your joints might pain you, and your thoughts could be fuddled into tomorrow."

"My thoughts are not fuddled," she said, giving the *f* particular force. "I am quite certain that I refuse to be married off to some handsome bounder. I'm eighteen. Do you know how young eighteen is? My grandmama lived to be eighty-three, and she was probably knocking a few years off that figure for vanity's sake. I want to live to be vain at eighty-three, though I'm no great beauty."

If she recalled that speech tomorrow, she might be embarrassed by it, though I found her words touching. I well knew how young eighteen was, and yet, I'd buried many eighteen-year-olds in Spain and France.

Old enough to take the king's shilling or buy their colors, but under English law, not old enough to marry without saying, *Papa, may I?*

"I like you," Miss Longacre said, making a clumsy effort to braid a hank of Atlas's mane. "You came here for Lady Ophelia's sake, and you stayed for Miss West's. When all those other louts were laughing about hysterical women, you were trying to find the scoundrel who bungled so awfully with Miss West. Mama says you are bad *ton*, but Papa says a ducal heir cannot *be* bad *ton*. We had a great row about that, among other things. I feel a touch queasy."

How the hell—how the rubbishing hell—could I extricate us from this situation? Atlas began to crop at the sparse grass. Bad form to graze when he was under saddle, but he was also due for his morning oats.

I could pretend that Miss Longacre and I had simply gone for a pre-breakfast promenade in the garden, but anybody could see us emerging from the trees. That same person might have noticed Miss Longacre's flask glinting up on the viewing platform. Worse yet, her condition would become obvious as soon as she opened her mouth, as would the fact that I had been private with an inebriated female first thing in the day...

Disorderly retreat came to mind. Leave Maybelle here to fall asleep while I quietly mentioned to Hyperia that somebody of the female persuasion ought to look for a missing hoyden in the vicinity of the belvedere.

Though somebody of the male persuasion might come along with nefarious intent. One woman had already been assaulted at this blasted house party. Then too, Hyperia was off charming Ormstead somewhere in the wilds of Kent. Given how eager Ormstead was to be charmed, she might be occupied for hours yet. I wasn't about to rely on Lady Ophelia's good offices.

"Miss Longacre?"

"You can call me Maybelle. You taught me the verse about the pintle past all understanding, not that I understand pintles in the general case."

"Would you like to become my wife?"

She left off twiddling Atlas's mane and studied me with earnest focus. "You aren't bad-looking, for all that white hair, and you are a ducal heir. Mama would weep, or pretend to, but Papa would loooooove to have a ducal connection. He didn't have to spell that part out. I'd be a duchess someday, if your brother failed to have a son. I'd be Lady Julian rather than Plain Miss Longacre, even if His Grace was froo... fruitful."

"All true, but you'd be married to a man who's rumored to be a traitor. To hear your mother tell it, I'm a bird dropping on the family escutcheon."

"You too?" She giggled like the schoolgirl she'd recently been. "I'm a disgrace, a tribulation, and I forget what else Mama said. You and I could be bird droppings together."

Bless her, she was truly unhappy being Plain Miss Longacre. "Do you seek merely to be Lady Julian?"

Her brows knit, as if the question required significant concentration. "You aren't proposing, but if you did, I'd have to decline. Not because of the coward and traitor bit, which is nonsense. Prancing popinjays, the lot of them muttering such things. Ormstead served, and he's not joining in the verbal assisin...assassin... the gossip. I don't want to die, you see."

She leaned against Atlas's neck, and I feared we had reached the lachrymose portion of the program.

"You appear in good health to me, miss."

"I am very healthy, except for my lamentably high spirits and my unguarded tongue, and I forget what else Mama doesn't like. My finishing governess said I have a good bosom."

I hurt for her, being assessed as if she were a heifer fattened for market. "You have an independent spirit, and in a young woman, that's often terrifying to those responsible for her wellbeing."

"I don't feel terrifying. I feel terrified. Ginny died, you know, and the doctor said it was God's will. Then Portia nearly died—bled for ages, went through fevers and everything—and then she did die, even though the fevers had let up. God's will again. God's will seems to require a lot of needlessly dead women. God is apparently keen on slaughtering all manner of fellows on the battlefield too—the same God for the French, the British, and all those other nations—despite the generals being the ones giving the orders. My will is to stay alive."

She looked up at the bright blue sky above the canopy of maples. "Sorry, God." She stuck out her tongue and made a rude noise.

What a charming drunk. "Is that why you offend anybody who looks like a marital prospect?"

She sighed, let go of the horse, and perched on a handy boulder among the rhododendrons. "I want to at least *like* the fellow if I'm to perish in bloody agony having his brats. Mama has a chart, with columns and rows. The bachelor names go down one side, and the columns include family standing, titles-if-any, number of properties, acres, wealth, ties to trade. Mama should have been a general. Your name is not on her chart, my lord, and you should thank your lucky stars."

As interesting as this discussion was, and as sad and endearing, the risk of discovery grew with each passing minute. Guests would seek the back terrace after breakfast, wander the garden before the day became too hot, and travel to and from the stable, orangery, and river path in dedicated pursuit of idleness.

Atlas continued to crop grass, while I tried to think like a reconnaissance officer, rather than like a cad who'd interrogate a captive when she was half seas over. Now wasn't the time to ask Maybelle why she'd lied about Hyperia's assailant taking off for the stable.

Now was the time to get the lady safely back to her boudoir.

The solution came to me as Miss Longacre drained the last drop from her flask.

"Then you don't seek to become Lady Julian?"

"I don't seek to become Lady Anybody, or Mrs. Anybody. When

I'm one-and-twenty, I come into funds of my own, and there's nothing Mama and Papa can say to it. They want me to think only of my settlements and forget what will come to me if I'm not married. I'm eighteen. I'm not stupid."

She was frightened and determined and an all-around fine young woman. "You're a bit tipsy, is all, and you sought the age-old and notoriously foolish comfort of the bottle, or flask as the case may be, but if you don't seek to marry me—my most grievous loss—then we must get you up to your rooms with nobody the wiser. Neither the other guests nor your parents are to know, do you understand?"

She scowled at her empty flask, which probably wasn't hers, but rather, Lord Brimstock's spare. "I don't understand anything. Why can't Mama just leave me alone?"

I withdrew from my breast pocket the small notebook and pencil I always carried with me—old habits died hard. I printed my message, because facile literacy among the stable lads was not a foregone conclusion, and tucked the note into the bar from which the left stirrup leather hung, such that an edge of white paper peeked out from between folds of saddle leather. I loosened the girth a hole, and ran up both stirrups and secured them so they would not flap against Atlas's sides.

I then tied up his reins so he'd not inadvertently get a foot caught and led him to the edge of the trees.

"Go get your oats, my boy. Don't tarry for more grass. Go where they can get this saddle off you and give you the proper brushing you deserve before you once again roll in the dust. Are we clear on your mission?"

Atlas swished his tail, as much of an affirmative reply as I was likely to get. I brandished my riding crop before his face.

"Go," I said, stepping back and pointing in the direction of the stable. "Shoo! Begone!"

Atlas trotted off a few steps, looked back at me, and then seemed to get into the spirit of the undertaking. Most equines enjoyed a good game of "loose horse," and Atlas was no exception. He was soon off down the bridle path by the river at a pounding trot and even kicked up his heels for good measure.

We waited barely fifteen minutes before Canning appeared, looking tired, but his usual good-humored self.

"Does my lord expect me to believe that the best rider on the premises had a mishap that resulted in torn breeches?" he said.

Miss Longacre stepped out from around the back of the belvedere. "Canny, you have come to rescue me!"

Canning looked from me to the young lady, who was doubtless starting to regret her folly. "I'm not the rescuing sort, miss."

"Yes," I said, "you are. Miss Longacre thought to enjoy the view from up top, but isn't feeling quite the thing. She doesn't want the other guests to see her under the weather. If you could discreetly fetch her lady's maid here—avoid the garden paths, keep to the trees —I will wait with Miss Longacre until the cavalry arrives. On that happy occasion, I will be nowhere in evidence, because I was never here and neither were you or Miss Longacre."

Canning was doubtless brimming with questions, but he was also very good at his job. "I'll fetch Miss Belvoir, my lord. She's an early riser and quite loyal to Miss Longacre."

He decamped at a jog, and the longest twenty minutes of my life ensued. Anybody could take a notion to explore the belvedere on such a fine morning. Anybody might notice that Miss Longacre and I were both late to breakfast.

"Where did you get the flask?" I asked her when Canny had been gone for about ten minutes. The vessel was plain pewter, no embossing and too capacious to be a lady's article for the hunt field.

"I found two flasks under my pillow when I went up to bed at nearly three in the morning. I refilled that one in the library. Might have spilled a bit. Came out here when the birds started up. Such a pretty sound, birdsong."

"And it did not strike you as odd that somebody would leave a quantity of spirits under your pillow?"

"Yes. Very odd, but I'd been arguing with one of the fellows—not Brimmie, not Banter. Somebody else was braying at me as if I haven't a brain in my head when all I asked for was a finger of brandy. One of the other gents got to sermonizing over cards. 'Ladies should never take strong spirits,' sayeth he. We survive patent remedies that are mostly brandy, take rum punch at Christmas, and enjoy a toddy with no ill effects, so why the stupid rule about ladies and strong spirits, which isn't really a rule, but just a saying used to keep us from tippling as all the fellows do?"

"Somebody gave you an opportunity to test your logic." And was that somebody watching from nearby as I wrecked his scheme to snabble a rich wife?

"I did not proffer logic," she said, putting a hand to her belly. "I argued facts. Women imbibe strong spirits—ladies do—but men pretend we don't, and we pretend we don't. I'm truly not feeling quite the thing."

"You would not be feeling quite the thing if you were a man who'd drained three flasks on top of wine with dinner and cordials over a very late night of cards. You are exhausted, in need of a quantity of water and lemonade, and you'd do well to become close friends with your toothpowder or a bushel of parsley. Don't let anybody talk you into laudanum or a patent remedy this morning. Sleep, time, and harmless liquids. A pot of China black when you've had some rest, and you're sure it will stay down."

Voices drifted through the woods, so I retreated to the shadows at the bottom of the staircase.

"You're very kind," Miss Longacre said as Canning appeared some distance off with an older lady at his side.

"I'm not even here, Miss Longacre. If you recall nothing else about this adventure, please recall that, lest you become Lady Julian and responsible for the whole burden of a ducal succession which I am duty-bound to take seriously." Or I should have been.

That seemed to sober her as nothing else had, and she was soon trundling off in the clucking company of her lady's maid.

"You can come out now," Canning said, "and I have a message for you from Lady Ophelia."

I emerged from the dank confines of the belvedere's foundation. "Hold your fire, for God's sake. Whatever Lady Ophelia wants, it can wait. That was a very, very near miss, for me and for the young lady."

Miss Longacre and her maid had broken from the trees and were strolling arm in arm across the park. For all anybody knew, Miss Longacre was taking the morning air—the maid's shawl obscuring her evening attire—before tucking into her breakfast. I wished her well and wondered what Hyperia would make of Maybelle's entirely valid reservations regarding marriage.

"Miss Longacre's lot isn't easy," Canning said, swatting a leaf from the toe of his boots. "Lady Longacre is ambitious for her daughter, and Lord Longacre hasn't sense enough to curb his wife's determination. Miss Maybelle needs some time to find her feet, is all."

"Like a filly new to training. Slow and steady makes for a trustworthy mount, while precipitous action can have permanent negative consequences."

Canning swatted at another leaf. "She's not a horse, my lord."

And I, thank the celestial powers, would not be her husband. "Do you know of a Portia or a Ginny?"

"Her cousins, they were like older sisters to her. They were close, though Portia and Ginny made their come outs one and two years ago, respectively. That was before my time, but the staff says Maybelle took their passing very hard."

Dead before they'd reached their legal majority. No wonder Maybelle was reluctant to enlist in the ranks of dutiful wives.

"Keep an eye on Miss Longacre, Canning, to the extent you discreetly can. While at cards, she took up the cause of women's right to drink strong spirits, and some fool thought to test her by putting two loaded flasks under her pillow. She refilled at least one of those flasks and will have a very, very sore head."

Canning's genial features lost their good humor. "For God's

sake... Too much liquor can be deadly, especially to the untried. That was a cruel and stupid thing to do."

"Also daring. Miss Longacre doubtless sleeps in the family wing, and her lady's maid, a chambermaid, a footman bearing coal, or her own mother could have intruded into her bedroom and found the culprit setting his bait." Unless the culprit had chosen his moment for when the family was embroiled in their argument.

"If it was a he," Canning said. "Some of the young ladies are none too fond of Miss Longacre. She has few friends."

"Because she had her cousins." As I had had Harry. "This is the damnedest house party I have ever attended."

"It's about to get damned-er, my lord. Lady Ophelia is asking to see you directly."

"Any idea why?"

"She wants you to escort her on some calls. Says it would be impolite to come all this way and not drop by to see friends in the area."

Hyperia had given me my congé, or tried to, but that was before I'd found the young lady of the house three sheets to the wind and bellowing vulgar verse to the heavens.

"I suppose I will find my godmother at the breakfast table?"

"With Brimstock on one side, Cleary on the other, and Banter sitting across from her. One has to admire her ladyship, albeit from a safe distance."

"Be glad you can maintain that safe distance, and my thanks for your assistance—again. You would have made a fine officer."

Canning guffawed, saluted, and marched off, and I was left to reflect that his diction was matched only by his discretion. He was probably loyal to the house, too, damn the luck, else I'd have tried to woo him onto my London staff.

As I made my way to my room, I passed an open parlor door. Miss Maria Cleary sat alone, her chair angled so she was in profile to me and facing a window onto the park. The morning light was such that I saw in her face the reflected beauty that she'd once claimed. Delicate features, thick hair gone as white as my own, regal bearing.

And yet, her head trembled slightly on a slender neck, her mouth was slack, and her shawl hung limply around her elbows. She was a ruin, while Ophelia, her contemporary, was a fine and lustrous antique.

Miss Cleary caught sight of me and beckoned. "Do come in, sir. Are you one of Mendel's friends?"

I might dodge a senior officer's orders, but I would never be rude to a lady. I entered the room and bowed. "Miss Cleary. Lord Julian Caldicott, at your service. I am acquainted with both Lieutenant Daniel Cleary and Mr. Mendel Cleary." I was acquainted with Miss Cleary, too, though she had aged considerably since before the war.

Five years ago, she'd given Ophelia a run for her money in the darling-senior-flirt steeplechase.

"The Caldicotts are tall," she said in a soft quaver. "Ophelia is tall. She is not a Caldicott."

According to family rumor, she halfway was, on the wrong side of the blanket a couple generations back. "Ophelia is my godmother. I'm her escort for purposes of this gathering."

"Do sit. I abhor a fellow who looms. Mendel looms and hovers. Like his father, that one."

I wanted to be anywhere but with this sad old lady, but then, so did apparently every other guest on the premises. They were assembled in merry pin down in the breakfast parlor, and I did not particularly want to be with them either.

"Mendel is devoted to you," I said, wanting to give credit where due. "How was your journey from Town?"

She sent a worried glance in the direction of her knees. "I'm not allowed in Town. Mendel says I need the country air. Nobody stays in Town these days anyway. Once grouse season starts, London is deserted."

Grouse season was still two months off. The king's birthday had passed, true, but the worst of summer's heat had yet to entirely decimate London's fashionable ranks. Did Miss Cleary know what month it was?

My sympathy for her expanded, such that I was no longer in a hurry to leave. "London is noisy and smelly in summer. Country air can be quite reviving."

She stole a glance at me. "Can it, really? Nobody calls in the country except the vicar. Vicar smells of camphor."

"Does he preach at you for all your wayward tendencies?"

My attempt at teasing earned me another worried glance. Prisoners had eyes like that; as did the elderly, apparently, when peering into the abyss of inchoate mental decline. Big, dark pupils full of bewilderment and a small, hopeless flame of rage.

"Vicar mostly wants money," Miss Cleary said. "I have pots of money. You mustn't tell anybody. Mendy looks after my funds for me. I should have married."

If she'd married, the pots of money would have become her husband's worry, assuming he yet dwelled among the living and assuming her pots of money truly existed. Her shawl was less than pristine. She wore neither gold nor jewels nor so much as nacre hairpins. Her house slippers were fit for the charity box.

"Lady Ophelia married," I said. "She suffered many griefs for becoming a wife and mother."

"You are her worst grief, my lord. She's quite clear on that. Always has been."

That observation stung, though it was the offering of a wandering mind. "I'm not that bad."

"You are very sweet to sit with me here. I don't suppose you'd see me back to my room?"

"I'd be happy to, unless you'd rather join the other guests downstairs?"

She gazed out upon the park, probably seeing Venetian breakfasts, ridottos, and gaiety long past. "I'd best not. Travel can be so wearying. We've been here a week, and still I am not at my best."

She offered me a sweet smile and rose when I gave her my hand. If she'd arrived with the other guests, she'd been on the premises three or four days.

Once I got her on her feet, she genuinely needed my arm to remain upright. We tottered into the corridor, and she aimed another smile, this one more determined than sweet.

"Lead on, my lord."

She obviously did not know where her room was, and neither did I. An inquiry to a passing maid solved our dilemma. Though our progress was stately, we did manage the ten yards to Miss Cleary's door.

The door whipped open when I would have lifted the latch.

"There you are, miss. Thank God." A woman of middle years and stout dimensions held the door open wider. "Please do come in."

She was attired not as a maid and must therefore be the companion—or nurse companion.

"Miss Cleary and I were enjoying a friendly chat," I said. "She's known me since I was in short coats." A slight exaggeration. "Lord Julian Caldicott, at your service."

An odd transformation came over the woman's features. She bobbed a curtsey best described as furtive.

"Thank you for your assistance to Miss Cleary, my lord. I'll see to her now."

Miss Cleary stood, hand on my arm, head bent like a penitent schoolgirl.

"I offered to see Miss Cleary downstairs. Perhaps you'd like to accompany us, Miss...?"

"Mrs. Waldrup."

"Wallie," Miss Cleary said softly. "Wallie is devoted to me."

"That, I am." Mrs. Waldrup's tone was genuinely fond. "We'll enjoy our breakfast on trays, my lord, though thank you for the thought." She took Miss Cleary gently by the arm, thereby removing Miss Cleary's hand from my sleeve.

"Perhaps we can breakfast together tomorrow," I said, an excess of gallantry, also an invitation to one of the few other guests who would not hold me in low esteem.

"Miss Cleary is seldom abroad in the morning," Mrs. Waldrup said, "though it's kind of you to ask. Come along, miss. You were very naughty to go exploring without me. All this travel has upset you, I'm sure. Let's have a tisane to settle your nerves."

"The raspberry," Miss Cleary said, brightening marginally. "I do enjoy my raspberry tisanes."

Mrs. Waldrup rearranged the shawl over Miss Cleary's shoulders and waited for me to take my cue.

I bowed. "Good day to you ladies, then."

I was halfway through the door when Mrs. Waldrup called after me. "My lord?"

"Ma'am?"

"You won't say anything to Mr. Cleary, will you? Miss Maria was only gone for a few moments, and she's safely returned, and Mr. Cleary does fret over her so."

The odd quality of Mrs. Waldrup's curtsey, the grimacing nature of her smile made sense. She feared being sacked. She was likely paid a pittance that she desperately needed, and she feared one momentary lapse in vigilance would cost her her post.

"Not a word," I said. "You may rely on my discretion."

Her relief was pathetic and also, I noticed, shared by Miss Cleary.

I took my leave, unsettled by the whole encounter, which had lasted perhaps ten minutes. Was a failing memory my first step toward the sort of timorous, retiring life Miss Cleary had been reduced to? Was I soon to regard a raspberry tisane as the highlight of my morning?

Torture at the hands of the French had been a terrifying thought, but the notion that I might end up drifting in a world without any mental or physical autonomy was a horror too vast to contemplate.

Whatever Mendel Cleary's other failings, that he was devoted to his aunt spoke well of him.

~

When I gained the privacy of my broom closet, I found a valise sitting at the foot of the bed. A day after my arrival, my luggage was finally on hand, and I was to unpack it myself.

"Brung your tray!" Atticus rapped on the open bedroom door while balancing the tray on his hip. "Thing's heavy if you don't mind my sayin' so."

"Set it on the vanity, please. Good morning again, Atticus." Even Arthur believed in polite acknowledgment of the people who prepared his food, looked after his clothes, and kept his house from falling down around his ducal ears.

Atticus kicked the door closed behind him, put the tray on the vanity, and made a fancy leg. "Good day, your toffship. I could unpack your duds. Idiot Taylor brung your trunk to Westmere's room, where it sat until idiot me saw it when I fetched the shaving water. Westmere don't have the blunt to put a family crest on his spare satchel. You have the same design on your ring."

Was temporarily misplacing my effects due to malice or incompetence? "The winged lion was on the Caldicott coat of arms when we held a mere barony. Another branch of the family uses three lion heads and a lot of other folderol. Bless you, child. You brought me eggs." And toast and ham and fat slices of what looked to be a ripe peach. "My compliments to the kitchen and to Cook specifically."

"Canny said to feed you up, and Cook is fond of Canny. She'd fix up a tray for Old Scratch hisself if Canny asked her to. Tea this time, because the coffee is all being drunk up in the breakfast parlor. Between cards at night for the gents and breakfast at dawn for the ladies, the staff be grumbling already."

Atticus wasn't grumbling, but neither was he decamping as readily as he might. A grumbling staff might take to cuffing the bootboy at the least provocation.

"Please deal with my luggage if you've nothing better to do," I said, taking a seat on the vanity stool. "Hang a sachet in the wardrobe before you put any clothing in there. The other sachet should go in the bottom drawer of the clothespress. If there's a third, that one goes on the bedpost nearest the night table."

He sniffed the little muslin bag of lavender sitting atop my packed clothes. "Pretty."

"Keeps the bugs away. Do you happen to know who was chaperoning the card games last night?" The eggs were hot and redolent of a tangy cheddar, the ham cooked to a turn, and the toast soaked in butter.

God bless a conscientious cook. As I made a breakfast sandwich from my feast, I realized that I was not eating simply because one consumed a morning meal. I was ravenous for good, plain fare. Famished, as I hadn't been for months.

"Taylor would know who was in the cardroom," Atticus said. "He had late duty last night. He's the only red-haired footman in all of Britain, to hear old Chessman tell it. Chessie's the butler, and he's a good sort." Atticus lifted one of my shirts from the trunk and fingered the cuff gently. "Some fine duds you got, sir. I'd be afeared to iron fabric this delicate." He held the sleeve up to the light, as if to peer through it.

"Bond Street tailors are the envy of the fashionable universe," I said, pouring myself a cup of steaming tea. "If you were apprenticed to a tailor, you might already know how to make such a shirt, though it could take you as much as two weeks of steady sewing. You'd spend your days sitting on a table by a window, praying for sunshine and good eyesight."

"And some jolly mates to work with." He laid the shirt out reverently on an open drawer of the clothespress, folded the sleeves this way and that, and then scowled. "I don't know how to do this."

For Atticus, that was probably among the hardest phrases to utter in the whole language.

"Like so," I said, tidying the shirt so it was free of wrinkles, then arranging the arms and cuffs in the traditional fashion. "The creases that form will not be visible once I put on my waistcoat and jacket." I showed him how to deal with satin knee breeches—yes, I'd brought a pair—and riding breeches, waistcoats, stockings, and trousers before finishing my breakfast.

I left two pieces of buttered toast and a thick slice of ham on the tray and silently lectured myself about putting off the inevitable.

"Are the ladies scheduled for any particular entertainment this morning?" I asked.

"Chasing the gents while appearing to ignore them," Atticus said, arranging my slippers beneath the clothespress. "Why put wings on a lion?"

"Because the lion is the king of beasts, and the eagle is the king of birds, so put them together—sometimes you'll see the winged lion with an eagle's beak—and you have an invincible creature."

"Birds can be shot outta the sky, and lions can end up in a menagerie. Pretty slippers." He waved my favorite pair of house slippers in my direction.

"My sisters are skilled with their needles. I'm off to find Lady Ophelia, and as soon as you've unpacked that trunk, I might ask you to pack it again, so try to recall how that was done."

"You're leaving?" He sounded disappointed, which was inordinately gratifying.

"I was never invited."

"But you're here, and Mr. West ain't, and Lady Longacre do set great store by everything being just so. If you leave, she'll be shy a bachelor."

"The lesser of two evils, apparently." I disdained to linger where I was unwanted, but neither was I comfortable abandoning Hyperia at a gathering where I'd found the daughter of the house soused and singing by dawn's early light.

To say nothing of a valuable horse going missing—*my* valuable horse—about which nobody seemed troubled save myself and the beast's former owner.

To say even less about Hyperia herself being assaulted by moonlight.

"I hope you're decent," snapped a female voice from the far side of my closed bedroom door, "though I've seen you and plenty of other fellows as God made you." Lady Ophelia charged into the room without further preliminaries.

"I was an infant when you had that privilege," I said, bowing. "My lady, good day."

"Is it? Is it a good day when my godson and escort cowers in his room rather than meet me over eggs and toast?"

"Are we dueling?"

Atticus found it expedient to focus on rearranging my footwear beneath the wardrobe.

"Out, boy," Lady Ophelia said. "Leave the door open. I don't care who hears me berating a thoroughgoing rascal for neglecting his duties."

Atticus shot me a look that said he'd stay if I needed him. A touching display of loyalty, perhaps, or a clever boy hoping to collect some gossip for the staff.

"If you'd take the tray, Atticus, I'd appreciate it."

He scampered off with his booty.

"They don't even send a footman to you." Ophelia took to pacing, her morning gown swishing as she prowled before the hearth. "By God, Betty Longacre has a nerve."

Betty? I could not credit my hostess answering to Betty.

"Her mother was the same way," Lady Ophelia went on. "All condescension and grace in the churchyard, but don't turn your back on her. Betty's ashamed, of course. Took her too perishing long to provide Longacre with an heir. No spare to be seen, so Longacre's brother hovers at his elbow like a vulture in winter. One understands where Miss Longacre gets her personality."

"She's grieving." I dragged a brush through my hair—my damnably white hair—and found a clean handkerchief to fold into a pocket. "She lost two cousins in childbed last year, and they were like sisters to her."

Too late, I realized my mistake. Ophelia came to a halt and studied me with narrowed eyes. "How would you know that? You were kicking your heels in France, and then caught up in the Hundred Days, and then... otherwise engaged."

"Canning, the footman, told me. He offered the family history in confidence by way of mitigation for Miss Longacre's lack of charm. She's not eager to follow her cousins to the grave."

"Nothing is more inconvenient to the polite world than a young lady attempting to think for herself. How well I remember..." Ophelia went to the window, which offered a dingy view of the roof of the conservatory and one corner of the back terrace. "Those deaths were not secrets, but why would a footman be interested in improving your opinion of Miss Longacre?"

"Loyalty to the family, I suppose."

Ophelia tried to open the window, which refused to budge no matter how she banged and tugged at the sash. "Hyperia West rode out with a groom and returned not fifteen minutes past with William Ormstead. Do you intend to let her slip away after all I've done to bring you two back together?"

"Yes."

Ophelia whirled to scowl at me. "Ungrateful gudgeon. You won't do better. Perry West isn't loud or hilarious, she's not dripping with jewels and titles, but she has a good head on her shoulders, and her mother isn't half mad."

"Hyperia is all that is lovely, and if Ormstead has sense enough to appreciate her, I wish her the joy of his attentions."

"Do you?"

I once again sensed I'd ridden into an ambush. "I most assuredly do."

Ophelia's expression became suspiciously pleasant. "Glad to hear it, because if they're of a mind to start courting at this house party, you will be witness to their billing and cooing."

"Hyperia has excused me from any obligation to her. I expect to leave for London tomorrow." Atlas could make the distance by sunset if he had to, but I'd asked much of him on our morning hack, and no wartime exigencies required that I demand heroic measures of my horse.

Lady Longacre's vanity did not signify compared to Atlas's wellbeing.

"And yet," Ophelia said, "here you are, because I have not excused you, and you aren't so far gone in your pouting that you'd strand me in these dismal surrounds without an escort."

I replied with the same exaggerated pleasantness she'd aimed at me. "Sparing my family and Society my unwelcome presence isn't pouting, and you have never been stranded in your life."

Something strange flickered across Ophelia's features. Not rage, not fear... sorrow, perhaps? Bewilderment? The emotion was too fleeting and complicated to be parsed.

"How like your father you sound. Even more than Arthur, you have the late duke's flare for martyrdom."

I'd learned from Papa that silence could be wielded for tactical purposes, and thus I held my tongue.

"You think you are Prometheus," Ophelia said, stalking up to me, "bound to the only rock of shame and loneliness in the whole of Britain. There's Maria Cleary, going nigh half-witted on me when she's six months my junior. She was always sharp as Toledo steel, Julian. Westmere has to leave because his mother *is* half mad, and he's been summoned home. She might well have tried to take her life again because some fool thought to withhold her laudanum.

"Banter prefers men, but he must do the pretty with a vengeance lest he end up on the business end of a hangman's noose. Cleary sent two brothers off to war. One came home lame, the other fell in with a pack of rotters and is said to be on remittance in Rome. Miss Ellison was visiting an aunt in Ireland for most of last year, and word is that the child she bore has been sent to a cousin in Wales. Longacre has only the one son, and the boy is dull-witted, to put it politely. Maybelle must marry a sensible man, or the family fortunes will sink precipitously."

What a sad litany for a group of people whom most would envy. "What has any of that to do with me?"

"First, you aren't leaving. Lady Longacre will now need you to keep the numbers from slipping further out of balance. She might recruit one late-arriving volunteer bachelor, but not two. Town is emptying out for the summer, and all the best bachelors are in demand elsewhere."

I disliked the sound of that. Staying because I was concerned for Hyperia and curious as to the whereabouts of my horse was one thing. Staying because Lady Longacre had a reason to tolerate me was quite another.

"What's second?" I asked with some trepidation.

"I require your escort over to Morelands."

The name took a moment to register. I associated the Morelands estate with summer playmates, long evenings racketing about on ponies with another ducal brood, and at least one peer and his wife who had regarded my father with genuine affection.

"You, my lady, are well equipped to travel five miles in a closed carriage without dragging me along." She should take Maria Cleary. Get the lady a bit of fresh air and scenery.

"So ride your horse."

"I've already put him very much through his paces this morning." I was resisting for form's sake, and also because some niggling unease had taken root where Ophelia was concerned. What was she up to this time?

Because she was always up to something.

"I was concerned for you," she said, "shut up all alone in that poky town house, lurking behind drawn curtains, your clothes hanging on you like winding sheets. You received nobody other than immediate family... But my concern was misplaced. You are simply too poutful and selfish to bestir yourself on another's behalf."

Poutful was not a word in any proper lexicon. "Godmama, you traveled to *Russia* when you were younger than I am now, for pity's sake. *In winter.*"

"I don't need you clinging to my skirts, you dimwit. Devlin St. Just bides at Morelands, and he could use the cheering sight of a fellow former officer."

The name landed like a mortar shell in the conversation. "Most former officers cross the street when they see me approach." St. Just would not. He was perceptive and good at convincing the unsuspecting that nothing bothered him. One could not call him shy, but neither was he as naturally boisterous and outgoing as his legitimate siblings.

"Her Grace is worried about St. Just," Ophelia said. "He weathered France and Spain, he dealt with the loss of the brother he was supposed to protect—as if one can protect a sibling and fellow soldier in wartime—and he has made being the bastard firstborn look easy, but he's not in good heart these days."

St. Just had come close to disgracing himself after Waterloo. Attacked a civilian on the horror that the battlefield had become when the fighting had ceased. The details were sketchy. He'd resigned his commission, and not much had been seen of him since.

"I'll come with you," I said, "but tomorrow I'm leaving for London, unless Lady Longacre herself *asks* me to stay."

"Well of course she must ask. Caldicotts don't grovel to anybody, ever, as I and the rest of the world had occasion to know. The coach is waiting for us out front."

I grabbed my hat, made sure my spare spectacles were in my pocket, and resigned myself to a tedious penance of a day.

My assumption in that regard, like many of my assumptions regarding Lady Longacre's house party, proved to be wildly inaccurate.

CHAPTER NINE

Colonel Devlin St. Just was black Irish on a robust, charming scale—
or he had been. The man I beheld in the Morelands formal parlor
was gaunt, dull of eye, and devoid of charm. In an odd way, he put me
in mind of the elderly Miss Cleary. St. Just was polite, too, of course,
though even good manners came across as an effort made for the sake
of his step-mother's sensibilities.

"Moreland is still in Town," the duchess said, "but we expect the
duke home any day. His Grace's parliamentary intrigues will ever
fascinate him, and then too, Westhaven seems determined to bide in
London this summer."

The Earl of Westhaven was heir to the Moreland dukedom, and a
perennial bachelor, much to his parents' despair and the matchmak-
ers' frustration.

Esther, Duchess of Moreland, was of an age with Lady Ophelia,
but cut from more majestic cloth. Whereas Ophelia was willowy and
languid, Her Grace, was dignified, statuesque, and gracious. Her
duke was legendarily devoted to her—*even at their ages*, as Ophelia
put it—and Her Grace had raised eight legitimate children as well as
two ducal by-blows conceived before Moreland had spoken his vows.

One did not trifle with the Duchess of Moreland, and attempting to toady to her was a worse choice yet.

She stunned me by treating me to a brief, fierce hug. "You are recovering," she said, running a maternal eye over me from boots to brow. "Not out of the woods, but on the mend. Don't let anybody try to hasten you back to the whirl, young man. Healing takes time."

That last was clearly intended for St. Just, who stood a little straighter at her words and gazed a little more intently at the ormolu clock on the mantel. He'd greeted me in the foyer with a polite bow, then offered his hand, a touching gesture of true welcome.

He swiveled his gaze to me like the horse artillery maneuvered its light guns into place, and his eyes held a silent, desperate plea.

"While you ladies catch up over the teapot," I said, "perhaps St. Just will reacquaint me with His Grace's magnificent stable? An hour in the coach has left me restless, and I have many fond memories of the Morelands hayloft."

Her Grace, a notably self-possessed woman, smiled at me as if I'd offered to pay off the national debt.

"Devlin, you will accompany Lord Julian. He'll be particularly interested in that chestnut filly His Grace wants to name Sunshine."

"Mama, I implore you, spare the poor horse such a curse. Come along, my lord. We have equines to admire."

St. Just and I managed to make our exit without breaking into a sprint, though the ladies were probably as relieved to get rid of us as we were to gain the fresh air.

"You're at the Longacre do?" St. Just asked. Even his voice had changed, becoming darker, as if the distance between normal discourse and laughter had increased twelvefold.

"Ophelia tricked me into attending. First, I was merely an escort, free to drop her at the gateposts, now I am to make up the numbers because Healy West failed to show, and some other fellow was called to his ailing mother's side."

Morelands was a country home in the grand style, and summer showed it to excellent advantage. Like most such estates, it strove to be self-supporting, and that meant the grounds included everything from a spice garden to a vast conservatory to a sprawling home farm.

St. Just had directed me through the back gardens, an interesting arrangement of formal parterres that gave way to more exuberant beds, a rose garden His Grace had planted specifically for his duchess, a maze trimmed to waist height, and various scent and color gardens.

"His Grace will miss the roses if he remains in London much longer," I said as we passed fragrant beds beginning to fade.

"He's intent on harassing my brother home from London. Westhaven is intent on having London to himself this summer. My money's on Westhaven, and I'm sure I will be dispatched to look in on him."

A hint of testiness underlay that recitation. "While you simply want to hide?"

"Hide? Is that what you call it?"

We followed a path out of the garden proper and into the park. "I call it not burdening my family or Society with my presence. The stink of my military failings has followed me home with a vengeance."

"I will never forget the stench of the battlefield at Waterloo."

"Nor will I." Worse than the scent of a mere rotting carcass or two, the scent of a hellscape that had to be experienced to be believed. The accompaniment had been the steady drone of flies and the moans of the wounded left out in the elements for days. Those who could still speak had begged for water, water, always water. "I expect the nightmares will haunt us to our graves."

We came within sight of the majestic barns and lush paddocks in which the Duke of Moreland took such pride.

"I sometimes worry that this is the dream," St. Just said, "and I will wake up to hear the bugler blasting "Boots and Saddles" and feel that combination of eagerness and dread that meant another battle was upon us."

"After the first time," I said, "it was all dread for me. Thank the benevolent powers I was relegated to staff duty after Harry died."

St. Just brushed a glance over me. *Harry's death* was a polite way to refer to that time I got myself captured by the French, failed to rescue my brother, probably spilled my guts to the ever-so-polite commandant, and then was more or less tossed from the chateau like a spent salmon to die peacefully of exposure in the mountains.

The commandant hadn't counted on the skills I'd gained as a reconnaissance officer. I could make fire out of dry wood and friction, and I could set willow snares in pitch darkness. I knew how to use the prevailing wind to improve the range of my hearing and could orient myself to the compass points by sun, moon, and stars. Trailing game had been second nature to me from boyhood on.

I had made it out of the mountains, eventually.

"There's something you should know," St. Just said, heading not for the stable, but for the paddocks. "Girard is alive, and he's in England."

I walked along for another few paces before I could find words—proper words, not mere profanity—with which to fashion a reply.

"I try not to think of him by name. He's the French commandant, the Frenchman, that damned fiend... Never a name if I can help it."

"But you think of him all the same."

"Less and less." I was not quite lying. Of late, I'd been haunted by, rather than obsessed with, whatever had happened at the ugly monstrosity of a castle on the border of France and Spain. The gaps in my memory plagued me, and my inability to save Harry would color every waking and sleeping moment no matter what else might befall me.

St. Just turned us down a grassy bridle path along the hedgerow. "Girard is actually half English. He was trapped in France as a youth during the Peace of Amiens. The French gave him a choice of starvation in a prison town or serving the army. He has inherited an English barony, and if you hear mention of Sebastian St. Clair, blow full retreat."

"He was so damnably civil to me," I murmured. "That explains the perfect English. I've never seen a colder pair of eyes." Lucifer would have eyes like that. Always measuring, always subtly probing whatever and whoever he beheld.

"We're not to kill him," St. Just said. "Wellington's orders. The war is over, and when it comes to St. Clair, the military is playing some deep game with the diplomatic ranks, or so we're told." That last was said with a ragged ghost of humor. "Time to get back to the waltzing and wagering, and toasting His Majesty, too, of course."

"It could be worse, St. Just. You could have been labeled a traitor and then dragooned into an inane house party where nobody talks to you, though you can hear them whispering behind your back before you've even left the room.

"When you want to slink back to the safety of your London lair," I went on, "you instead find your former almost-fiancée is among the guests, and some fellow thought it amusing to try to accost her by moonlight. She heel-stomped the blighter, and he slunk off before I could pummel him. Then you win a horse in a fair, albeit toweringly stupid, wager, but the damned creature goes missing, and on the same day—this very day, as it happens—you find the belle of the assembly inebriated and singing lewd songs in the belvedere."

And then find another belle, albeit from bygone days, at sea in a very different sort of wilderness.

I nearly did not recognize the sound that issued from St. Just—a laugh, harsh, percussive, more of a bark than a sound of merriment, but I had amused him.

"Then," he said, "you are dragged across the countryside by your very own god-harpy to visit the infirm in the person of myself. You poor, put-upon dear."

I hit him on the arm, and he grinned—truly smiled at me with a bit of the old rascally charm—and the chronic ache in my heart—guilt, sorrow, regret, loneliness, what did the label matter?—shifted to something equally sad but a touch less bitter.

～

"Lady Ophelia isn't a harpy, but she's not to be trusted. Can you sleep?" I asked when we'd traveled half the length of the mare's paddock. Several foals grazed among the mamas, and I easily picked out the flame-red filly Moreland sought to afflict with the name Sunshine. Most young horses gamboled and cavorted and generally enjoyed high spirits between napping, cropping grass, and spending time with Mama.

This little creature galloped around the paddock at a blazing run. She had the knack of gathering her quarters under her so each stride launched an equine rocket across the grass.

"I can sleep," St. Just said, taking up a perch along the fence, elbows on the top rail, one boot resting on the bottom. But for the immense sadness in his blue eyes, he would have made a handsome picture. "I don't sleep well. Laudanum terrifies me, but it works, more or less. If I'm tired enough, I can get in a few good hours. Thunderstorms make me bilious."

"They unnerve me. I want to hide in the wardrobe like a small boy who has overheard his parents in a bitter row." Which I had, and frequently about me.

Another sidelong glance. "Their Graces always took marital differences behind closed doors, and Her Grace got the old man sorted out fairly early in their dealings. The duke still drops out of formation from time to time, but never for very long. There aren't many like our duchess."

That St. Just loved and admired his step-mother boded well for his future. Whom did I love and admire in the same fashion? I could not recall the last time my own mother had hugged me, though she expected her cheek to be kissed on appropriate occasions. Lady Ophelia's affection was of the presuming sort, and my sisters...

I loved them, but they had lives that did not include me, a reality many a soldier returning from the war had to face. For twenty years, the Corsican had provided Britain with an excuse to swell her military resources, but all that prowess came at a tremendous cost. The country was now buried in debt, drowning in economic chaos, and overburdened with excessively fit men whose singular skills were marching, drinking, and killing.

"The duchess is concerned for you," I said, resuming our walk. "I am concerned for you, if that makes any difference. Lady Longacre's house party is a penance wrapped up in a tribulation decorated with a misery, but I did sleep well last night. Perhaps it is time to look in on Westhaven in Town."

"I hate Town."

"What do you love?"

"My family." St. Just's answer was prompt and emphatic.

We approached another verdant, rolling paddock, this one populated with mature fellows doing enthusiastic justice to the grass. Moreland was a horseman in the old-fashioned, democratic sense. MPs might wait weeks for an appointment with him, but the stable lads likely had his ear simply for the asking.

"We all love our families," I said, "even as they drive us to Bedlam. I sometimes think I hear Harry's voice, but it's just my mind taunting me. What makes you happy?"

One of the geldings, a leggy chestnut, lowered himself into the grass in the particular, knees-first manner of the equine, then commenced rolling and kicking into the air until he succeeded in flopping from one side to the other.

"That makes me happy," St. Just said, watching the horse repeat the maneuver. "That healthy beast doing as he pleases, not a care in the world beyond hoping for a patch of clover to lend variety to his snacking."

"Then spend time with the horses and avoid house parties at all costs."

He walked along beside me as the chestnut stood and gave himself a good, hard shake. "I was invited to the Longacre do. Sent regrets. I've sent a lot of regrets in the past year. Their Graces worked so hard to ensure that Maggie and I were accepted everywhere, and now..."

Maggie—*Lady* Maggie—was the other ducal by-blow, and

another female with whom one did not trifle. She was all that was correct and lovely and witty, but illegitimacy or the duchess's example had also given her an impregnable sense of reserve. If and when she married, it would be after a long and determined siege on the part of a truly devoted swain.

"Now," I said, "all that acceptance you enjoy as a result of your ducal patrimony feels like shackles. Commit a little treason, St. Just, and you'll be free of those constraints."

He studied the horses in the paddock. The chestnut was going through a get-acquainted ritual with a bay that involved blowing into each other's nostrils, a little pretend-nipping, and then a friendly sniffing about the tail.

"Did you commit treason?" he asked in the same tone he might have inquired after my mother's relentlessly robust health.

"I honestly don't know. The sequence of events, as best I can recall, is as follows: Harry slipped out of camp on some mission nobody will say much about. I followed out of fraternal concern, because it wasn't like Harry to keep secrets from me. I'd got him out of more than one scrape, and he'd done the same for me. He was picked up by the French and did not put up a fight."

"Because," St. Just said, "by then he knew you were on his tail, and he sought to spare you captivity and its attendant woes."

Officers captured out of uniform were fair game for torture, and nobody's reputation for extracting information from the unwilling rivaled Girard's. He had been a dark legend among British forces, though no price had been put on his head. Perhaps somebody with a jaundiced sense of justice

had known of the English title to be slung about his neck if he survived the war.

"Harry might well have grasped that I'd followed him, but I'm good at tracking discreetly. I did put up a fight when they spotted me —standards must be maintained, despite Harry's more sensible example. He and I were held separately, and I was eventually told that he'd died honorably."

I hated saying those words, because Harry should not have died at all. Not like that. "I cannot recall the entirety of my captivity," I went on. "I'm not even sure how long I was in French hands and how long I wandered around trying to find my way back to British forces. My sense of time was distorted. Girard kept me where I had no window and could not see the sky. Candlelight or darkness were all I knew, and patterns of sleeping and waking were purposely rendered unpredictable. A little bit of that, and a man loses all sense of time and not a little of his wits."

Particularly when food and water were also withheld for uncertain periods, then produced on a schedule that felt as if it had no rhyme or reason.

"Girard's genius," St. Just said, "was not in physical torture apparently, though he or his superiors would resort to that on occasion. He excelled at breaking men's minds."

"He certainly dealt a few blows to mine, though he was always polite, always correct. I cannot recall any physical torment, though I recall hunger, thirst, darkness, cold, and endless uncertainty. Then Girard took to having his guards wake me up whenever I began to drop off to sleep, and I came completely unraveled for a time."

I had not spoken of these details to anyone, and I did not want to speak of them now, but still words took form.

"When I was at my worst, I saw Harry before me plain as day, then my mother, then fellows I'd known to have fallen in combat. Why not just kill me? They'd killed Harry. Later, it became clear that I'd tipped Girard off regarding planned British troop movements. I doubtless forget on purpose some exchange he and I had, some damning disclosure I made, but the recollection refuses to come into focus."

St. Just was quiet for a time while the horses in the field went back to the important business of grazing.

"Perhaps you made no such disclosure."

"General Huddington's advance party was all but slaughtered, St. Just. They were on a glorified goat track I'd discovered a few weeks previous to my capture. Who else knew of that way to reach one of the higher, less traveled passes?"

"Every shepherd for fifty miles in any direction," he said, studying the horses. "Every scout and reconnaissance officer sent to inspect the track after you. French reconnaissance officers, Spanish Bonapartists. Many an advance party was ambushed as we crossed Spain and into France, and very few of them attribute their losses to anything but bad luck."

He was being kind, and also stating a real, if unlikely, possibility. "I don't know what happened," I said, "but I have been judged in the court of public opinion and found wanting. My family is loyal for form's sake, not because they have faith in my innocence. As far as they're concerned, I failed Harry. I should have gone back to camp and informed my superiors, who might have worked out one of those prisoner exchanges that were never supposed to happen."

"And seldom did happen. Is this clouded past why you sprang Miss West?"

Yes, in part. "Her Grace knows all, I take it."

"Between Papa and Her Grace, there are no secrets in polite society for long. You might consider paying a call on Christian, His Grace of Mercia. He was held at the chateau at the same time you and Harry passed through its doors."

I'd had a nodding acquaintance with Mercia, who remained something of an enigma. He'd bought his colors despite having a lofty title, a lovely duchess, and no direct heir of the body.

Why do that? "Mercia will not enjoy revisiting his wartime experiences," I said. By all accounts, the duke had been physically tortured and never once disclosed anything of value to the French. For his pains, he'd earned himself a useless hand and the undying admiration of the London crowds. Perhaps he regarded that adulation as useless too.

"Mercia is coping," St. Just said with another slight smile. "As you are. We've probably hit the limit of our parole, and Her Grace will want to see us both stuffed with sandwiches. If I call on you in Town, will you be home?"

"To you, yes, but please don't think to inflict any of your pretty sisters on me. If they come around, other ladies might take a notion to follow in their charitable footsteps, and I am not up to flirtation." Loyalty to Hyperia forbade me that pleasure, even if I were interested in it.

"I will come as the lone scout," St. Just said, "assuming Her Grace lets me out of her sight. Who else is at the house party?"

I recounted the list—Cleary, to be pitied for one brother on remittance and the other making a slow recovery from injury. Ormstead, doing his best to catch Hyperia's eye. Brimstock, on the hunt for a well-heeled wife. Banter with troubles of his own. Westmere, decamped to see to a mother too fond of the poppy. Colonel Sir Thomas Pearlman, mad at the world by force of habit.

Various young ladies who'd had a more or less unsuccessful Season or Seasons.

"And your host and hostess?"

"Lady Ophelia says the Longacre heir is somewhat wanting for intelligence. Wedding Maybelle to a worthy fellow has thus become a matter of dynastic necessity. Maybelle accurately surmises that marriage, or the motherhood that marriage portends, is the death of many women. She is not at all enthusiastic to become one of the martyrs who secures the family's survival at the expense of her own."

"I see you are very much still on reconnaissance, my lord." St. Just ambled along the fence line more slowly than he'd struck out from the house. "Life should not be a matter of dodging mortal peril."

"Particularly for a young lady of eighteen." Or a young man of eighteen, seventeen, sixteen... The recruiting sergeants had been fixed on filling quotas, not on counting a lad's teeth.

St. Just stopped at the corner of the paddock and looked back on the fit, happy creatures at their ease.

"I come this way often," he said. "A walk around the paddocks means I don't bother the lads tending to the stable, and I avoid the gardeners, and yet, I'm within sight of the house if Her Grace gets to fretting about me. I don't recall seeing that chestnut in with this group previously."

An odd sensation prickled over my nape. "The chestnut who was rolling so vigorously five minutes ago?"

"That fellow," St. Just said. "Good-looking specimen. Rolling and offering his card to the other fellows at the club. If he's a regular, why do that? I'd have remembered him. The grooms might have moved him from another paddock, but I patrol the perimeter... I *walk* the fences regularly, and I don't recognize that horse."

St. Just knew his horseflesh. He'd ridden dispatch with legendary success, and for those officers, their ability to remain attuned to their mounts was often the difference between life and death.

"St. Just," I said, studying the now dusty chestnut, "I don't suppose Morelands yet has any ponies on the premises?"

"Of course we do. Aging pensioners from Evie or Jenny's girlhood."

"Before we go into lunch, might you indulge me in a little experiment?"

~

"But what about the white stockings?" Lady Ophelia asked before the coach had even cleared the Moreland gateposts. "You said Cleary's chestnut had four white stockings, one of them rice-powdered or painted or something to match the others. Did this horse wear makeup?"

"We could not tell. The beast has been in tall wet grass, splashed in mud puddles, and otherwise obscured the evidence. He has a white star and four white stockings, one slightly shorter than the others, but England is full of chestnut horses with slightly mismatched white markings."

"Did he know his name? His name was... Copernicus? Ptolemy? What did you say his name was?"

Ophelia was like a hound on the scent, and it occurred to me that my godmother was an intelligent woman overly afflicted with boredom. The gossip and matchmaking and pointless socializing were expected of her, but Copernicus and Ptolemy were not familiar names to most Englishwomen of good breeding.

"His name is Trafalgar, if he's Mendel Cleary's horse, but he showed no particular interest in that name." I doubted even Atlas responded to his name per se. He paid very close attention to the rattle of oats in a bucket or to my tone of voice when I greeted him, but what was a name to a horse?

"Not Cleary's horse," Ophelia retorted. "*Your* horse. This is another prank in poor taste, mark my words. You should have had that gelding saddled and ridden him right back to Makepeace."

"I can't know it's the right horse, Godmama. Until St. Just can confer with his stable lads and inquire of his immediate neighbors regarding a missing gelding, we've come across a mere coincidence."

The coach swung out of the winding Morelands drive and onto a bumpier track.

"Cleary cannot afford to wager away a good riding horse," Ophelia said. "Or so Lady Longacre would have me believe. He's land-poor and house-proud. He expected to have your spectacles from you, but ended up having to hide his horse. What did you and St. Just discuss?"

I did not want to belabor the situation with the chestnut gelding, but I was even more reluctant to bear tales regarding St. Just's troubles.

Which left... my troubles. "St. Just warned me that a certain French officer of whom I have very disagreeable memories has washed up on English shores. Seems the misfortunes of war landed him in France during the Peace of Amiens, but he's actually half English." The paternal half, the one everybody seemed to think counted the most, though I was reminded of Miss Longacre's cousins dying in childbed.

What of the parent who risked her life to produce every child?

"That would be Lord Sebastian St. Clair, I suppose," Ophelia said on a little grimace. "The gentlemen's clubs are full of wagers about how long he'll be permitted to survive. He has a barony styled after the family name and no heir, so the fine fellows of St. James's might give him time to procreate at least. You are not to challenge him, Julian. I won't have it."

I could not imagine the circumstances that would prompt me to risk my life or another man's life on the field of honor. I was done with killing. Of that much, I was certain.

"If St. Clair is titled," I said, "he'd be within his rights to refuse a challenge from a commoner such as myself, and he'd probably enjoy turning the *Code Duello* against a former prisoner." Truth to tell, I did not want to blow out even *his* brains. The war was over, as St. Just had said.

"Rather than kill him, why don't you get some answers from him? Interrogate him as he interrogated you? Ask him where Harry is buried so we can at least bring the boy home for proper planting in the family plot."

The day was lovely, if a trifle warm, but I was tempted to take out one of the wool lap robes, wrap it around me, and pull it up over my head.

"The war is *over*, my lady. If Arthur is inclined to exert his influence to learn of the whereabouts of Harry's remains, we will leave that to the family duke."

"You will have to face St. Clair, Julian. He'll pop out of the bushes in Hyde Park or bump into you at some horse auction."

I considered telling Ophelia that I'd finish our journey up on the box, listening to John Coachman's tales of his days as a prizefighter.

"If St. Clair is foolish enough to show his face in polite society, he won't be gracing the mortal sphere much longer. Too many good men suffered too much at his hands. I might be a traitor, but he surely is."

"I know his auntie," Ophelia said, gaze on the peaceful English countryside so many had died to defend. "She claims he was orphaned in France, made to choose between death and dishonor at a young age. She's quite fond of him. She's the only family he has left."

Was this a backhanded attempt to comfort me, who had not been given a choice between death and dishonor?

Or perhaps I had. Perhaps Girard—I refused to think of him as some English baron strutting about his ancestral manor and having an *auntie*—had left the knife in my cell so that I might end my own existence. I had never been sure, but he'd taunted me with the very blade I'd carried in my boot when I'd been taken captive. That little weapon had saved my life once I'd begun scrabbling my way out of the mountains.

"Would you disown me if I abandoned Lady Longacre's house party?" I asked.

"Yes. You cannot go running back to London just because St. Just passed along a little military gossip."

"Why didn't you pass along the gossip first, my lady?"

"Because I did not know if the Traitor Baron was also your personal French nightmare. More than one of the Corsican's officers treated English captives ill, or do I mistake the matter?"

Did anybody else appreciate what a gifted thespian Lady Ophelia was? "You wanted to deny me one more reason to remain safely behind my curtained windows. I'm not a coward, Ophelia."

She muttered something that sounded like *would that you were.*

I pulled down the shade on my side of the coach, tilted my hat over my eyes, and attempted to feign sleep on the washboard abominations that passed for the King's highways. That Girard was circulating in London Society, moving under what amounted to safe passage from Wellington himself, troubled me.

Girard alone had answers that I both needed to have and dreaded to learn. Where were Harry's remains? Had Girard allowed me to escape, or had even his citadel of suffering slipped into chaos as British forces had advanced into France?

What had I told him—*if anything?*

The afternoon was barely half gone, and yet, the day had been challenging and not... not boring. Not tedious at all. From the missing horse to Miss Longacre's early morning aria, to St. Just's surprising disclosures, the day had not been boring at all.

I still had some of my reconnaissance skills—I could follow tracks, navigate unknown terrain, and think on my feet—but my ability to put together information from disparate sources was rusty. I wanted to gallop off to London and tie Girard to a chair until he'd given me the answers I deserved. Somebody was bound to put period to the man's existence, despite all of Wellington's orders to the contrary. Wellington might be the greatest of national heroes, but he was not a god.

With enough bitterness and brandy, some half-lame, half-sane former lieutenant would take a notion to end Girard's existence. If I was to question the Traitor Baron, time was of the essence.

And yet, I wasn't ready to have that conversation, assuming Girard was willing to be confronted. One could refuse callers, go to ground, and pull the curtains closed, as I well knew. A week ago, I'd been content to immerse myself in bawdy ancient poems, and here I was paying social calls in broad daylight, albeit wearing spectacles and wrestling with an intermittently pounding head.

Another skill one learned as a reconnaissance officer was caution at all times. Why was Girard still alive? What had earned him a virtual pardon from Wellington himself?

As we pulled up before Makepeace's stately façade, I realized I would rather remain at the house party, a pariah without portfolio, than deal with the larger questions waiting for me in Town. This odd gathering of idle, unhappy people would soon be over, and there was time enough later to deal with the older demons haunting me.

"Something's afoot," Lady Ophelia said as I handed her down from the coach. "No footmen to meet us, nobody idling on the veranda. Who do you suppose is in trouble now?"

"As long as I'm not in the crosshairs..."

But I was... again.

CHAPTER TEN

"They've been at it for several hours," Hyperia muttered. "Turning the house upside down over a stupid pocket watch."

She'd been reading in the grand Makepeace foyer, the logical place to bide if she'd wanted to accost us upon our return.

"Whose pocket watch?" Ophelia asked as I drew her mantle from her shoulders. No footman or underbutler appeared to take the garment from me.

"The purloined item originally belonged to Mendel Cleary's grandfather." Hyperia spoke softly, as if she were imparting state secrets. "Cleary was quite up in the bows about having the guest quarters searched and the maids and footmen questioned."

"Rude of him," I muttered, my arms full of Ophelia's silk wrap and my hat still on my head. "I don't suppose anybody has had a look through Cleary's quarters?"

Hyperia took my hat off and set it on the chair she'd been occupying. "Of course not. Cleary claims he left the watch on his vanity when he went to the stable this morning, and by the time he returned to his room after lunch, the heirloom was missing. Lady Longacre agreed to set the staff to searching the public areas."

The day needed only this.

I thrust Ophelia's mantle at her and snatched my hat from the chair. "Both of you, listen to me. Search your own rooms. Start with the obvious hiding places, the ones you'd choose if you wanted a cursory examination to bear fruit. Under the mattress, in your jewelry boxes, beneath your pillows, in your Sunday boots. Conduct your searches without witnesses."

"Jules, have you taken leave—"

"Do it," I said, "and pray God I can reach my own quarters before—"

Lord Longacre appeared at the top of the steps. "My lord, my lady. I see you've returned. Miss West, Lady Ophelia, I need a word with Lord Julian in private, if you will excuse us."

I passed my hat to Hyperia and mouthed the words, "Search my room first," then jaunted up the steps with an energy I did not feel.

"Her Grace of Moreland sends greetings," I said, mustering a smile for mine host when I reached him. "Is something amiss, my lord?"

"You know damned well something is amiss." He stalked off in the direction of the family wing.

My day had begun with similar accusation from Mendel Cleary, that I knew what was amiss, and was in fact, the instigator of the problem.

I'd had enough of that rubbish, and I was no longer a green lieutenant fearful of provoking a senior officer.

"What I know," I replied without raising my voice or moving so much as one inch, "is that Lady Ophelia returned from a call on your ducal neighbors and found no footman to assist her from the coach, no butler to take her wrap, no maid to inquire if she'd like a tray to tide her over until supper. She will remark upon the indifferent hospitality at Makepeace unless some plausible explanation for these oversights is provided immediately."

I could mimic Arthur's hauteur when attempting to twit him, but I'd never done so previously for any other purpose. Arthur and I bore a resemblance, though he, like the rest of our siblings, was dark-haired, while my own locks had been chestnut brown.

Then too, I was slightly taller than His Grace, and I used that height to stare down at Longacre. My head hurt, I was both hungry and thirsty, and I was not in the mood to be accused of a theft I hadn't committed.

Another theft, counting my own blasted wayward horse.

Longacre stalked back to me, though a hint of caution had come into his gaze. "I told my wife we were making a tempest in a teapot. If I had tuppence for every time she's lost an earbob or Maybelle has misplaced a bracelet... but the item in question belongs to Mr. Cleary and is of great sentimental value. He's insistent that the house be searched from top to bottom."

We stood outside what appeared to be an informal parlor. Two large, anemic ferns in shiny brass pots took forlorn comfort from an east-facing window. The chairs did not match, though all were uphol-stered in green, and the carpet showed some wear.

A curate, steward, or impecunious second cousin might be received in such a room. I availed myself of it and waited for Longacre to join me.

When he deigned to do so, I closed the door. "Exactly what has gone missing?"

"A pocket watch said to belong to Cleary's grandfather. A family legacy, motto inscribed on the inside of the cover. Chased gold, gold chain."

"I've seen him flash it about. The chain is longer than most and not made of gold."

Longacre sat and rubbed a hand across his forehead. "How could you know the composition of Cleary's watch chain?"

"By how it swings. The links aren't heavy enough to be gold, and I can't see Cleary, who is notably jealous of his coin, indulging in that expense. If he had fit the watch with a genuine gold chain, it would be as short as possible without violating the dictates of fashion."

Longacre rose and paced to the window, brushing past the ferns and sending a cascade of withered leaves to the carpet. "You are so damned clever. Cleary suggested you are unhappy about the missing horse and sought retribution by nicking his heirloom."

"Cleary also claims I stole my own horse, though I couldn't have picked the beast out of a herd at the relevant time and still have no idea how to identify Trafalgar's saddle or bridle. I'll be curious to hear what he has to say when I tell him that the missing horse is swishing flies in a paddock over at Morelands."

Longacre cracked open the window. "Please God, not Morelands. The last thing we need is His Grace of Meddling riding roughshod over my wife's social gathering, and he'll do it too. Moreland means well, but he's rubbishing officious when he gets to playing magistrate. Lord Lieutenant of the Universe at Large."

Moreland was former military, the father of ten, and did not suffer fools. "Stealing a gold watch is a hanging offense. The situation calls for thoroughness, if a crime has been committed."

As I made that staunch declaration on behalf of law and order, I desperately hoped Hyperia and Ophelia were ransacking my room. My objective was to keep Longacre talking until they'd had time to recover the watch.

"Has it occurred to you," I went on, "that Cleary is unhappy about losing the horse and seeks to make a fool of me with this missing watch?"

"Yes," Longacre said, his back to me in a spectacular display of rudeness. He braced his hands on the windowsill and leaned out into the afternoon sunshine. "Yes, it has. Or perhaps the footmen, who have taken Cleary into dislike, are getting into the spirit of gathering and moving precious objects about on a lark. With your permission, I'd nonetheless like to have your quarters searched."

That I was for once shown proper consideration made me wary. "I was gone for most of the day. Why not search first and spare me this interview?"

Longacre turned and braced his hips against the windowsill. The slanting sunbeams revealed thinning hair and the start of jowls, though he was still an attractive man.

"You would know if your effects had been searched, my lord. My wife tells me you are doing without a valet and, unlike Cleary, managing well enough on your own. If I had sent Brimstock or Ormstead to search your effects, you'd see that a boot was moved half an inch or that your pillows were not exactly where you'd left them. Any other guest would attribute the disturbance to the passing efforts of staff, but Lady Longacre says you haven't had so much as a footman in your room to build up a fire."

Meaning her ladyship's rudeness was deliberate and not some miscalculation on the housekeeper's part.

"You would still be within your rights to search any room in your own home, sir." What had made him cautious, when we both knew the watch might well turn up in the drawer of my night table?

Longacre ran a hand over the drooping fronds of the nearest fern, creating yet another mess.

"Maybelle has barely come out of her rooms all day," he said. "She joined the company for luncheon, ate enough to feed a sparrow, said a total of two words, and returned to her apartment. I love my daughter, but..."

He did. I had to grant him that much. "But?"

"But I do not understand the female of the species, my lord. Maybelle is loath to leap into matrimony. Her two best friends, her cousins, the girls she was closest to in the whole world, were snatched away from her, and she mourns their loss. I told Lady Longacre that Maybelle needs time, and Lady Longacre countered that we need a sensible, solvent son-in-law and then grandsons. One would think I am at my last prayers."

Or that one's prospective widow hadn't much in the way of a jointure. "What has this to do with Cleary's watch?"

"If I took the liberty of searching your room without your permission, then you'd hear of it, or worse, Lady Ophelia would hear of it. She and my wife are already hissing and growling at one another over your presence here. We're to banish Lady Ophelia from all guest lists going forward, et cetera and so forth."

"And should you offend my dear godmama," I said slowly, "she will at some opportune moment deliver the cut sublime to Lady Longacre or, worse yet, to Maybelle. Maybelle's chances of a good match plunge yet further, and then Maybelle and her mother start feuding—all over a stupid watch that probably keeps bad time."

Was Lady Longacre sufficiently determined to get rid of me that she'd risk offending Lady Ophelia?

"The watch isn't the point," Longacre said. "I simply want to find the damned thing and get on with this house party. We're to have country dancing this evening, of all the inanities."

"You've searched the public rooms?"

"To no avail."

"The staff quarters?"

"Had the butler and housekeeper undertake that distasteful task. If the footmen disliked Cleary before, they'll spike his tea with wormwood when they learn he suggested they'd perpetrate a theft."

Longacre was, in a roundabout way, asking for my help. But at what price? "If the watch is found in my room, what will you do?"

"Quietly ask you to leave."

"Because then, Lady Ophelia has no excuse for escalating the war with Lady Longacre?"

He made a face as if the milk had gone off. "Lady Ophelia won't have the excuse that I insulted you directly if you give me permission to undertake the search—or if you leave of your own volition in the next hour."

~

Leaving camp of my own volition was how I'd started down a road that had led to allegations of dereliction of duty, treason, and moral turpitude. Leaving of my own volition—buying my officer's colors without consulting even Arthur—had been another ill-informed decision.

After a period of convalescence—if staying up all night wandering the family seat could be called that—I'd left Caldicott Hall of my own volition to bide in London and wander a far smaller domicile.

I'd been leaving of my own volition with disastrous results for years.

The hour had come to eschew that tactic. "I understand that my departure would solve a problem for you and several others. Nonetheless, the time has passed when I could quit this gathering as a travel escort having done his duty. I'm now here arguably to make up numbers that have grown less balanced since my arrival. If I'm shown the door in disgrace, or if I leave with my tail between my legs, then I have a problem."

"What problem? You go back to lurking in London, which idleness has apparently contented you for months."

Idleness—my days and nights refusing to abide by any rhythm, my powers of concentration not half what they should be, my family coming around timidly to make awkward conversation for the duration of two cups of tea, my head alternately pounding and swimming with disembodied memories...

Idleness of that variety could eventually lead to madness, did his lordship but know it.

"Consider matters from my perspective, Longacre. If, after attempting a short outing in the countryside, I resume my lurking under a cloud of gossip—another cloud of gossip—then my family will be concerned. My mother and brother will interest themselves in my affairs, and I might well be taken up by the sororal press-gangs for another tour at the family seat. That plan will not serve. The next time I repair to Caldicott Hall, I will do so on my own terms and without the taint of further scandal riding pillion."

I wanted to leave, but I wanted even more to guard what little remained of my good name—to say nothing of keeping an eye on

Hyperia, who was too willing to dismiss an assault as a stolen kiss gone awry.

"You were mentioned in the dispatches once or twice," Longacre said, apropos of nothing. "Cool head, quick thinking. Nothing too profuse, but to be mentioned at all says Wellington took note of you. You aren't stupid."

Wellington had been punctilious about giving credit to subordinates where due, and Britain had loved him for it. We'd needed heroes, needed reasons to preen and rejoice between defeats and casualty lists. His elegant, precise dispatches had provided that.

What I needed was a nap in a dark room, a tall glass of lemonade, and to find the blasted watch. "Are you asking my opinion, my lord?"

"Of necessity, I am."

"Then I suggest that you and you alone search my room with no witness save myself. Make the search without fanfare."

Longacre appeared to consider my proposal. "Do I find the watch or not?"

"That depends on whether you believe I stole it. I met Cleary in the stable this morning, at a time when he claims that watch was sitting in his room. I then went for a hack and had some difficulty with my horse. By the time I was ready to come in to breakfast, Lady Ophelia had determined that I was to escort her to Morelands. I had no opportunity to steal the watch, unless I moved very quickly. But then, I don't know which room Cleary occupies—I am housed in staff quarters rather than in the guest wing—and more to the point, *I have no motive* for taking the watch."

"What of the horse?"

To blazes with the blasted horse. "I do not need or want another riding horse, my lord. Cleary should never have offered the wager he did, and stealing a watch would in no way return the horse to me. Cleary should never have fleeced the other fellows at cards and should never have played so recklessly at battledore, and yet, nobody is asking him to leave."

"Much more of this nonsense," Longacre said, starting for the door, "and I will be the one lighting out for parts distant. No time like the present, my lord. If Cleary knows what we're about, he'll demand to witness the search, and that rather defeats the purpose of the exercise."

Damnably valid point.

We met Hyperia and Ophelia all of two yards from the door to my room.

"There you are!" Hyperia said, all smiles. "I was hoping for your escort in the garden before supper, Lord Julian. Will you oblige me?"

While Hyperia spoke, Lady Ophelia caught my eye and gave a slight shake of her head.

Cleary had apparently hidden the watch a bit too well. "I will be happy to walk with you before supper, Miss West. Shall we say about eight?" Assuming I wasn't shackled in the wine cellar in the next hour.

"Splendid."

"Until then." I bowed, she curtseyed, Ophelia and Longacre ignored us, and then the moment was at hand to see me labeled a thief, a liar, and a fool.

Though after diligently searching my quarters, Longacre could not find the watch. I continued to rifle my effects for half an hour after his puzzled departure, and I didn't find the blasted thing either.

~

"I could send a note to one of your sisters," Hyperia said as we ambled along a rhododendron walk. "Have them summon you back to Town on pain of ducal disapproval. Nobody could blame you for heeding a family writ."

"Arthur already disapproves of me. If he had a couple of sons in the nursery, I might well be racketing about the Continent with all the other remittance men."

"I hear Rome is fascinating."

You too, Hyperia? "Rome and the Italian states generally are a mess." Most of the Continent was a mess, for that matter, and Britain at least qualified for muddled status. "The Corsican left the Italians with a taste for republicanism while appointing his infant son King of Rome. Napoleon forced the Austrians out of the north of Italy, but now the Austrians are back. Half of Italy's national treasures are gracing foreign capitals and private collections, and poverty has returned with a vengeance. I have no wish to go to Rome."

Or back to London, not yet.

"What do you wish for?"

The rhododendrons formed a majestic border twenty feet high on either side of the path. The flowers were enormous, and the bushes had been pruned such that Hyperia and I wandered between walls of green, bold pink, white, and rose. Along with the tangy scent of woods and earth, the air held a hint of the clove-carnation fragrance of the blooms.

"I want this," I said. "A peaceful stroll with a lovely lady, the natural beauty of my homeland all around me, the robins at their evensong, and a good meal in the offing. What of you?"

"I want to find that watch in Sir Thomas's jewelry box."

How fierce she was. "He'd claim I put it there. What does Ormstead think has become of the watch?"

"He says you'd be a fool to have taken it, and Cleary would be a fool to feign its theft."

"Cleary has argued with a footman, sown ill will among the bachelors, and lost a fine horse in a stupid wager. I'd say his credentials as a fool are well established. When you are not defending my honor, Hyperia, what do you want?"

Out in the garden, the guests were assembling for a meal al fresco. The falling dew brought their chattering and laughter to us as if from a great distance. The company would move indoors for dancing when full darkness fell, though our capering would be limited to country dances. At the conclusion of the gathering— assuming we did not descend into an outright melee in the next ten days—we'd be treated to the stifling, interminable spectacle of a formal ball.

"Let's sit," Hyperia said, leading me by the arm to a bench on a shadowed bend in the path.

When I took my place a decorous foot away from her, she scooted closer. "Don't be like that."

"Don't be gentlemanly?" I expected Ormstead to come trotting from the undergrowth at any moment. A lapse of manners on my part would not sit well with him.

"Don't be formal. For so long, Jules, what I wanted was for you to come safely home. Then you did, and what I wanted wasn't what you wanted. Now..."

I owed her this opportunity to air her disappointment in me. England's grounds for judging me were questionable, but Hyperia had every right.

"Perry, I'm sorry. I am not the same man who went off to war. You must believe that marriage to an alleged traitor is much less than you deserve. Half this gathering thinks me capable of thievery. The other half thinks I'm daft."

"You are neither. Which opinion offends you more?"

I considered her question while birds flitted overhead and a lone bovine bawled in the distance.

"Either a loss of honor or a loss of my wits could see me again deprived of my freedom. The criminal is put to death or sentenced to penal servitude for a time certain. In a few cases, he's transported for life, but those are rare. The man judged mentally defective, on the other hand, is never given a reprieve from bondage. His liberties are stolen from him, and getting them back is nearly impossible. Of the two, I'd rather be a criminal and have hope, than be declared insane and condemned to eternal despair."

Hardly a cheering topic. I wasn't about to tell Hyperia just how intimately I'd become acquainted with mental instability while in France. Those experiences came for me in nightmares that left me screaming into the darkness.

Then too, there was that little problem with my memory.

"You ask what I want," Hyperia said. "I have what I want—you are home safe and well, more or less—though now I am left to convince myself that what I wanted was simply marriage to a good fellow, some healthy children, and a happy dotage."

"Those are worthy dreams, Hyperia."

"No," she said, "they are not. Maybelle has the right of it. To marry and have babies is no great plan for happiness or meaning, Jules. Society tries to tell the ladies it is, but society tells men a very different story. For a lady, wifehood and motherhood are a privilege, a literal consummation devoutly to be wished, despite the fact that wedding vows render a woman's personhood forfeit and put her life at risk. Many men chose war over domesticity. Is war such a merry undertaking, I wonder?"

"The Corsican would have had us all speaking French, Hyperia."

"Not after we wrecked his navy, he wouldn't."

She was right—up to a point. The Battle of Trafalgar in 1805 had put period to Napoleon's navy and thus to his ability to invade England. Within a few years, though, he'd been rebuilding, and the decision was made to ally ourselves with Portugal and attack France by battling our way across Spain.

I verbally fell back and regrouped. "War is no sort of merriment at all."

"And neither is matrimony for most women, but what choices do we have?" She fell silent, and so, thank heavens, did the distant cow. I was prepared to let the conversation die and cast about for some topic other than war, thievery, and our broken understanding.

"Ormstead kissed me, Jules."

A flare of rage lit up inside me, quickly doused by self-derision. Clearly, Ormstead hadn't made a proper job of the undertaking, but who was I to judge him?

"He kissed you with your permission, or I'll sort him out, Hyperia."

"With my assent," she said, "and he didn't take undue liberties."

No groping, then. No fumbling, no trying to lift her skirts less than a week after some fool had assaulted her. Prudent of him, and yet...

"His kiss failed to move you."

"Oh, worse than that. I did not particularly care one way or another if he sought to do more than kiss me. I simply waited for him to finish."

Was I to pity Ormstead? Because I nearly did. "Why tell me this?"

"Because you all but threw me at him this morning. Such maneuvers are neither necessary nor appreciated. I like William, but I don't... That is, allowing him to develop aspirations in my direction when I cannot return his enthusiasm would be unkind."

Liking can grow into attraction. Give it time. He's a good man.

I was clearly not a good man, because I kept those platitudes to myself, though they were all probably true. I wanted Ormstead to be a good man for Hyperia's sake and for my own.

"I nonetheless want you to dance with Ormstead tonight."

"Why?"

"Because you delivered a solid stomp to the foot of the fellow who accosted you barely forty-eight hours ago. If the culprit is among the guests, he might sit out the dancing."

"Or dance only the sedate figures."

"I doubt we'll be permitted many of those, and pray God we're not expected to remain up until all hours promenading, stomping, and chasséing." My eyes no longer ached—bless the approaching darkness—but my head was still throbbing.

"I am to watch for any gentleman who sits out all the dances?"

"Or dances until his gait goes off, or he limps from the dance floor." A distinctive trill of laughter drifted through the hedges. "Maybelle is apparently feeling more the thing."

"She has no choice, Jules. A poor showing at luncheon, followed by a lie-down that lasted all afternoon... Gossip will soon attach to her ill health, and she cannot afford to risk that."

Hyperia was in a determinedly gloomy mood, though I could not blame her. I rose and offered her my hand. She stood without assistance, then slipped her fingers around my arm.

"I had not realized the extent to which ladies must comport themselves like reconnaissance officers," I said. "Set one foot outside camp, and assume you are in enemy territory. Every shed, tavern, and livery stable is the scene of a potential ambush, and you can't water your horse without first drawing a weapon."

"More or less."

Perhaps that watchfulness might bear fruit. "Please do what you can to get the various bachelors on their feet, Hyperia. Whoever took liberties with you might not have realized I was in Ormstead's company. He and I were on a darkened terrace, apart from the other guests. Any varmint who wants to see me accused of assaulting you is my enemy."

"Jules, it's not worth—" A particularly loud rustling in the bushes silenced her, and her grip on my arm became firmer. "What was that?"

An odd attempt at a birdcall followed, a cross between an owl and a drunken nightingale.

"Atticus, show yourself."

"I daren't." Very softly. "Meet me in the kitchen garden in a quarter hour, milord. I'll be by the pea vines."

"Go," Hyperia said, "though if I'm to dance myself to exhaustion, I will expect a full report."

"I'll see you back to the other guests like a proper escort, and Atticus can eat his fill of peas while he's waiting for me."

"I don't fancy peas." A hissed whisper. "A quarter hour, no more, or Cook will swat me silly."

The bushes rustled again, and I wondered how much Atticus had overheard. I returned Hyperia to the milling guests, and a scrubbed and smiling Ormstead asked her for a turn along the roses. She went with convincing good grace, and I made a discreet progress to the pea vines.

"She loves ya," Atticus said. "Fair gone on ya."

"Miss West pities me, and being tenderhearted, she mistakes long association for fondness. Do you have the watch?"

In the gathering shadows, Atticus's teeth gleamed white. "That would be this watch?" He held up a golden orb, and I snatched it out of his hand.

"A watch like that could be pressed into use as a signal beacon. Don't flash it about."

I opened the lid and made out an inscription on the inside. The chain was overly long and light for its length. I tried to hand it back.

"I don't want it," Atticus said, paws in the air as he stepped two feet from me.

"So where and when did you find it?" I asked, relieved beyond measure that he had.

"Not here," Atticus said. "The footmen like to smoke out here."

I tucked the watch into my breast pocket and followed him into the dim, humid interior of the glass structures along the south wall. He opened a door, and we were once again in the cool night air and outside the garden. The only sounds were crickets and nightbirds, and had the terrain rolled just a bit more, I might have been back in Spain, meeting with an informant and watching for certain death behind every bush and tree.

Instead, I was in Merry Olde and wondering why in the hell anybody would bother to ruin what little remained of my reputation.

CHAPTER ELEVEN

As soon as the hue and cry had gone up earlier in the day, Atticus had seized upon a convenient oil can and, under the guise of tending to my neglected window, gone straight to my quarters. He'd found the watch rolled into a pair of my cotton stockings.

"What made you look there?" I asked as we tarried in a gazebo perched on the bank of a trout pond. "Why my stockings?"

"Canny hides his medal and letter of commendation in his socks. He pretends he doesn't want the medal to get dusty, but in truth he doesn't want the rest of us gawking at it."

"A man's past is private." Or should be. Perhaps Canny the footman didn't want to be reminded of the days when he'd been Canny the feared and respected sharpshooter. "Good work, in any case. The question remains how to get the blasted watch back to Cleary's rooms, and don't tell me you'll do it. You cannot be seen anywhere in the vicinity of his apartment if you're also looking after my quarters."

"You got no faith, guv. I can be quick as a cat and twice as quiet." Atticus leaped up onto the gazebo railing and spun gracefully.

"You can be transported for thievery, and I doubt you'd enjoy the hazards of the voyage or the hard labor. What about Canning? The footmen are in and out of guest rooms at all hours. If he can stand guard, I can return the watch."

I hated to spread the risk such an activity represented, but for all I knew, Cleary had set a booby trap. If he couldn't catch me hiding the contraband, he'd ambush me when I returned it.

"Canny takes the coal up every evening. He could be your lookout."

Perfect. "He's not in the ballroom?"

"Nah. He don't go in for gettin' champagne spilled on his livery while the dowagers pinch his bum. The younger footmen like the ballroom work. Some of the chaperones are happy to pay for a bit of romping and rogering."

Oh, the Quality. "If Canning and I can return the watch discreetly, and only on that condition, please tell him I want to do it tonight. I am already in your debt, Atticus, and in his as well. I can rely on other resources if need be to accomplish the task, but I'd rather not."

Atticus hopped down from the railing as nimbly as he'd ascended, landing with barely a sound. "You don't ditch a lady and then ask her to go housebreakin' for ya, guv." He sat on the gazebo's railing, his feet resting on the seat of the wooden bench facing the pond.

I took a more decorous place on the bench opposite. Merciful powers, I was tired, and I had yet to show my handsome face in the ballroom.

"I did not ditch Miss West, and I would not ask her to return the watch."

"Then you'd ask your auntie."

"Lady Ophelia is my godmother, at least for official purposes."

"She's got a lordly nose like yours, and wouldn't nobody be transporting her unless she wanted transporting. I like her."

"I do too—or I did. Hadn't you best be getting back to the kitchen?" I wanted a moment to enjoy the solitude and quiet of the pond, or the relative quiet. A pair of bullfrogs had begun serenading the evening, and their homely songs, like the lowing of the cattle and the singing birds, soothed my soul.

When natural darkness went silent, a prudent man took notice.

"You like Miss West." A casual observation on Atticus's part.

I sensed in his words the puzzlement of inchoate adolescence, though he was young to be contemplating wooing—or romping and rogering. But then, childhood belowstairs was nearly nonexistent, and he was a noticing sort of lad.

"I like her very much, but married to me, she'd be burdened by association with my wartime failings, and she doesn't deserve that."

Atticus leaned back, tore a twig off the nearest tree branch, and lobbed it into the pond. The ripples flowed outward, like the whispers of a spreading scandal.

"We won," he said. "We lost a lot of battles, but we won the war. Five years from now, nobody will care that the Frenchies got you for a time. You'll be just another old soldier, telling stories that are only half true."

Five years on, I'd be the age my father was when he married, but Atticus would still be a boy, while I already had white hair. The bullfrogs continued with their nocturnes, and the sweet notes of a fiddle tuning up drifted from the manor house.

"I don't know what the truth is about my time in captivity. I went a bit mad for a time." The admission came as both a relief and a surprise.

"Like a tomcat in a hamper? Fair loses his mind when the lid closes."

Loses his dignity too. "Something like that." The reality had been exactly like that at times, shut away in complete darkness, only the occasional scurry of a rodent marking time and assuring me that I hadn't died. Perhaps I did not want to confront Girard for fear I'd kill him, or stash him away in an oubliette of my own making.

I had had enough of killing, particularly killing for the convenience of kings, emperors, and the lords of the City who'd made a lucrative job out of playing both sides.

Atticus had apparently forgotten that he was in a hurry to return to the kitchen, and perhaps because he represented my younger, happier self, I kept talking.

"I can't recall all of what happened behind the French lines, but my memory is more problematic than that."

"Did you take a knock on the noggin?" The boy was merely curious and not ghoulishly so.

"I can forget *everything*. My name, what country I dwell in, which language I'm to use and why... I can speak coherently when these spells are upon me, but everything that I am, everything I've done, slips from my recall."

"Did the Frenchies do that to you?"

"No. It just... happens. Has been happening since I went up to university. Then some hours pass, or I nap, and when I wake up, it's all back." Except for the time at the chateau. Some part of that horror yet eluded my memory. No other explanation presented itself for what had clearly happened there.

The first two times I'd lost my powers of recollection, I'd attributed the lapse to strong drink, overexertion, sexual exuberance, lack of rest... all the excesses young men embrace so recklessly. The third time, I'd been at Caldicott Hall, and Arthur had seen me in my befogged state.

I hadn't known who he was, why he felt entitled to scold me —*Stop playacting, Julian. Your humor eludes me*—or where I was. Some fancy country house belonging to a rude fellow who was almost as tall as I was.

I'd gone off to war, confident that vigorous activity and a soldier's discipline would put the problem to rest. More fool I.

"I fear the condition is worsening."

I'd had a spell of forgetfulness at the chateau—I could recall the lapses themselves once they passed—but something worse must have happened, some further erosion of my powers. Unlike every other instance, when the lost information returned that time, the puzzle had been short a few critical pieces.

Atticus tossed another twig into the water. "I'd like to forget every birching I've ever suffered. I'd like to forget that time the footmen put me up to stealing a sip from Cook's cooking sherry. Putrid stuff, and people drink it *on purpose*."

I'd never tried to explain my malady to anybody other than medical professionals, though various family members had seen its effects, and Hyperia knew the bare facts.

"I don't merely forget what day of the week it is, Atticus. I forget my name, my age, my nationality, where I am... Everything is gone right down to the name of my first pony or if I ever had a pony. I also forget that I'm prone to such lapses when I'm in the midst of them, so each time it's like I'm losing my mind all over again."

I had discreetly consulted physicians, and they'd been of no help. One old herbwoman had suggested I was eating something that induced an imbalance in my humors others were not prone to. Salvia, cannabis, opium, and many other plants affected the mind, so her theory had been some comfort, though I could find no association between my diet and my memory lapses.

"I carry a card," I said softly, "in my pocket." I took it out, though the light was too dim to read what I'd written. "I'm never without it." The card had been Hyperia's idea, like sewing a soldier's name into the collar of his uniform. Though few with any sense carried much money on London's streets, I'd affixed some pound notes to the card in an abundance of caution.

"What's it say?"

"*You are Lord Julian Caldicott. You have written this card to remind yourself that your memory sometimes fails in its entirety. The lapses pass within a few hours. You have merely to be patient, and all will be well.*" I'd also written my direction and my brother's particulars on the card, though I'd never had need to consult it.

Since returning from France, I'd yet to suffer a bout of forgetting.

"So you can't woo Miss West because you're dicked in the nob?"

"That's part of it. She knows about the memory lapses, but five years ago, I had an extra older brother standing between me and the title, and after every lapse, my recall eventually returned. Now I am the spare, and I can no longer be confident of a complete recovery from a bout of forgetting."

"Like you're an old man. Old men get married all the time."

"I'm not an old man." Though, for all I knew, in another few years, I'd be as dotty as one—or worse. I'd be like Miss Cleary, waiting for my favorite tisane and losing track of the very room I slept in.

"You should tell Miss West," Atticus said, hopping off the railing and rubbing his rump with both hands. "She might not care. She woulda married you before you bought your colors, wouldn't she?"

"That's different, and when I told her not to wait for me... she had the option of bestowing her favors elsewhere."

"Except she didn't. Ormstead's making sheep's eyes at her now." Atticus slid gracefully down the banister of the few steps leading up to the gazebo landing as lightly as that cat he'd referenced earlier.

"If Ormstead is wooing Miss West, that is none of your affair, my boy." Or mine. I rose from the bench, though I was reluctant to give up the night for the thumping and chattering of the ballroom. "Tell Canning to meet me in the guest wing in an hour." I could put the watch in Cleary's jewelry box, where no maid or footman ought to have peeked.

"I'll tell him, and won't nobody overhear me when I do. You should let Miss West know you've gone off your head worse than before."

"I don't tell anybody that, and if I'm lucky, my memory will improve over time."

Atticus tossed a final stick into the water. "From what I seen, you ain't lucky, guv. You're smart, you cut a dash, you got some blunt, and you're a decent fella, but you ain't lucky."

When I offered him no argument, he slipped away into the night, and I resigned myself to the dubious charms of Roger de Coverley and his loud, sweaty ilk.

~

The old skills had not deserted me. I made my presence known in the ballroom, pretended to enjoy a flute of champagne, and looked in on the cardroom long enough to know Ophelia and Hyperia were trouncing Banter and old Sir Pericles at whist. I asked the lone red-haired footman for directions to the gentlemen's retiring room and prepared to commit reverse larceny.

Canning met me at the top of the main staircase. "Starting to get loud," he said. "We'll be bringing out the cheaper champagne within the hour and watering the punch."

Country dancing, by its nature, was thunderous. Four dozen feet thumping and glissading in rhythm had the same power and punch as a marching army crossing a bridge. One feared for the bridge, and for one's nerves.

"Loud is good," I said, "unless the noise drives Cleary from the ballroom. He wasn't playing cards."

"You'd best be careful, my lord. He might be looking in on his auntie." Canning's observation was less than complimentary. "He looks in on her frequently."

"He's either a devoted nephew," I said, "or he's trying to impersonate one. This is his room?"

"Aye." Cleary was billeted exactly where a doting nephew would ask to be, right next to Miss Cleary's apartment.

Canning retrieved a bucket of coal and a bucket of ashes from the nearest alcove while I mentally reviewed my position. These rooms were at the end of the corridor, facing the home wood rather than the garden. Weak light came from beneath the door to Miss Cleary's parlor, while the room across the corridor and Mendel's room showed no illumination.

"Whistle if trouble is afoot," I said. "Laugh, pretend to be tipsy. I shouldn't be above two minutes. 'God Save the King' means all clear." Thirty seconds might suffice, but I wanted to do a little nosing about while I was in the neighborhood.

I slipped through Mendel's parlor door and found his apartment to be a mirror of his aunt's. The parlor was small, comfortable, and devoid of human touches. No flowers, no window cracked open, no riding jacket slung casually over the back of a chair.

The bedroom was a different story. Mendel was managing without a valet—or maybe he was imposing on the good offices of Brimstock, Ormstead, and Banter's valets—and his room was going untidy about the seams. The jewelry box was open, the contents a pile of sleeve buttons, cravat pins, and rings. One door of the wardrobe hung ajar, a pair of tall boots beside it. The right boot had flopped over at the ankle, while the left was held straight by a boot tree.

Shameful abuse of expensive footwear. A quick gloss of fingertips over the soles confirmed that they were Hoby boots, but that hardly proved anything. I wore Hoby's work, as did much of Mayfair.

The bed was made, though a discarded shirt topped the quilt. A top hat sat on the sideboard, wrinkled gloves beside it, Mendel's shabby riding crop across the brim. At least when it came to his attire, Mendel was not given to ostentation.

Hearty laughter came from the corridor, followed by a murmur of masculine voices. I slipped the watch into the heap of gewgaws in the jewelry box and cut a swift, silent path to the balcony. A little acrobatics on my part, and I was soon on the next balcony over and silently counting to one hundred in French.

The voices faded, and the door to Cleary's room opened. The clank of a poker against andirons followed—Canny, just doing his job —and I let myself into Maria's bedroom. The chamber was dark and filled with antiphonal snoring. Mrs. Waldrup was ensconced in a reading chair near a dying fire, and Miss Cleary was in the chair opposite her. An empty decanter sat on the table beside Mrs. Waldrup's chair. A book lay open in her lap. Two empty glasses glinted in the light of the embers on the hearth.

Bless their hearts. Would that I could have joined them.

I made my way into the parlor and waited for Canny's signal.

This room also had a fire, which rendered it quite warm, and allowed me to see what I had not noticed on my earlier visit. The chair backs were topped with lace doilies, probably Mrs. Waldrup's work. The serviceable shawl had been folded on the sideboard.

A vase of roses graced the mantel, and beside them sat a framed sketch.

I knew not what inspired me to examine that sketch, but I knelt with it by the fire and expected to see some little rendering of flowers or kittens. A decorative memento brought along by a traveler to give temporary quarters a touch of home.

The sketch was quite good. Either Maria had been a talented artist, or she'd commissioned a small portrait of her nephews in boyhood. The younger two might have been peas in a pod—albeit one pea plumper than the other—while the oldest already showed signs of the arrogance that would make him such disagreeable company later in life.

Arthur had a fine opinion of himself, but he wasn't arrogant. Our sisters would have dealt swiftly with any pretensions in that direction.

I recognized the middle brother from our time together on the Peninsula. Daniel Cleary had the gift of rubicund good cheer, and even a maimed foot hadn't stolen that from him. Mendel, by contrast, peered out of the frame with impatience, as if even sitting with his younger brothers was an affront to his youthful dignity.

Twit.

A quiet baritone importuned the Almighty regarding a happy, glorious, victorious monarch, and I set the sketch back on the mantel. Curiosity sent me back into the bedroom, where I lifted the lid of Maria's jewelry box. She'd worn not so much as a brooch or bracelet when I'd come across her playing truant, and her jewelry box, while sizable, housed only a few rings and one string of pearls.

An older lady of means should have some pretty baubles about, reminders of younger, more sociable times. Where was her painted fan? Her engraved watch? Her keepsake brooch?

I lifted the velvet-covered false bottom of the jewelry box, expecting to find answers to my queries, and a quantity of gold winked back at me, though none of it was wearable. A pile of sovereigns sat atop equally impressive stacks of bearer bank notes made out against an account at Wentworth and Penrose's institution.

Pots of money, indeed, and like many an aging eccentric, Maria kept hers—a small but impressive sampling of hers—where she could reassure herself daily of its safety.

The ladies slumbered on as I replaced the false bottom, closed the jewelry box, and quit the room. I retrieved the shawl from the parlor and draped it across Maria's lap, then returned to the corridor. I was pretending to have paused before a pier glass to retie my hair into its queue when Canning joined me, his coal swapped for a second bucket of ashes.

"I thought the gentlemen's retiring room was along here somewhere," I said.

"Around the corner to your right, my lord."

"Thank you."

He winked and took the left turning, which I had reason to know would lead to the footmen's stairs. "Happy to be of service."

I took the right turning, though my thoughts remained with the two ladies, dreaming so peacefully in their chairs, where the stomping and chattering from the ballroom barely registered.

Poor Maria might well have a devil of a head come morning, but for now, she was at peace.

"And may flights of angels sing you to sleep," I muttered, then realized that I'd cited an epitaph for a mad, dying prince. I mentally revised my sentiment to a cheery *nighty-night* and prepared to be seen by many trustworthy witnesses in the gentlemen's retiring room.

CHAPTER TWELVE

I did not need the facilities in the retiring room itself, so I stepped across the corridor to what had become its annex. The gentlemen's swearing and tippling room, perhaps.

"The violins are bloody flat, I tell you," a sprig seated by the window said, corking his flask with a decisive blow of his gloved fist. "I cannot abide country musicians."

"Miss Ellison's bosom isn't flat." That came from Brimstock, who sat in a wing chair in a corner of the room.

The place looked to be a library without books or a gaming room without a billiards table. The requisite shelves were built into the far wall, heavy furniture was arranged about the room, and a potted lemon tree added a touch of greenery by the French doors. A fresh breeze wafted in from the balcony, though the air bore the slight odor —and sting—of tobacco smoke.

As I came farther into the room, I saw that Brimstock's bare foot was propped up on a hassock, a towel with what I presumed to be ice wrapped over his arch. His jacket was off, as was the jacket of the musical genius by the window.

"Did somebody step on your foot, Brimstock?" I pretended to

examine the decanters marching in height order along the sideboard.

"Longacre's rubbishing colt," Brimstock replied. "Ruddy thing is a demon, and I told mine host as much. Should be sentenced to hard labor with the draft mares. They'll sort the little shite out."

I took a ham and cheese sandwich from the tray before the decanters. "How did Longacre respond?"

"Claimed I'd offered him an inspired idea, and he wished he'd thought of it."

"Broomstick likes some meat on a woman's bones," another coat-less scion said from a window seat. His cravat had been tied in the most elaborate, lacy confection I'd ever seen on a gentleman's person. The pin securing it boasted a sizable amethyst. "Brimmie probably dreams of draft mares."

Mozart snickered.

Brimstock lifted a drink from the table by his chair, saluted, and sipped. "You know what they say about soft cushions," he replied.

The order of the evening seemed to be to shrug out of one's coat, get off one's feet, and insult women. I could manage two out of the three. I draped my coat over the back of the chair pressed into service for that purpose and took a bite out of my sandwich.

"Will you offer for Miss Longacre, Brimstock?"

He shifted the towel to peer at his injured foot—or show off the purpling bruise—then reapplied the cloth and sat back. "We still have more than a week of this ordeal to endure, Caldicott. One doesn't surrender one's freedom lightly."

"You won't surrender your freedom at all," Amethyst said. "You'll simply add the fair Maybelle to your stable. She isn't bad-looking, and she has settlements."

"Has a sharp tongue too," Mozart muttered. "I cannot abide a woman with a sharp tongue."

Men did this, and for the sake of justice between the genders, I hoped women did it too: assessed marital prospects as if acquiring new furniture. *That armchair looks comfortable, but puce upholstery is too high a price to pay for comfort. Another chair perfectly matches*

*the aubergine sofa, though anything stuffed with horsehair will itch
and rustle abominably.*

"Miss Longacre," I said, "is understandably reluctant to follow
the example of not one but two young cousins who died as a result of
giving birth. They survived a year of matrimony apiece, from what
I've been told." I took another bite of my sandwich rather than lapse
into outright sermonizing.

The tulip shot his lacy cuffs and fluffed his cravat.

Mozart cleared his throat. "If Eve hadn't gone about flirting with
snakes, then the ladies might have an easier time of it."

"If Adam had been a proper escort and on hand to fling the snake
out of the garden," Brimstock said, "we might all have an easier time
of it. None of this sweat-of-our-brow and perpetual-toil nonsense.
Somebody find me some fresh ice. This lot has melted."

Raking apparently made a fellow more broad-minded than I'd
realized. I tugged the bell-pull—the bruise was nasty—and wandered
out to the balcony. If Brimstock was flaunting his injury, he might
well have come by it honestly.

Mendel Cleary lounged with a hip propped on the railing, his
shirt white against the evening darkness.

He caught sight of me, straightened, sniffed, and brushed past me
through the French doors. He muttered the word *thief* so quietly only
I would hear him.

"Pay him no mind." The tip of Ormstead's cheroot glowed
momentarily red. "Longacre suggested to him that he'd won enough
at cards for the nonce. He's pouting."

"I believe the manly term is 'seething.'" *Brooding* was too calm a
term for Mendel's turbulent mood.

From the balcony, we could see down into the glittering, semi-
sunken ballroom. The strains of violins in close harmony—sounding
perfectly in tune to me—drifted up on the night air.

"Mendel Cleary doesn't have an easy time of it," Ormstead said,
blowing smoke rings. "He's inherited spent acres, one brother toils
away as a glorified clerk at Horse Guards, the other came home from

the war and became a wastrel. There's old Mendel, trying to marry wealth before he has to sell off his hunters and his art, though he has all the charm of a temperance crusader on the topic of gin."

"Dear Mendy doesn't seem to mind putting out coin for decent boots, gold sleeve buttons, and Bond Street tailoring." I finished my sandwich and dusted my hands over the railing.

Ormstead tapped the ashes from his cheroot into the abyss of darkness beneath the balcony. "I do not want to talk about Mendel Cleary or his perishing watch."

I glanced behind us. Cleary was shrugging into his coat and doing up the buttons. Off to pout somewhere else, and good riddance.

"You want to discuss Hyperia West," I said, "but I am not the person you should be talking to."

"You and she were all but engaged, my lord. She would have wed you."

"She would have wed the man who went off to Spain, full of his own consequence and ready to teach those upstart Frogs a lesson."

Ormstead watched his smoke rings drift into the night. "We were such fools."

"We were exactly what we had been raised to be." Arrogant little pawns who'd excelled at taking orders without question. "Talk to Hyperia. She's so smart, she even knows how to hide how intelligent she is. She loves a good verbal donnybrook, and she's a demon in a steeplechase."

"If you are that fond of her, why not marry her?"

"It's complicated, but suffice it to say that I wish her only the best."

Mendel had quit the room behind us, and a footman was arranging more ice on Brimstock's wet towel.

"Marriage is the least complicated undertaking in the world," Ormstead countered. "You care for each other, there's desire too, and marriage provides the means to further both sorts of interest while creating a home for the inevitable offspring. The institution makes perfect sense to me."

"While making sense of the woman herself takes a little more work. Best of luck."

His cheroot smoke was bothering my eyes, and the topic... The topic bothered my heart. "I must make my obeisance before Lady Ophelia," I said. "Lord Longacre will be along directly to send the stragglers back to the ballroom, and I don't fancy another scold from him."

I retrieved my coat from the heap draped over the chairback and wondered what exactly I *did* fancy. Oddly enough, I no longer wanted to be the popinjay who'd pranced off to war, convinced that because he could read, ride, and shoot, he was God's gift to the British military.

But I wanted that popinjay's innocence, I wanted his damned brown hair, I wanted...

I'd apparently picked up the wrong coat. I could have forced my arms into the sleeves, but the cut was too narrow in the chest. I was sorting through the heap of other possibilities when Mendel Cleary returned. Only then did I notice that he was wearing a garment cut too loosely for his frame.

"I'll need a bath after this," he said, unbuttoning the jacket, "but at least you didn't put mine on." He balled up the coat and tossed it at me. I passed him the one that didn't fit.

I put on the correct coat and patted down the pockets to make sure no stray watches had been secreted therein.

"An easy mistake to make," I said, prepared to once again attempt civility. "No harm done." A few wrinkles needlessly added, but no harm.

Cleary smiled at me, a genuinely pleased, good-humored smile. He buttoned up his coat and nodded. "No harm at all. Good evening, my lord."

He jaunted from the room, leaving a puzzled silence in his wake.

Brimstock wiggled his toes. "So Cleary can smile. One had doubts. Who will refresh my drink?"

Mozart obliged, and I made my excuses. But for Cleary's rudeness on the balcony, my reception had been cordial enough. More to the point, I had been seen by numerous witnesses who could explain why I'd absented myself from the festivities.

I grabbed another sandwich, bowed to the company, and made my way back to the ballroom, the long day catching up to me yet again. Bone-weariness was a part of life on campaign, and I'd hoped to put that sort of mind-flattening fatigue behind me. I was nearly that physically tired now and also worn in spirit.

Marriage was simple to Ormstead. Caring, desire, vows, *et voilà*. Domestic bliss. Would that it were still so for me.

I left Ophelia to her admirers after about a quarter hour of fetching punch for her and the other chaperones, then tendered my excuses.

"No stamina," Ophelia said. "That's the problem with young men today. They simply lack bottom. Off to your beauty sleep, then, and leave me to enjoy this cheerful company."

Some old gallant blew her a kiss, she simpered, and I made my exit. I promised myself that whatever else was true, thirty years on, I would not waste my evenings on whist and flirtation when I could instead be reading a good book by the fire with an old friend and a good vintage.

Though who would that old friend be?

I took a sconce down from the corridor a few yards from my room and was surprised to see a faint light already leaking from beneath my bedroom door. Atticus would not have waited up for me. Canning was refilling coal buckets and trimming sconces.

Which left...

I pushed open the door and strolled into my quarters. "Really, Cleary, if you must plant contraband in a man's rooms, you ought to get it right the first time."

He ceased rifling beneath my mattress, straightened, and jerked down the hem of his evening jacket. "If you've destroyed my grandfather's watch, I will have satisfaction from you."

"For the last time, I did not take your rubbishing watch. I had little opportunity and no motive. The same with the horse. Whatever crusade you are on to vilify me must end."

"Your own actions have vilified you from now to kingdom come," he sneered. "All I want you to do is leave. You forced your presence on people who should not have to deal with you. You refused to slink back to Town as you ought. You had to appoint yourself investigator-at-large over some stolen kiss, then meddle at battledore. I can't help that I excel at cards, but you could certainly have left this gathering the day you arrived."

He stalked across the room until he stood nearly toe-to-toe with me. No odor of drink came from his person, but a vein was throbbing at his temple.

"You had to go poking your nose into matters that don't concern you," he went on, apparently blessed with one kind of stamina. "You fraternize with the staff and imposed yourself on my aunt. That you'd commit larceny for entertainment is all too plausible... Now I hear you've gone to tattle to Moreland, and next thing, he'll be over here oozing ducal consequence and asking awkward questions."

No, he would not. Moreland was too busy meddling with his heir's bachelorhood, and as far as I knew, His Grace was still in Town.

"Why," Mendel said, marching for the door, "why in the name of all that's honorable can't you just *leave?*"

He was truly incensed about his precious watch—or the schemes he'd had involving the watch—but something else caught my ear. He longed to challenge me. Yearned to face me over pistols or swords or bullwhips...

"You think I won't meet you, Cleary?"

"I know you won't. The great warrior has come home broken in mind and body, crying off from his engagement, idling behind closed curtains in London. He hasn't the courage or mental fitness to take up arms again."

I gestured toward the door. "I haven't the foolishness to risk my life for the sake of a watch I did not steal, much less destroy. I bid you good night."

He parade-marched out, the picture of masculine indignation, bootheels thumping on the floorboards. I closed the door behind him and flipped the lock. Atticus knew to knock, and I wanted no more reprisals of Cleary's intrusion.

He should find the watch in his jewelry box before morning, and if that did not put an end to his malice toward me, perhaps I would quit the gathering early. He could insult me the livelong day, and that was no matter.

If he'd insulted Hyperia, though, or even Ophelia... I could not ignore slights to the ladies, and that might well be his next tactic.

I wasn't too weary to care, but I was too weary to ponder Mendel Cleary's rudeness any further. I hung my jacket over the back of the room's sole chair, scuffed out of my dancing pumps, and began the ritual of my nightly ablutions. Not until I was hanging up my evening kit in the wardrobe did I realize the true magnitude of my difficulties.

For a few moments, Mendel Cleary had worn my jacket, and in those few minutes, he'd apparently found the card in my pocket. That was the reason for his uncharacteristic smile and the comment about my mind being broken. He knew the full extent of my mental infirmity and would likely use it against me at the first opportunity.

Why? Sir Thomas had grounds to hate me. Lord and Lady Longacre were certainly entitled to resent me. I deserved the enmity and suspicions of many, but from Mendel Cleary, to whom I should have been no more than a distasteful curiosity, I had earned undying loathing.

And I did not know why.

~

"I thought today we'd pay a call on Sally Hortonson," Ophelia said, stirring her chocolate. "Such a lovely family, if a bit loud. We could bring Maria with us and get the poor dear a bit of fresh air."

Encouraged by my reception among the gentlemen last night, I had braved the breakfast parlor at an early hour. Cleary had yet to blight the morning with his presence, and Sir Thomas was probably riding about the countryside, vanquishing brigands to build up his appetite.

"As it happens, Godmama, I thought I'd return to London today." Mendel Cleary's bald enmity was making up my mind on that score. He would continue with his machinations until I was thoroughly disgraced if not banished from the gathering and Society itself.

Hyperia had already asked me to leave, probably anticipating exactly the course Cleary was bent on pursuing. I had anticipated trouble from Sir Thomas, but Hyperia knew society better than I did. If Cleary desisted, Sir Thomas might take up the hue and cry against me.

Part of me desperately wanted to stay, to be simply another semi-bored, semi-diverted guest at a country house party. Hyperia felt safe, or so she claimed, but I was still uneasy on her behalf. We never had discovered who'd accosted her.

Another part of me was tired of fighting a rear-guard action against enemies whose ire I did not deserve.

I kept these conclusions to myself, because Ophelia and I had company. Sir Pericles—cane resting against his chair—pretended to read yesterday's London newspaper, and Miss Ellison was carefully spreading jam on her toast. Canny stood vigil by the groaning sideboard, and Amethyst, cheeks approximating the shade of new asparagus, had banished himself to the company of a swaddled teapot at the shady end of the table.

Lady Ophelia set down her cup. "Talk of leaving is nonsense, Julian. You are here to stay, else I shall have to racket about all on my own. Who knows what trouble might find me? Besides, the sky is less than promising, and if you get caught in a downpour on your way back to Town, you might well end up with an ague."

If she only knew the conditions I and the entire army had endured in Spain and France.

"A bit of weather never hurt a true soldier," Sir Pericles observed, turning the pages of his paper. He'd been knighted shortly after Moses had presided over the defeat of the Amalekites, but the old boy's hearing was apparently still in good order.

"When you've drained the chocolate pot," I said, taking a place across from Ophelia, "I will escort you to your room. We can discuss the matter further at our leisure."

Miss Ellison passed me the jam. "I hope you stay, my lord. With a ducal heir underfoot, the other fellows are a bit more on their mettle, though only a bit."

Ophelia preened at this support, and I was a little heartened too. Miss Ellison knew what it was to fall from grace in Society's eyes and what it was to embark on the long trudge back toward acceptability.

"Thank you for that," I said, taking up the jam pot, "but others do not share your kind opinion, and our host and hostess were never expecting to add me to the guest list."

Lady Ophelia gently swirled the chocolate pot, a porcelain confection glazed all over with red carnations, and poured herself a second cup, or a third. Who knew how long she'd been waiting to ambush me?

"Lady Longacre will be short two bachelors if you decamp," Ophelia said. "I have it on good authority that Healy West has decided not to make the trek here and has sent his regrets."

I tucked into my eggs and mentally counted to twenty in German. "Healy West is not a fellow to leave his sister unaccompanied in the wilds of Kent."

My comment earned the notice of the ailing Amethyst, who sent a bleary squint in my direction.

"I am qualified to serve as the lady's chaperone," Ophelia said, stirring her chocolate vigorously, "and Lady Longacre has a connection to Miss West as well. You are nonetheless needed here, Julian, and here you will stay."

Well, damn. Ophelia had got wind of Ormstead's interest in Hyperia, and this was to be my penance. Healy had doubtless received an offer from Ophelia to stand in as the guardian of Hyperia's virtue, and Healy, being nobody's fool, had wasted no time sending regrets.

Hyperia joined us before I could protest further. She looked tidy, pretty, and dear, and she smiled genially as I rose to greet her.

"I am famished," she said. "The country dances always leave me with a lingering appetite."

Sir Pericles peered out from behind his paper. "Trouncing your elders at whist seems to appeal to you too, young lady."

"Oh, quite, but you did put up a notable fight, Sir Pericles. Do sit down, Jules. I can fix my own plate."

She piled eggs and a few slices of ham on her plate—God bless a lady with an appetite—and took the place beside me.

"Julian is once again announcing his intention to desert the gathering," Lady Ophelia said. "Tell him he's needed here, Miss West. Men require constant supervision, else they take odd notions."

Hyperia poured herself a cup of tea before I could perform that office. "Lord Julian must do as he sees fit, my lady. This house party was not on his schedule, and we have imposed on him significantly already."

Point to Hyperia, though her remark had Sir Pericles harrumphing behind the Society pages.

I was contemplating a second serving of eggs—they were hot, and I had passed over the ham, though the aroma wafting from Hyperia's plate was tempting—when Mendel Cleary strode into the room.

He exuded brisk good cheer until he realized I was among the guests at the table. Like a bad fairy whose pretty disguise disintegrates at the stroke of midnight, his gaze narrowed, his posture stiffened, and his mouth became a flat, disapproving line.

"The company will excuse me," he said. "I have abruptly lost my appetite."

I was halfway through the thought, *Good riddance, again,* when Lady Ophelia was on her feet.

"Young man, I will not excuse you."

Miss Ellison became fascinated with her tea cup. Hyperia patted my thigh beneath the table.

"Then I beg your ladyship's pardon," Cleary retorted, "but you cannot expect me to break bread with a thief, a traitor, a liar, and a varlet. That person..." He jerked his chin in my direction. "That disgrace to the male gender should offend all who behold him."

Cleary was not wearing his grandfather's watch, though he did have on a signet ring, sleeve buttons, and a cravat pin. He'd doubtless found the watch, but was persisting in the fiction that it had been stolen. If I'd had any doubts previously that his ire toward me was manufactured, he'd put those doubts to rest.

"Mr. Cleary, you insult my friend," Hyperia said quietly. "Your behavior is not that of a gentleman, and the only party for whom you stand as a conscience is yourself. You owe me and Lady Ophelia, if not Lord Julian, an apology for your lapse of manners."

Oh, Perry. I wanted to clap my hand over her mouth, and to... hug her. Her words were well meant, so loyal and firm, but Mendel was turning the same rosy shade as the carnations on the chocolate pot.

Cleary appeared to get hold of himself, though at the sideboard, Canny's posture had become that of the soldier at attention. The change was subtle and grand and reminded me of many a morning before battle.

"The only apology I will make," Cleary said, nodding slightly to Ophelia and Hyperia, "is to offer my condolences to you two ladies on the loss of your common sense. Lady Ophelia has brought a scoundrel into our midst, and you, Miss West, are too hen-witted to see her error. Lord Julian Caldicott needs to return to London, and if you truly cared for him, you'd be shooing him out the door."

Sir Pericles had lowered his paper and was staring fixedly at Cleary. Amethyst looked baffled, and Miss Ellison's pale cheeks had acquired two becoming dabs of color.

I rose with a sense of inevitable doom. Doom that had been pursuing me since the night I'd trailed Harry from camp, doom that had followed me out of the mountains in France and right back to London.

"Please apologize to the ladies," I said. "Your differences are with me, Cleary, though I know not why you've taken me into such personal dislike."

Increasingly, I did not care about the why. Some people were simply entitled snobs, and many of those objectionable sorts hailed from the gentry ranks. And yet, Cleary was a devoted nephew, a conscientious landowner—in as much as he could be—and a possible suitor for Miss Longacre's hand.

He was more than the strutting twit making my life so difficult, and I was more than the fellow who'd come to such sorry straits in France. The thought was a relief and wanted further pondering, but for the moment, Cleary had my full attention. He had insulted the ladies, but still, I would not call him out.

Neither, however, would I quit the battlefield.

"The ladies have become your pawns," Cleary said, "and if you will not leave in the next hour, *my lord*, then you will give me satisfaction instead."

Sir Pericles was the first to recover from that salvo. "Cleary, you exceed all bounds. I don't care if Lord Julian personally rowed the Corsican to France from Elba. *There are ladies present.*"

Cleary had *counted* on the ladies being present, though I knew not exactly how or why they figured into his scheme. Perhaps he thought I'd defend their honor when my own wasn't worth the bother?

"Apologize," I said. "Not to me, but to the ladies." I did not tell him that I'd been planning to leave, because quitting Makepeace now truly would forfeit my honor.

"You should apologize for breathing," Mendel retorted. "Name your seconds."

He was committing mortal sins against gentlemanly deportment by failing to give me an opportunity to apologize and by insulting the ladies in public.

"I'll serve," Sir Pericles said, rising and passing Lady Ophelia his newspaper. "Lord Julian's father would have expected it of me, though I must say this is all a damned lot of nonsense. Nonsense that Lord Julian, whatever his myriad other failings, did not start."

Canny was still staring resolutely at nothing. He could not second me, having no gentlemanly pretensions, but I suspected he wanted to.

"Please apologize to the ladies," I said. "Your differences with me aside, they are owed your respect."

Mendel smiled the same sort of smile he'd offered me last night when we'd exchanged coats. "Do they *know*, my lord? Do they know that you have become as daft as my dear old auntie? That your memory is as leaky as Napoleon's naval blockade? *I know*, and I will see to it that all of London does, too, unless you tuck tail and run like the coward you are."

Calling me a coward to my face, before witnesses, qualified as bad melodrama, and yet, the threat Cleary wielded was real. My memory problems could taint my family with rumors of madness, and even ducal standing would not eclipse such a failing.

"With whom should Sir Pericles consult?" I asked quietly. Perhaps the seconds could sort this business out, or perhaps, upon reflection, I'd find it expedient to visit Rome for a few decades.

"Brimstock and Banter. Ladies, I bid you good morning."

He offered them a jaunty bow, helped himself to a croissant from the sideboard, and left as if he hadn't a care in the world.

Sir Pericles thumped his cane against the floor. "Damned lot of nonsense. Choose swords, my lord. Harder to cheat. That one has the look of a fellow who'd fire early and blame his mischief on a faulty weapon."

On that cheering note, he, too, quit the breakfast parlor, as did I, lest my eggs and toast make an untimely reappearance.

CHAPTER THIRTEEN

My escape was thwarted by Lady Ophelia marching after me.

"Julian Caldicott, you will listen to what I have to say." She came on relentlessly, and manners forced me to pause at the foot of the grand staircase. "What on earth was all that about?"

"I will be damned—and I do mean damned—if I know, my lady. Mendel Cleary hasn't simply taken me into dislike. Annihilating me has become his *raison d'être.*"

"I hadn't pegged him for a hothead." She started up the steps. "He saw you were at table and began launching Congreve rockets of rudeness in your direction. Not done. One can make no sense of it. He's been Maria's prop and stay, he sent two brothers off to war, he's managing his acres as well as may be... A suitable *parti*, though not a catch. What could possibly justify such behavior from a man who jealously guards what standing he has?"

"Perhaps he'll commence with a spot of blackmail," I said, accompanying her up the steps. "He found the card in my coat pocket last night."

"Card? Are you cheating at cards now too? Is this what you dashing blades think passes for sport these days? I despair of the younger generation. Cheating at cards and calling one another out between the toast and the second pot of tea?"

"Please do not mention food. I refer to the card I carry for reference at those times when my memory falters." When my powers of recollection departed altogether.

"Whatever that has to do with anything." Ophelia paused before the door to her apartment. "Cleary does not want to annihilate you, except perhaps socially, but he does want you gone from Makepeace."

The words *this is all your fault* begged on their aching knees to be spoken. "He knows I have problems with my memory, my lady. I want to be gone from Makepeace, but I cannot permit his threats to send me into a disorderly retreat."

She opened the door, grabbed me by the wrist, and dragged me into her sitting room. Like her friend Maria, she'd added a few touches to an otherwise unremarkable parlor. The flowers on the sideboard were her signature roses. A French novel lay open on the love seat, and a pair of exquisitely embroidered slippers had been half tucked beneath a reading chair.

"Your memory problem. Remind of the particulars, Julian."

"I've told you about it," I said, confident of that much, because I'd told only her and Hyperia outside of immediate family. Arthur had begrudged me even those disclosures. "I have spells of forgetfulness. They pass, but when I'm in the midst of one, I cannot remember my own name."

She began fussing with the roses. "You've tried moderating your drinking?"

"The problem is not drink and not diet, that I can discern. The problem is a fundamental weakness in my mind. When the plague of forgetting descends, I don't know where I live, what church I attend, or who my nearest relation is. I wrote out a card to keep in my pocket, one that explains the situation to me in my own hand."

"And Cleary found the card. Have you discussed this memory problem with your mother?"

What had Her Grace's opinion on the matter to do with the price of cheese in Cheshire? "I have not, not specifically. Arthur probably has." The duchess was his ally and his hostess for the nonce.

"You should. This sort of thing might run in families, like webbed toes or red hair. Your brother might not know the particulars of some enfeebled uncle, though the duchess would have heard about it. If the flawed lineage was on the maternal side, she will certainly be aware of the details."

Whether I had mentally unsound antecedents interested me not one bit at that moment. "More pressing matters demand my attention for the present. Do you know if Cleary has dueled before?"

She withdrew one wilted specimen from the bouquet and tossed it into the dustbin. "What does that matter?"

"Because the choice of weapons is mine, and if he prefers swords, I'll choose pistols and so on."

She drew herself up, and I was reminded that Ophelia was a tall woman and imposing when she wanted to be. "You will do no such thing, Julian. Harry's death was tragedy enough. Arthur can't lose you too."

Some part of me acknowledged that she was raising a valid point —or she believed she was. As the ducal spare, my existence was justified to the extent that I was an insurance policy for my family against escheat.

That policy had been voided in France, alas. "Arthur will just have to marry and beget his own heirs," I said. "He's the conscientious sort. He'll have the heir and spare in his nursery in less than five years, once he makes up his mind to tend to the matter." Though why hadn't he already done so, paragon and peer that he was?

I expected return fire from Ophelia, remonstrations and lamentations. References to degenerate youth and fading damsels. She picked up her French novel and sank onto the love seat.

"Arthur loves you," she said, "and he took Harry's death very hard. If you don't care for the succession, please consider that your siblings believed for a time that they'd lost both you and Harry. Then

Arthur got word you'd escaped. We were frantic. Weeks went by with no more news, and we thought only of you and the possibility of your survival. Mendel Cleary's stupid games aren't worth dying for."

This was news. "You believed I'd *perished* at French hands?" And Hyperia would have been among those suffering such torments, too, but she'd never mentioned this little hell of uncertainty to me.

"There was... confusion," Ophelia looked abruptly elderly and tired. "First, we thought you had been taken captive and killed. Then word came that, no, Harry was lost to us, then you *and* Harry. Wartime communication leaves much to be desired, and Wellington was intent on driving into France with all due and deliberate speed. Notices to families of officers taken prisoner while on unsanctioned maneuvers were not a priority. Then you rose from the dead, Julian. You are not to throw that miracle into the faces of your siblings because some strutting ass takes a notion to annoy you."

Cleary had insulted me, Ophelia, and Hyperia and threatened me as well. If Ophelia would only consider the matter calmly, she'd see that Cleary was also threatening my family's standing.

"We need not duel to the death."

She put her face in her hands, as one did when sorely grieving, then sat back. "You stupid boy. A man who breaks every rule of etiquette at the breakfast table would gleefully run you through when you lay bleeding on the ground. You must not give him the opportunity."

"Then I must ensure that if anybody is left bleeding on the ground, it's Mendel Cleary."

I departed on that note, sure of my logic, not at all sure of my chances. I was yet to be denied the solitude of my room, though.

Hyperia came up the steps looking like the Wrath of Mayfair. "Jules, I don't care about insults or honor or Mendel Cleary's stupid taunts. You cannot kill him. He deserves a thrashing, maybe even wounding, and I am tempted to see to the matter myself, but you must not kill him."

Had I not loved Hyperia in some fashion since my youth, I would have fallen in love with her in that moment. Ophelia feared I'd get the worst of any encounter with Cleary, while Hyperia assumed I'd prevail. Ophelia expected me to dodge off. Hyperia would have served as my second.

"You won't tell me to light out for Portugal in the next hour?"

She sent a fulminating glance down the steps. "Are you daft?"

"Well, yes, in one sense." I withdrew into the nearest parlor, the one where I'd found Maria Cleary playing truant. "Do you recall the card I carry in my coat pocket?"

"Of course."

"Cleary found it, and that's why he could maunder on about my little problem before that assemblage at breakfast. He knows, Hyperia."

She went to the sideboard, opened a few drawers, and came up with a pair of embroidery scissors. "You've been to war and suffered untold horrors. Memory lapses, nightmares, and periodic doldrums are nigh predictable for such as you."

She began snipping away at the ailing ferns, cutting off dead fronds and tossing them into the dustbin, untangling healthy foliage so it caught the fullest complement of sunlight and curved in graceful arcs. She tested the soil with her finger.

"Overwatered. Easy to do with ferns. I'll have a word with the housekeeper, and perhaps you should have a word with Cleary's banker."

"Buy up a few of his mortgages?"

"Of course. Use the weapons you have, Jules. You haven't been out in Society much in recent years, and he's a handy bachelor. You're behind the starting line in the social footrace, despite your standing. Cleary is received all over Town, but he hardly moves in exalted circles."

"He will be more effective moving on the fringes if he decides to spread nasty talk about me." And he had the best kind of nasty talk to offer—the truth. "He'll mutter about my mental incompetence, tainted blood, and treasonous tendencies."

Snip by snip, the ferns were looking more the thing. Hyperia rotated one plant half a turn one direction so the side that had been facing the window now faced the room and shifted the other plant a quarter turn the other way. She moved both a few inches closer to the light and used the hearth set to sweep up the detritus from the rug.

A nothing of a domestic moment, but her care for the ferns and her ability to put them to rights soothed me. I would miss her. I *had* missed her, terribly, and I was going to miss her even more in years to come.

But I was alive to miss her. I could do my missing of her in England. We could remain friends, the better for me to torment myself with proof of her future happiness. All comforts, of a sort.

"Will Cleary truly slander you?" she asked, dusting her hands and returning the scissors to the drawer. "Will he presume to spread gossip about a ducal family when he's just another land-poor squire trying to find an heiress to court?"

"Yes, and he'll go about it like a sniper, lurking in cardrooms and making his muttered asides count, then drawling a few confidential assassinations of my character at the club or while shopping for gloves on Bond Street."

She surveyed me with the same critical eye she'd turned on the ferns, and I had half a mind to ask if she wouldn't mind taking those scissors to my overly long hair.

"You excel at tactics, Jules. At deduction based on a few pertinent and usually-overlooked facts. I know you were good at intelligence work, because Arthur bragged that you'd finally found something at which your skill excelled Harry's."

"I was better than Harry at Latin." Also Greek, and languages generally, but I'd gloated over that skill in private.

Hyperia cracked a window, letting in a slight breeze that gently riffled the ferns and would help them dry out. "And you are better than Harry at surviving, for which God and your native ingenuity be thanked. You cannot kill Cleary, but I know you will sort him out. Look to your strengths and to his weaknesses."

Good advice, though after a demand for satisfaction, one was given little time for pondering strategy. A duel was God's opportunity to pronounce judgment on an otherwise unsolvable question of honor and best undertaken with dispatch.

War was doubtless justified with sophistry of the same ilk.

"I don't have much time, Hyperia. My affairs are in order, what affairs I have, and I doubt the seconds will be able to effect a rapprochement."

She gazed out across the park. "Cleary was clever in that regard, wasn't he? You are challenged, but you have committed no specific slight to his honor. If you apologize for your non-crime, you admit guilt. If you refuse to apologize, he can blow your brains out. I suspect his objective is simply to run you off."

"Lady Ophelia agrees with you. Something about my mere presence has upset Cleary past all bearing."

Hyperia went to the door, which we'd left mostly open. "Be careful, Jules. Should anything happen to you, Cleary's days would be numbered. If I didn't send him to his eternal reward, Ophelia would."

"I am careful by nature." So careful, I'd gotten myself captured by the French, cast into permanent disgrace, and challenged to a duel that still made no sense to me.

～

Intelligence work for the military was both active and independent. While the regular soldier sat in camp cleaning his weapons, dicing, and longing for letters from home, the intelligence officers were out in the countryside, lingering over a pint at the local watering hole or putting a few casual questions to the grooms at the livery.

We rode and hiked over miles of terrain without being seen. We moved at night as easily as we did in daylight. We did not exactly come and go from camp as we pleased, but we had far more autonomy than the usual run of officer.

This sortie to Makepeace was reviving my appetite for movement. To gallop my horse for more than the genteel length of Rotten Row, to ramble through woods and park and village, to breathe fresh air and hear the cattle lowing... My body was rejuvenated by the environs, and thus I sought the out of doors when Hyperia left me.

I needed to approach Ormstead, because relying exclusively on old Sir Pericles as my second would not do, but that discussion could wait until I'd settled my thoughts. A change into riding attire was in order, and if I was lucky, the rain would hold off for a couple of hours while the overcast remained.

Atticus met me at the door to my broom closet. "You going to shut Cleary's gob permanent-like?"

"Talk travels fast." I let myself into my room, which I'd taken to locking in my absence. "Was Canny indiscreet?" He'd be the logical conduit between the breakfast parlor and the servants' hall.

Atticus followed me through the doorway. "Canny were fuming something fierce. He don't much care for Cleary, and he does like you. Said Cleary were completely beyond the pale, and Miss West and Miss Ellison were present, as was Lady Ophelia. Canny were insulted on behalf of the house, but he was plenty mad on your account too."

Atticus began making the bed while I retrieved riding attire from the wardrobe. "You are not to insert yourself into these proceedings, Atticus. Bystanders can be injured at a duel. Shots go wide, horses spook, the seconds take up arms... The whole business is beyond stupid." Military officers weren't supposed to duel with each other, but they had, and to frequent tragic effect. I had served as second on four occasions, once for Harry.

"Will milord choose pistols or swords?"

"I haven't decided. Cheating is easier with pistols."

"By firing early, you mean?" Atticus smacked one of the thin pillows. "Why not choose fists? You have some reach on him, and you're quick."

I'd also had two older brothers, and Harry had been lightning fast with his fists. "I cannot risk a blow to my head."

"Canny said Cleary were blathering on about you being dicked in the nob. That's dirty tactics, that is." The pillow got a hard right cross followed by a left jab. "Airing a fellow's linen to rile him up, but Canny said you didn't rile."

"The ladies were present." I *was* riled nonetheless, and yet, a part of me rejoiced to know I could still be enraged, however frustrating the provocation. I'd been drifting about in my own life, hiding behind heavy curtains and insomnia and boredom.

A man in a temper was alive in at least the emotional sense. A man who let that temper rule him wouldn't stay alive for long.

"You going riding?" Atticus asked, shaking out the worn extra blanket and refolding it at the foot of the bed.

"I am, and if I'm lucky, I'll run into Ormstead in the stable yard. Please tell Canny not to do anything stupid on my account. Cleary's quarrel is with me." I hung my morning coat in the wardrobe and took down my riding jacket. "You aren't to do anything stupid either."

Atticus tucked my house slippers by the bed. "I could have a little peek at Cleary's room."

"No, you could not. Snooping could get you sacked. We've discussed this." I dragged a comb through my stubbornly white hair and sat on the vanity stool to pull on my riding boots. "You think dodging Cook in a bad mood is a tribulation, then try finding work when you've been turned off without a character."

"I'd go to London," Atticus said, opening the wardrobe and eyeing its contents. "Anybody can find work in London."

"No, they cannot. Every former soldier has come to Town, as have the families displaced by enclosures, as have all the weavers and spinners put out of work by the factory looms. London hasn't room to house any of them, so finding a safe place to sleep is nearly impossible unless you have a domestic post or an apprenticeship. Do you know anybody in Town?"

The boy closed the wardrobe. "I might. I was born there. My mama was from around here, though, so I was sent out this way when she died, and when I was seven, I came to Makepeace."

At the age of seven, he'd been more or less sold into servitude, though without articling him to any profession. The parish earned a bounty, Makepeace got cheap labor, and Atticus lost any connection he might have had with his mother's family or friends, along with the hope of entering a skilled trade.

Though he seemed happy enough, and nobody was trying to put a bullet through his heart.

"If I had a look through Cleary's room," Atticus said, "I might find some vowels, or naughty letters, or something he stole from Lady Ophelia, just for example."

I rose, nigh desperate to be out of the house and away from even this well-intended, conniving stripling. "Nobody would believe the good squire had suddenly taken up stealing from old ladies. He fleeces only the gents who ought to know better. Away with you. I'll lock up after us."

Atticus sent me a sulky look. "You shouldn't have to lock up. So you can't remember everything all the time. Does Cleary have a perfect memory? His auntie certainly don't. He cheats at cards, and nobody's trying to snuff his candle. When the footmen get to spatting, they settle it with threats."

"I am not a footman." I took a final look around my quarters. Locks could be picked, and noting the location of every item in a room was old habit.

"Canny explained how it works belowstairs," Atticus said. "Taylor has been a footman longer than Canny, so he's mad that Canny might be made the underbutler. Taylor was in a temper one day over a compliment Miss Longacre paid to Canny, so he says he'll tell Lord Longacre that Canny wrote his own character to get the post here. Canny says go ahead and tell that bouncer, but I'll tell Miss Belvoir that you were making sheep's eyes at Florence down at the posting inn. Everybody knows Taylor is sweet on Miss Belvoir and that all the lads make eyes at Florence, but Taylor ceased making trouble for Canny faster than you can say old Boney's an ass."

"So they conduct a war of threats?" Such drama belowstairs. "It's a wonder anybody has time to sweep out the hearths."

"Not a war," Atticus said, skipping out the door. "It's like tomcats, ya see. You have to let Cleary know you aren't to be trifled with."

"That's the point of trouncing him with pistols or swords," I said, closing and locking the door. I plucked a single long strand of hair from my head and tied it around the locking mechanism.

"That's smart," Atticus said. "A man who isn't to be trifled with knows to do things like that. Nobody will notice a hair wrapped about the latch, or if they do, they'll think it got snagged from a coat or cloak."

"A long-haired fellow's trick," I said, "but a dark thread works better, provided it's fine. Promise you will stay out of trouble, Atticus. Don't promise you will stay out of trouble and mean you promise to not get caught. This is not your fight."

A mulish glint came into his eyes. "Tomcats kill birds and mice and squirrels and bugs. They don't go about killing *each other*, for all the noise they make."

"Now you're a natural philosopher. Back to the kitchen with you, and if I'm gone before morning..." I produced a sovereign from my inside pocket. "For luck and good service rendered."

He caught the coin, looked like he wanted to berate me at length, then bolted off down the corridor.

I watched him go and considered the wisdom of tomcats, because Atticus had put his finger on a strategy worth considering.

～

I'd sent the stable a request to saddle Atlas, and I did not intend to keep my trusty steed—or some overworked groom—pacing up and down before the horse trough. Ormstead and I met at the top of the terrace steps, though, and the sooner I spoke with him, the better.

"My lord." He offered me a nod. "Bit of a dull day for a hack, but you might still beat the rain."

To perdition with the rubbishing weather. "Cleary demanded satisfaction of me at breakfast."

Ormstead's open, handsome face underwent a transformation—disbelief, astonishment, disapproval, and then the blank features of one trying to ignore the drunk making distasteful remarks by the men's punchbowl.

"What did you do to provoke him?"

"Wrong question. He insists I've stolen his watch, which I did not. He makes vague references to my treasonous past, which the army itself has concluded doesn't exist. He also threatens to make public a lingering memory problem that's afflicted me since university. Now that he's announced my personal tribulation to the world, he says he'll spread word to all of Mayfair unless I quit Makepeace on the hour. He made these accusations while Miss Ellison, Miss West, and Lady Ophelia were present."

Though interestingly, neither our host nor hostess had witnessed them, nor had Miss Maybelle.

"*Not done*," Ormstead said, pacing off across the terrace and then returning. "Not done to involve the ladies, though you can't ignore the encounter, given the witnesses. I gather you're on your way back to London?"

Another wrong question. "I am on my way to enjoy a pleasant hack before the rain starts. I was hoping you'd serve as my second."

What I'd hoped was that Ormstead would take my part, would curse Cleary straight to Hades's front gate, demand to second me, and condole me on the inconvenience of meeting such a scurrilous foe.

As Harry would have done, may he rest in peace. As Hyperia *had* done.

"Second?" He rubbed his chin. "You can't ask some other officer? Sir Thomas, perhaps?"

The wrong questions were piling up by the moment. "Sir

Thomas will root for the opposition. Sir Pericles heard the exchange and offered to support me on the spot."

Ormstead leaned over the balustrade and plucked a pink rose from a rambunctious cane. "I suppose if Sir Pericles will lend his consequence to the matter, I cannot refuse to aid you. Pistols or swords, and have you tendered an apology?"

"For what would I apologize?"

He busied himself with getting the flower threaded through the buttonhole on his lapel. "For any slight that might, in the heat of the moment, have been perceived to offer offense of any kind, et cetera and so forth. You know how it's done. A lot of words that add up to nothing."

"A lot of words that add up to I am a coward and deserve to be shat upon by a rude, land-poor squire who enjoys making false accusations, who delights in publicizing a man's private miseries, and who regards violence toward women as passing entertainment."

Ormstead's boutonniere refused to lay at the correct angle on his lapel. He kept nudging and tugging until the flower fell to the flagstones.

"I'm not saying the situation is fair, my lord. *Do* you have a problem with your memory?"

"Rare, temporary, and complete lapses."

He let the flower lie on the stones. "Then you might have pilfered his watch and not recall the prank."

Had Harry suggested as much, I would have plowed my fist into his gut. "The lapses are *temporary*. I have that general drawing-a-blank feeling, but the blanks fill in. They always fill in, and I did not steal that watch any more than you did." The blanks were enormous, and they apparently did not *always* fill in anymore.

"My recommendation would be pistols. You are doubtless a good shot with small arms, while Cleary has likely handled only long guns. You both fire into the air, and the matter is done. I am willing to stand about looking grave while you do it, provided Sir Pericles seconds you as well."

I retrieved the discarded flower from the flagstones as Ormstead headed for the house. "If anything happens to me, you'll look after Hyperia?"

His gaze went from the little flower to my face. "My dear fellow, I hope to be looking after Hyperia regardless of how your situation sorts itself out with Cleary."

How generous of him, to stand about looking grave while I risked my life because some popinjay had appointed himself the at-large exterminator of military veterans with flawed recall.

I wasn't about to wear the flower that Ormstead had discarded, but neither would I allow the blameless bloom to wilt from neglect. I cut around the side of the house and entered the conservatory by a side door, all the while wondering if perhaps I shouldn't allow Cleary to put period to my existence.

I took a seat on a bench among potted lemons, camellias, and more yellowing ferns while despair became a writhing demon in my mind. My life stretched before me, a series of gatherings at which I was unwelcome, in a world that accused me of betraying my brother and my country, in a society that lived to point fingers and whisper in corners of my failings.

Arthur would expect me to marry in another year or two, and the hell that future presaged for me and the lady both... For me to marry would be pointless, and I must explain to Arthur why, or he'd throw prospects at me until, from sheer exhaustion of the nerves, I assented to wed some vicar's toothsome pride and joy.

I surveyed a mental battlefield on which all sides sustained horrendous losses and none gained ground. A wasteland, a no man's land of sorrow and suffering.

If Cleary prevailed in our duel, he'd have to take a repairing lease on the Continent, like his wastrel brother. That left one brother still in England to oversee the family affairs, but perhaps I should save Cleary the trouble of traveling.

I would not retreat to London, but I could retreat from life itself. Men died "cleaning their pistols" from time to time, a nine days' wonder, always pronounced a tragedy even if the fellow was drowning in debt, addicted to the poppy, and wanted for hanging felonies.

I had entertained these sorts of thoughts before, but in previous fits of despair, the temptation to end my life had been a peculiar, morally repellant mental experiment in self-indulgence. Death was acquiring a horrid sort of appeal now, despite the fact—or perhaps because of the fact—that I was finally stirring from my postwar torpor.

I would never be able to put events in France behind me. Harry would never again beat me at chess. Hyperia would eventually marry Ormstead—the unkindest cut—and Arthur would find a good home for Atlas.

Why not spare myself and my family all those years of misery and just get it over with?

A little scandal and tragedy for them, a lot of peace for me. I had thought from time to time that Harry had had a certain luck, dying a hero's death, then I'd be ashamed of myself for thinking such thoughts.

I wasn't ashamed of myself for thinking them now.

CHAPTER FOURTEEN

I held the thorny little rose in my hand and let the bleak thoughts wash over me, not particularly caring if they pooled in my mind or ebbed away as they had on previous occasions. I needed to find some water for the rose, and from some corner of the darkness trying to engulf me, I heard Harry telling me that if I sought to end my life, I'd have to get off the damned bench, find a gun—I had none in my possession—and get someplace where the mess wouldn't be any bother to others.

I had gained my feet when I heard the doors between the house and conservatory open. Towering greenery obscured my view of the intruders, but I'd know Cleary's voice anywhere.

"Let's find you a bench, shall we, my dear?" He spoke as the doting nephew, all hearty good cheer.

"You are always so thoughtful, Mendy. Where would I be without you?" Maria was on another outing apparently, this time with a proper escort. "Do you suppose they're still serving breakfast? I might like to sit with the other guests for a change."

Mendel laughed gently. "Dearest Aunt, we had breakfast not an hour past. Let's have a seat, shall we?"

Maria had not been at breakfast. I could be a complete amnesiac and still trust that fact.

"But, Mendy, I'm peckish. All this fresh country air has put an appetite on me."

"You cannot possibly be peckish, pet. You did justice to a plate of eggs and some excellent ham before no less audience than Sir Pericles and Lady Ophelia. Have you directed Mrs. Waldrup to start packing your things?"

Was Cleary intending to depart? And what the hell did he mean when he referred to Maria sharing a meal with Sir Pericles and Lady Ophelia?

"But, Mendy, we just got here. I vow we haven't been here a sennight yet, and no house party lasts a mere few days. In my day, we'd keep company in the summer for weeks at a time and even longer if the gents removed to the grouse moors."

Maria's voice held a pleading note beneath her bewilderment. *Why has the world stopped making sense?*

"The time does fly when we're enjoying ourselves, doesn't it?" Mendel replied, which was no sort of answer to the questions Maria had indirectly posed. "I do think this outing has done you good. You've had a chance to catch up with a few old friends, pay a few calls. That was the point, wouldn't you agree?"

A thorn bit my finger. I opened my fist and tried to open my mind. How well I knew that pleasant, patient, humoring tone. Knew the feeling when questions went unanswered and a conversation leaped from topic to topic without a thread of continuity. I knew that smothering, helpless despair when reality refused to behave as reality was supposed to.

I had tried, in my dark cell, to mark time by the meal schedule, but in hindsight, I suspected Girard had purposely overfed me when he wasn't underfeeding me. Meals had been too far apart or too close together, then the pleasantly polite French commandant had dismissed the evidence of my own body.

You English have such appetites!

You are not hungry for our fine French potatoes and ham?
Have some more wine. A second glass never hurt anybody.
Though it had likely been my fourth or fifth glass.

"Mendy, do you think I might bide with Lady Ophelia for a time? She and I have hardly had a moment together, and I did so look forward to renewing our acquaintance."

Mendel sighed so gustily the leaves of the lemon tree should have quivered. "Ophelia told you just the other day that she's off to Edinburgh next. Says the summer's heat isn't as bad up north. Were you thinking of accompanying her all the way to Scotland? I'd miss you terribly, and Mrs. Waldrup might not be up for the journey."

Ophelia had no plans to visit Scotland, and Mrs. Waldrup was hale enough to bustle the length of the Camino de Santiago without a single faltering step.

I listened to another quarter hour of Mendel's caricature of devotion. He exuded long-suffering good humor, even as he twisted Maria's reasoning powers before her eyes. She trusted him, she had nobody to gainsay him, and she was apparently dosed with some patent remedy masquerading as raspberry cordial frequently enough that her mind could gain no traction against him.

All the while I eavesdropped, memories of France bombarded me. Girard had spoken to me thus, when I'd been so far beyond exhaustion, into the closer reaches of madness, and he had presented himself as the voice of honest compassion. I had lost a brother, I was disgraced—*la guerre est si injuste!*—I was famished and parched and without a friend in the world... and Girard had sated me with lies and manipulation.

The enormity of his evil—and his genius—sank into my awareness like moonlight filling the landscape. A vague memory surfaced of Girard asking me about a British defeat in Spain in which I'd supposedly taken part. He'd inquired after meals I'd enjoyed that I'd forgotten I'd consumed. He'd exchanged a laugh with the guards over my fine singing voice when I'd had no recollection of regaling anybody with a recital.

He'd been slowly, gently, inexorably driving me mad... And, for a time, he'd succeeded.

Cleary was bent on the same course with his aunt, though his objective wasn't anything so noble as the defeat of a wartime enemy. I'd sort through my options where Cleary was concerned later. My present challenge was to absorb what I'd deduced regarding my imprisonment.

I kept my appointment with Atlas and laid the pink rose on the rim of the water trough, stem trailing in the water. Rain was inevitable—the sky had become, if anything, more threatening—and that suited my mood.

After the requisite walk and trot, I let Atlas have his head, and he thundered along the river at a joyous, blistering gallop. Despite the burdens I carried, despite everything, I delighted in the exertion and the glory of his sheer animal power.

This was yet mine to enjoy, as was much else.

The first drops of a cool, misty rain fell as I patted Atlas's sweaty neck and turned him for home. The rain showed no inclination to turn violent, and I'd spent many an hour in a damp saddle. I considered again the conversation I'd overheard in the conservatory, as well as the nagging feeling that I'd missed something important about the whole business.

We came within sight of Makepeace sitting on its bucolic rise, and a low rumble of thunder sounded off to the south. The Channel was making this weather, as the Channel made much of Kent's weather.

I hadn't seen the flash of lightning, but I'd felt it in my mind.

Girard had lied about so much and lied so very, very well. I had been meant to think he'd extracted some vital facts from me in a conversation I could not recall—facts that had led to avoidable British deaths.

For the first time, I entertained the serious hope that no such conversation had ever occurred.

You are human, non, my lord? And I am very good at what I do. So a little detail slips here and there. Greater men than you have been slipping details to me for years. This is war. Have some more wine.

I swung down from the saddle, in no hurry to reach our destination. The possibility that my memory had not suffered further deterioration held up no matter how I changed the angle of my inquiry. Girard had had other prisoners—he was a dark legend for his interrogation skills—and why not attribute to me—a mere courtesy lord—a treasonous slip that might, in fact, have belonged to the Duke of Mercia, a celebrated war hero?

Or to my own brother?

My theory had the feeling of rightness, of being not merely plausible, but impregnable from any angle. Girard was, after all, a British peer, and he'd well know the benefit of sparing a duke public humiliation. For all any of us knew, I would not have survived to tell any different tale than the one that suited Girard's purposes, and I and my good name would have been lamentable casualties of war.

I had not committed treason. Not inadvertently, not under the torments Girard had devised, not when half mad or in the midst of a memory lapse. The military, public opinion, and even Girard himself would never exonerate me of the charge, but I finally knew myself to be innocent.

I walked beneath the trees, my soul washed clean by the soft, summer rain, Atlas plodding placidly beside me. We reached a high border of wet, glossy rhododendrons. I led Atlas into their sheltering depths, leaned against his sturdy neck, and went completely to pieces for the first time since returning to the green and pleasant land of my birth.

~

By the time I returned from my ride, the ripples on the Longacre house party pond were already gliding outward. The groom Chubb took Atlas from me and gave me the sort of dolorous, respectful glance usually reserved for men who'd volunteered to participate in a forlorn hope.

"We'll rub him down proper, my lord, though it looks as if you've troubled to cool him out."

"Thoroughly. An old campaigner like Atlas isn't bothered by a little rain and mud." *And neither am I.*

"Some are like that—go better on a muddy track. We'll coddle him a bit just the same."

My stock in the stable had risen apparently, but then, Mendel Cleary was not well liked among the staff, and for all Chubb knew, I was soon to face my Maker.

My boots squished with every step, and my clothing was sodden, so I entered the house using the same conservatory door from which I'd exited nearly two hours earlier. Once again, I was cast into the role of eavesdropper.

"Miss Belvoir is a lady's maid," Canning said, exasperation threading his words. "She's not a tavern doxy. If you'd ever set foot beyond the village green, you'd know the difference."

"You're jealous, is all. The ladies know that fire on the roof means plenty of flames in the furnace even if I am just a footman."

I could not see Canny's conversation partner, but *fire on the roof* implicated Taylor, the red-haired footman, who had apparently been indiscreet with Miss Belvoir.

"Save your damned flames for when nobody's looking, for God's sake. If you care for the lady, then you protect her good name. Her post is all Miss Belvoir has, and Maybelle or her ladyship could sack her without a character for merely holding your hand. For that matter, they'd sack you for the same offense."

"You think you know everything just because you took the king's shilling and have bided in London. You don't know shite."

I expected fisticuffs to ensue, which would put me in the delicate posture of having to decide whether to let these two go at it or intervene.

Canny drew a long, audible breath in through his nose. "I know what it's like to make a rolling calamity of my life. To trust to fate, the wrong people, and my own ingenuity at the exact worst moment. If you and Miss Belvoir are to have a future, then you plan carefully, save every penny, and hope that you can train to be a house steward, because as sure as God made sheep, it is holy writ that footmen and lady's maids do not marry."

Canny delivered his homily wearily, as if the rolling calamity were still in progress.

Puzzling, that. He was a decorated veteran of the wars, and he kept his commendation hidden away. The sharpshooters were entitled, if anybody was, to tell tales of their acumen and bravery. Canny hadn't brought up the war once. I'd had to drag his past from him, and he'd parted with only essential facts.

I wasn't the only man on the premises with serious personal regrets.

"She loves me," Taylor retorted. "She loves me, and we're going to France, where we can live for a song."

"*Sait-elle parler française?*"

Can she speak French? And the question had been rendered with a creditable accent.

"Damn you, Canning. You think you know everything." Footsteps, and then the door to the house closed none too gently.

Another audible inhale and then a muttered, "Bloody hell."

I stepped forth from behind the potted lemons. "Try having a word with the lady. They are usually more sensible than we are."

Canning frowned, no pretensions to deference in his expression. "Sense was in short supply at breakfast, my lord, and you've apparently chosen not to gallop for Town."

"Have you joined the committee counseling me to depart?"

He scrubbed a hand over his face and gazed off in the direction of Taylor's retreat. In profile and without the footman's manufactured good cheer, Canning was an attractive man of an altogether more formidable sort. Why was Miss Belvoir mucking about with a randy redhead when Canning was on hand to disport with?

The question answered itself in the next instant: because Canny would not encourage the connection. Just as he was hiding his commendation, he was hiding much else. The longer I studied him—the soldier's bearing, the lean height, the proud features—the more certain I became of my conclusions.

"If you must meet Cleary over pistols or swords," he said, "then it's worth your life to be careful. He manipulated you into this duel, and he does not play fair."

"You refer to his cheating at cards?"

"He doesn't cheat, but he can keep count of the cards in his head." Canning tapped a blond temple. "Cleary has an abacus up here, apparently, though that doesn't help him balance his ledgers. Thinks he's special, does Spendy-Mendy. Mind your back with him, my lord. He'll claim his foot slipped, and he never meant to fillet you, that the gun's mechanism misfired, that he misheard the count. He is no gentleman."

And you are no footman. "I appreciate the warning. I don't suppose you'll be minding the sideboard at luncheon?"

"I will, for my sins. The younger lads prefer to do the stepping and fetching at supper."

Footmen serving supper would be more visible to the guests, more likely to make a friendly impression when bringing an extra serving of buttered peas or topping up a chaperone's wine.

"Then I will see you at lunch. We're dining in the gallery again?"

"Aye, and I'd best get back to the kitchen before Cook murders our Atticus." He withdrew into the house, leaving me the privacy of my thoughts. He'd forgotten to bow in parting, more proof that Canning was not to his livery born.

I was peeling my wet shirt over my head, absently enjoying the invective Atticus aimed at gents who disrespected good boots, when a detail from the conversation in the conservatory came back to me. I sat on the bed, my wet shirt in my hands, felled not by possibility this time, but by certainty.

As a reconnaissance officer, I had had many agendas. What

stores were available locally with which to provision the army? Wellington had very strict policies against pillaging, unlike the French, but he would barter with and buy from civilian sources on occasion.

I was also to look for the best path across a given valley or plateau, one that would afford the men shade and cover, but allow the column to stay together and set a good pace as well.

The cardinal question, though, was always, always, *What are the French up to now?*

Where are they going? What strategy will they employ to get there? What are their vulnerabilities and strengths? How can we make life harder for them with the least difficulty for us?

One of my commanding officers had begun every interview with a single question: *Tell me how to win the war, Caldicott, or how to win our little part of it for today.*

With my shirt dripping onto the worn carpet, and Atticus waxing profane in the depths of the wardrobe, I saw how I could win my little part of today's war. Victory was a matter of paying attention to details and dealing with facts in the right order.

I was damned good at both, and to blazes with pistols and swords.

$\sim$

The gallery had been arranged as if for a whist tournament, with small tables scattered about the room, and all the fires lit in deference to the dreary weather. The sideboards were set up as buffet stations— soup and bread here, sandwiches there, sweets at the far end of the room. Taylor manned a punchbowl, while Canny guarded the tureen.

Ophelia spotted me as soon as I entered the room, as did my host, who delivered a convincing cut sublime by riveting his attention to an unimpressive landscape he'd likely seen a thousand times before. Sir Thomas went for the cut infernal, studying his watch at length, rather than so much as glancing my way.

Cleary tried for a cut direct, glowering at me, then pointedly looking away, but not before I'd winked at him.

"Are you daft?" Ophelia muttered. "You don't wink at your potential murderer."

"I am not daft, though thank you for the vote of confidence."

"You went riding *in the rain*, Julian," she wailed softly. "Your health is unreliable, and you go out in the dirtiest weather and trot about in the mud. Are you hoping to die of a lung fever before Cleary's bullet carries you off?"

Her ladyship was trying for vinegar and starch, but her eyes held worry. She cared for me in her way, and she probably even meant well—most of the time.

"I needed to think without interruptions. I've chosen my weapon."

I had kept my voice down, but such was the heightened awareness of the company that Osgood Banter looked my way. Brimstock lifted his glass in my direction, and Maybelle nodded to me from across the room.

"Did I hear aright?" Cleary asked from a good ten feet away. "What's it to be, pistols or swords?" He had to be truly desperate to ask that question publicly. Dueling was frowned upon, stupid, *and* illegal.

"I was having a private conversation with my godmother, Cleary."

"You excel at private maneuvers. I still think you tried to abscond with Miss Longacre."

"No," said Maybelle evenly, "he did not."

Another question answered. Hyperia entered the room from the door at the far end and, oblivious to the turbulence in the air, smiled at me before the whole assemblage.

My second had arrived. I smiled back and faced my foe. "You continue to insult me in public, Cleary, to taunt me and to comport yourself as no gentleman should. Either apologize to Lord and Lady Longacre for your asininities or leave."

"Oh no, no, no," Cleary responded with great good cheer. "You are the blight on the guest list, sir—not that you were ever *on* the guest list—and you will take yourself back to London or to the pit itself, but I'm not going anywhere."

The room fell silent, while Hyperia settled herself into a comfortable armchair with a good view of the combatants. She arranged her skirts and turned limpid green eyes on me. Such calm, such confidence in those eyes.

Such faith in me.

"Very well," I said, "but only because you are determined on this drama, Cleary. The choice of weapons is mine, and I choose words."

I'd surprised him. First touch to Lord Julian.

"Have you lost what feeble wits you yet possess?" Cleary drawled.

A fast recovery. "I sometimes do lose my wits—we all do, come to that—but then I find them, and I am in possession of them now." Most of them, anyway. "I have chosen words as my weapon, and before these good witnesses, we will duel with words until truth vanquishes all challengers."

Lord Longacre bestirred himself to leave off appreciating the art. "We are trying to enjoy a *pleasant social gathering* here. Must you two carry on so?"

Lady Longacre looked torn between the hope that we would carry on a great deal more and the wish that this was anybody else's house party.

"Oh, we must," Cleary said. "We truly must. Here's a truth for you, my friends. This so-called gentleman carries a card about in his pocket, reminding him that he has lapses of memory and forgets everything including his own direction. Now he wants you to take his half-witted word over the word of a gentleman."

Hyperia helped herself to a petit four from the dish on the table next to her chair. "Lord Julian has lapses of memory, true, but they are lapses. His recollection is soon restored, while honor, once departed, is gone for good. I'd like to hear what Lord Julian has to say."

"As would I," Maybelle said.

"I'm curious as well," Miss Ellison said, her shiner being mostly obscured with discreet cosmetics.

"Then say on," Lady Ophelia added. "But mind you both, I'm getting peckish, and I do not favor cold soup on a rainy day."

I spared a glance at Canny, who was at parade attention, ladle in hand. He looked tired but resolute, as any soldier would in the midst of a forced march. He gave the slightest nod, and I had the permission I needed to finish what Cleary had started.

"Mendel Cleary travels with a very large amount of money," I began, "though the funds aren't his. The bearer notes are drawn on Miss Maria Cleary's bank. My guess is, that money was to be offered as ransom funds to appease the villain who meant to abduct Miss Longacre."

Maybelle had the grace to blush, and the heightened color was quite becoming.

Hyperia caught on in the next moment. "But that means..." She stared hard at Maybelle. "You recognized him and tried to throw us off the scent. Why?"

Rather than put the lady in Cleary's crosshairs, I answered. "Because if Maybelle had been kidnapped, she would have been ruined, and ruined ladies are all but impossible to marry off. Her lot at Makepeace in that case would have become unbearable. A clever woman—and Miss Longacre is very clever—might well have used the knowledge of Cleary's felonious scheme to inveigle him into marriage on her terms, a white marriage with a huge widow's portion would have been my guess."

Brimstock was not half so handsome when his mouth was hanging open. He shut it with a snap. "How did you know it was Cleary?"

Maybelle tapped her midriff. "Mr. Cleary's watch chain is ridiculously long. Between the moonlight and the torches around the summer cottage, I saw that chain quite plainly."

And Cleary, perhaps suspecting her game, had found an excuse to stop wearing the watch.

"Was it to be marriage on your terms, Maybelle?" I asked.

Cleary tried to affect polite boredom, while Amethyst and Mozart looked to be making a whispered wager over by the ancestral portraits.

"I hadn't made up my mind," Maybelle said. "A man who will scheme like that and then bungle the business... I would have kept him as a last resort."

"This is ridiculous," Cleary snapped. "Every fellow here wears his watch on a chain, and they all look the same by moonlight. Aunt Maria is eccentric and prefers to keep a fair amount of cash with her. She always has."

"Your plan," I said, "was to abduct Miss Longacre, then save the day by offering to prevail on Aunt Maria to provide the ransom in cash—or perhaps you'd present that money as your own. In any case, you would have been paying yourself with Maria's money. If you were truly ambitious—and you are—you would also have graciously offered to marry the ruined Miss Longacre and doubtless have demanded generous settlements to compensate you for taking pity on her."

Lady Longacre subsided into a reading chair. "Is this true?"

"He's daft, I tell you," Cleary retorted. "Mad as a hatter, forgets his natal day and family name. The money is Maria's, and this conversation has descended into farce."

"Then you don't have a healing bruise on the arch of your foot?" I asked. "Perhaps you'd like to prove that you don't?"

"I admit nothing." Cleary might be able to bluff his way past speculation and hearsay, but not physical evidence. A slight shift in his posture, a flicker of fear in the depths of his blue eyes were all the confession I needed.

"Then keep your powder dry, as it were, for now. Instead, might you explain why you brought no valet, no footmen of your own, no personal servants save for what amounts to a man-of-all-work, who's mostly biding in the stable?"

"Why duplicate staff when Aunt Maria must bring her retainers? I sought to ease the burden for my hostess by keeping our party smaller."

"Then you turned around and demanded Canny's services," Lady Longacre said. "One finds the contradiction puzzling."

Hyperia held the dish of petits fours out to me, and I took a sweet purely because she'd offered it.

"I'm not puzzled," I said. "Cleary wanted privacy when he attended his aunt. I'm fanatical about my privacy, too, for different reasons. Poor Maria has more patent remedies on her vanity than Wellington has honors in the whole of Apsley House, and her companion, a dear lady, is entirely cowed by Mendel's constant threats to give her the sack."

I approached Cleary as I munched on my treat—raspberry, of all the ironies. "When you shoo Mrs. Waldrup off, you spin a tale of confusion and falsehoods around your aunt such that she has no idea what day it is, whether she's had anything to eat since waking, or what county she bides in.

In short, you torture her."

Canny winced. Lady Ophelia looked to be eyeing the breakables.

"These are the mendacious imaginings of an ailing mind," Cleary said. "I refuse to answer them."

Ophelia stalked to my side. "Then you won't object when I take Maria back to Sussex with me, will you? You will not mind in the least when my solicitors have a look at her ledgers. You will smile and nod and be relieved to have the doddering old dear off your hands, won't you?"

Sir Pericles was looking thunderous, and not at me, for once.

Cleary nodded at Ophelia. "Of course Aunt Maria is welcome to visit her friends, but I warn you, she is growing forgetful. Any disruption in routine only makes her worse, and she relies on those patent remedies. She would not be dissuaded from attending this house party, and I hadn't the heart to put my foot down, more fool I."

He was not a fool—Maria relied on those damned remedies to the point of addiction, and by his design—but he had miscalculated. Even Napoleon, one of the greatest military minds of all time, had eventually miscalculated.

"You could not risk letting Maria out of your sight," I said. "But you hadn't counted on running into your own brother here at Makepeace, had you?"

A stillness came over the room, and Cleary looked to be calculating the distance to the door.

"Do go on," Lady Longacre. "I know my guest list, and Mendel and Maria are the only Clearys here."

"Of course you know your guest list, my lady. But do you know your footmen?"

CHAPTER FIFTEEN

"You can't prove any of this," Cleary said, though he was doubtless voicing a hope rather than a conviction.

"Actually, I can." Good former reconnaissance officer that I was. "You had a significant argument with the footman Canning, a notably able and hardworking fellow. We were told you attempted to requisition Canning's services, but that was not the only topic of your disagreement with him."

Canny gave me another slight nod.

"You and Canning," I went on, "bear a resemblance. More to the point, Canning might be the slender twin of your other brother, Daniel Cleary, with whom I briefly served. You were concerned—terrified, in fact—that I would see the resemblance and realize that your indebted brother was slowly working off his obligations right here in Kent, rather than kicking his heels on the Continent."

My conviction in this regard was based on evidence that in hindsight—always in hindsight—had been sitting in plain view.

Canny kept a low profile around the guests, avoiding the ballroom, allowing the other footmen to earn the vails and recognition.

He avoided even casual romantic entanglements.

He kept his letter of commendation, which would disclose his full name, from prying eyes.

He had trotted out a line of correct French with no effort at all.

He knew precisely how Mendel prevailed at cards, and that had to be something of a family secret.

He had the subaltern's ability to anticipate a superior's needs and perform his office with graciousness that never shaded into fawning. That skill might have been honed when he'd donned livery, but he'd acquired the rudiments on campaign with the Rifles.

Then there was Maria's sketch of her nephews—two peas in a pod plus the rotten apple. Daniel was more stolid than Canning, but their features were nearly identical.

The final scrap of evidence had been the sniffy inhalations. Mendel and Canning had the same sort of disapproving huff, just as Harry and I had had the same laugh. That was the insight that had befallen me as I'd sat on my bed, serenaded by the music of Atticus's cursing.

Lord Longacre leveled a sniffy look of his own at Cleary. "Your brother's creditors would have taken him to the sponging house if they'd known he bided in England, and you would have been forced by decency to pay his debts."

"A good theory," I said, "but Canning's debts are debts of honor. Mendel maintains that Canning fell in with a bad crowd. I suspect, on the contrary, that Canning was all but thrown to the very same hands from whom Mendel had won a pretty penny. Mendel knew that Canning would soon be fleeced of every groat, a return of the courtesies Mendel himself had offered to those men. Mendel planned to win twice. The first time at cards and the second time when his brother was hounded from England's shores with creditors on his heels. Canning could not have intervened on Maria's behalf from Rome, if he'd even known what was afoot."

Canning remained by the sideboard, but he was staring at his brother rather than at nothing in particular.

"You *gave me* passage to Rome," Canning said. "Claimed it was all you could spare, and took Trafalgar as surety. Then you went and gambled him away. I love that horse. He saw me through battles, kept me warm, carried my gear when I was too weary to stand upright. And you..."

Canning was friendless, in debt, and suffering from the same sense of disorientation every soldier brought home from the war. The thought that his charger had been well provided for had probably been a glimmer of comfort. If anybody had treated Atlas so cavalierly in my absence...

"Mendel was warning you," I said. "You rowed about Aunt Maria's situation, and Mendel was telling you that any attempt on your part to rectify her circumstances, and you'd be mourning more than the loss of your horse."

"I didn't do anything with the rubbishing horse," Cleary said.

"You gambled him away," I replied, "which you had no right to do if Canning was making timely payments against your loan. Trafalgar's rightful owner intervened, for which we do not blame him. I am not here to discuss stupid wagers over battledore. My objective is to explain why you systematically attempted to shame me into leaving the gathering."

We had reached the gravamen of my case, so to speak, the point at which truth would prevail or blow up in my face.

Lord Longacre looked at the clock, while Lady Ophelia glared daggers at Mendel. If Canning didn't black both his eyes, Lady Ophelia well might.

"Do you deny these charges, Cleary?" Longacre asked.

Cleary surveyed the gathering, likely probing for allies, or even for those skeptical of my claims.

Bollocks to that. "Before you answer, allow me to finish for benefit of those assembled. Had I recognized Canning as your brother, then Canning might well have applied to me for assistance with Maria's situation. Canning could have asked me to cover his debts or to investigate how he came to be so quickly in over his head at the clubs to which his own brother had given him entre. Canning might have confided his suspicions about that brother to a fellow soldier who is hesitant to judge others for their foibles. I was a threat on several fronts and should have been easily dealt with.

"Blame me for abducting Miss Longacre," I went on, "blame me for stealing a watch that is doubtless yet among your effects, blame me for a missing horse you never should have wagered away, blame me for the rain. Do that emphatically enough and long enough, and the most disinterested observer will eventually harbor a few doubts. Do that to a man already dwelling under a cloud and remind everybody of that cloud as often as you can, and you will nigh ruin him."

"Except," Hyperia mused quietly, "Mr. Cleary appears to have ruined himself. How ironic."

"Pathetic," Ophelia muttered. "In my day... In *any* day, such behavior cannot stand."

Miss Ellison rubbed her eye, and Miss Longacre sent her parents a look that presaged many a donnybrook if the wrong course was taken.

Our host apparently heeded that warning. "Lady Longacre and I will understand, Cleary, if the press of business means your coach awaits you out front in the next half hour."

Canning advanced on his brother. "Spendy-Mendy doesn't have a coach. He uses Aunt Maria's. If Lord Julian is right, then Mendel has been running his households with her money, and because Mendel won't listen when somebody explains that fields must be marled every few years, his land is played out, and he can't get decent rent for it. He'll be running his estate with her money too. Auntie has funds aplenty, and Mendel has plans for all of it. He couldn't spare me two groats and wouldn't let me even look in on Aunt Maria when she and I were sleeping under the same roof."

"Look in on her now," I said. "I'm sure Lady Ophelia will be happy to go with you, and do have an honest conversation with Mrs. Waldrup about all those patent remedies."

Ophelia aimed a magnificent glower at Mendel. "Send this strutting heap of rubbish to the coast in my coach. John Coachman will tolerate no mischief, and for the good of the law-abiding public, his siblings, and the aunt he's been fleecing for years, I want Cleary out of England in the next twenty-four hours."

Cleary tried sniffing. He tried hauteur and then martyred silence. Nobody was having it. He'd been routed, foot, horse, and cannon, and by mere words.

"Begone," I said. "Send word to Daniel of your whereabouts and send him a power of attorney, but take yourself hence, and don't come back until your brothers—and your aunt—see fit to forgive you."

He stalked from the room, and something passed from Mozart's hand to Amethyst's. "I cannot abide a cad," Mozart said. "Might we make a start on that soup?"

~

"I wanted to search Cleary's luggage before he left," Maybelle said. "His lap desk might have held a ransom note printed in a crabbed hand and threatening my doom if the money wasn't handed over."

I walked beside her on the crushed-shell paths of the garden. Two hours after Mendel Cleary had been banished to the Continent, the sky was a quilt of cloudy gray batting seamed with gold. My eyes weren't overtaxed, and Maybelle clearly had something private to convey to me.

She was sensible—most of the time—and shrewd, but she was also young and without much experience of life's darker corners.

"You underestimate the danger Cleary posed," I said. "He was relentlessly cruel to Maria, all the while appearing to be a doting nephew. He stole from her and even, in a sense, from his own younger brother. He more or less kept Maria drugged, and if his finances couldn't be brought right, Maria's life could well have been forfeit. If you had been able to identify your kidnapper—by voice, mannerism, or watch chain—he might have done away with you too."

A pillow held over the face of a woman far gone with the poppy would have been the work of a moment for a man in his prime. I hoped for the sake of Cleary's family that he wasn't that depraved, but the memory of him crooning lies to his enfeebled aunt left me in doubt.

His campaign to topple Maria's reason and steal her wealth had taken months to put in place and pursue. Patience in a villain doubled the impact of his evil, as I well knew.

"I'm back to where I was," Maybelle said, "regardless of Cleary's schemes. I did not *take* in my first Season. I do not want to take. I want to live to be one-and-twenty and then make my own choices, insofar as any woman can."

I gestured to the bench where Hyperia and I had sat just a few days earlier. "You have gained ground. Your parents chose Cleary as a suitable prospect to court you and mind the family finances. What will your parents say when you remind them of that? Cleary's bobbing neck-deep in the River Tick, cruel to his brother, criminally avaricious toward his aunt—at best—and your mother would have been delighted to see you marry him. If her confidence isn't shaken by that blunder, then you must shake it for her."

Maybelle sank onto the bench. "I hadn't thought of that."

"When the moment is right," I went on, taking the place a foot from her side, "you can indicate that Brimstock tried to inebriate you. He was another of her ladyship's brilliant choices." As were Amethyst, Mozart, and Banter. I should have known better than to expect much from Ormstead.

"Brimstock only provided the temptation. The foolishness was all mine."

Ye gods... My sisters had never been this naïve. "The whole time you were playing cards with him, arguing with him, and perhaps flirting with him, he was refilling your glass. If you weren't cup-shot by the end of the evening, you were close to it. Brimstock isn't evil, but he's shallow and self-centered."

"He has growing up to do, I agree. Ormstead's not bad."

"Ormstead disappointed me, but I think you'll find his interest lies elsewhere."

The nature of this conversation, somewhere between confidences and gossip, put me in mind of the trust I had enjoyed with my siblings. My sisters, in their way, were skilled at gathering intelligence, and Lady Ophelia was too. Harry had compared notes with me on any number of topics, though Arthur remained above it all—of course.

"Ormstead wants to court Miss West," Maybelle said. "I cannot fault his taste. What of Banter?"

Quiet, dapper Banter had been the only guest to actually apologize to me, and he'd made a hash of it.

Have known your oldest brother forever, and you deserved a fair hearing at least. Wasn't about to second that strutting popinjay. Told him so and he laughed. Should have known then and there. Sincere apologies.

He'd offered his hand, and I'd accepted that courtesy, because he'd at least made an honorable effort.

"Banter has his own reasons for wanting to avoid matrimony," I said. "State your case to him honestly, where you cannot be overheard. You might well spend the next two years pretending you are growing fond of one another—or growing fond of one another in truth —and then when you come into your funds, you can decide your own future."

Lady Ophelia would have approved of that bit of strategy. I thought it rather clever myself.

Miss Ellison strolled by, one arm linked with Mozart, the other with Amethyst, though he wore a garnet pin today. She waggled her fingers at me, and I waved back. She was another soldier returned from the wars and was apparently finding her footing at this house party, despite all predictions to the contrary.

"You won't tattle?" Maybelle asked quietly when the trio had passed. "About... the song?"

"Never. A gentleman doesn't. If you want me to have a word with Brimstock, I'll do so. He's an idiot, and leaving that much temptation under your very pillow was a mean, stupid thing to do."

"He was ungentlemanly, but then, I was unladylike for reasons we need not belabor again." She fell silent as if some great pronouncement were welling up from the depths of her soul. "You are a gentleman. These people, my own parents, tried to make you think you were not, but they were wrong, and you are a gentleman."

"Thank you." I was also not a traitor. I could no more prove my innocence than anybody else could prove my guilt. No matter. For now, self-exoneration was comfort enough.

Maybelle looked like she might do something bold and sweet, like kiss my cheek, which would not do.

I rose and pretended to admire the geometric walkways and rioting roses. "Shall you bide here in the garden, or would you like an escort back to the house?"

"I do believe I will go visit my mare," she said, getting to her feet. "Mama says the Duchess of Moreland has invited the whole party over for luncheon tomorrow. Colonel St. Just is in residence for the nonce, and he quite likes my Tatiana."

St. Just liked his peace and quiet more, but that was his battle to fight. "Please give the colonel my regards. I believe that's Banter coming down the steps of the terrace."

Maybelle smoothed her skirts, looked over her shoulder at Miss Ellison and her brace of bachelors, and made straight for Banter, who greeted her with an exceedingly pleasant smile.

~

"You are determined to leave?" Hyperia asked.

She'd intercepted me on the terrace, just a dozen steps shy of the house.

"I am. Lady Longacre made it plain that I am abundantly welcome to bide here for the rest of the two weeks, but I've had enough excitement." Her ladyship had all but begged me to stay, now that I'd made her gathering the most-talked-about house party of the year. In her eyes, I was restored to full honors as a bachelor of independent means and ducal connections.

Despite my white hair, my dubious past, and my lingering infirmities. Society was nothing if not fickle.

"I'm glad you came," Hyperia said, slipping her arm through mine and directing me—for that's what she was doing—to a grouping of chairs and benches arranged in the shade of an overhanging balcony. "Very glad. Cleary should be in Calais by this time tomorrow, and I wish the French the joy of his company."

He'd have to kick his heels in the port city until official traveling papers could catch up with him, meaning his creditors had a chance to catch up with him first.

Such a pity. "If I know Daniel Cleary, he won't send along any passports until Cleary has surrendered a power of attorney. Daniel has a keen appreciation for proper documentation and will doubtless work his way up through the ranks at Horse Guards."

Hyperia settled on a stone bench in the shade and patted the place beside her. "What of Canny? He won't have made much progress against his debts on a footman's wages."

Canny and I had had a quiet talk over a couple brandies. A terrible breach of fashionable protocol, but a tolerable lapse for two former soldiers compared to attempted kidnapping, larceny, and extortion.

"When his aunt is feeling better, Canny will approach her for a loan, provided his brother Daniel does not object. Canny would not accept a loan from me, but neither did he forbid me from making inquiries among the gentlemen who hold his markers." I would buy up those markers and ensure Canny had a reasonable chance to meet the repayment terms, even without a loan from dear Maria. "He did accept a rather generous vail from me, every penny of which he earned."

"By not judging you."

"He went beyond that, Hyperia." I had some time to ponder the details, and Canny's subtle hand had become apparent. "He made sure that I had basic considerations such as food and clean linen. He saw to it that I had at least one dependable support in the boy, Atticus, who is frightfully clever. He took a hand in sorting out squabbles belowstairs, and he was every bit as chivalrous toward Miss Maybelle as I was. He's a good fellow, and life hasn't been easy for him."

When Canny had recovered from the week's events, I would offer him a position as my London house steward. The butler's nose might be out of joint, but the cook and housekeeper would thank me.

"You are ready to mount your charger and ride off into the sunset?" She posed the question briskly, so I answered in the same tone.

"I'm ready to be quit of this place. I was never supposed to tarry here. I am glad to have spent time with you, though." I kept to myself any questions about Ormstead, who had been fair-minded enough until being fair-minded had cost him more than words.

"Turn your head, Jules."

"I beg your pardon?"

"Turn your..." She pushed my chin gently to the side, the better to study my profile. "There's some gold here," she said, drawing a finger along the fine hairs at my temple. "Faint, but I don't think I'm imagining it."

"Gold?"

"Baby blond. Paler than wheat. A sun-on-the-water hint of color."

"You're sure?"

She tugged me by the wrist into the stronger light on the terrace and brushed a thumb over my temple. "If it grows in that color, you'll be as blond as a Viking."

My middle had gone oddly fluttery. I would make a very good Viking. I had the height for it and the breadth of shoulder.

"What about the other side?" I waited an eternity while Hyperia strolled around me and brushed her fingers through my hair.

"The same," she said. "The new growth has a smidgeon of color. Must be the sunshine doing you some good."

Somewhere in the past few days, I had ceased to care about my hair. The issue had never been vanity, but rather, *recovery*. If my hair was gaining some color, there was hope for the rest of me—even the parts that hadn't stirred since I'd stumbled down the French side of the Pyrenees.

"You're sure?"

"My eyesight is good, Jules." She appropriated the end of my queue and held it up so that the ends of the mature strands were side by side with the new growth at my temple. "The difference is clear when I compare new and old growth. Shall we alert *The Times?*"

She was smiling at me and forgetting to hide the luminous abundance of her beauty. She had done the scientific thing—a direct comparison—while I had only peered at myself by candlelight, hoping to see a return of my formerly chestnut locks.

"Hyperia, might you do me a favor?" I posed the question before common sense could snatch away my courage.

"Of course."

"Kiss me."

She took me by the sleeve and steered me back beneath the overhanging balcony. "You're sure?"

"Just a kiss." We'd kissed any number of times, a buss in greeting or parting, a mistletoe nothing, a friendly smacker.

She stood so her back was to the wall, and I could step away if need be. Then she went up on her toes and kissed my cheek. More than a peck, less than overture.

"Well?"

I assayed my reactions and found no distaste, no reflexive shrinking away. I found no overt desire either, but perhaps that sort of yearning, like a glimmer of gold in my hair, would steal back over me bit by bit. Hyperia's kiss had been a small, sweet, sad loveliness, and I had borne it if not eagerly, then at least I had borne it calmly, a victory of sorts for me.

May it be the first of many.

"Well, thank you," I said. "I could not have asked anybody else."

She patted my chest. "You won't be asking me again either. I might take it amiss." Her tone was light, her words were a warning. Friendship did not give me the right to mislead her.

I owed her some sort of explanation, and now—finally—I had the courage to proffer one. "Not every ailment I brought home with me from France has obvious symptoms, Hyperia, and no, I don't have the pox. It's a different sort of malaise, affecting my... my humors."

My mortification was nearly eclipsed by amusement at my own expense. I had succeeded in surprising the ever-assured Miss West.

"Gracious." She blinked up at me. "Gracious angels defend us, Jules. Don't tell Arthur. He'll banish you to Switzerland for a repairing lease where they'll bathe you in ass's milk and force you to stride up and down the mountains all day. Your humors. Well. I thought I was the problem. You might have said."

She was both pleased and dismayed. The dismayed part was touching, also embarrassing. "I'm saying now, and if we don't soon change the subject, I will never be able to face you again."

She touched my hand. "See that you do—face me again. Spare me any more speeches about my independence and your prospects, Jules. I know I'm not to predicate any decision or action on your availability, suitability, or proximity, but let's not be strangers."

"We are friends, Hyperia. Very good friends, and I hope we always will be." On some fine and future day, I might admit to hoping for more than that, but today was not the day to be reckless and greedy.

Today was a day to be grateful for honest friendship.

~

I parted from Hyperia on a smile and a bow and entered the house intent on packing. If I left in the next hour, I could cover half the distance to London before darkness fell. I wasn't precisely keen to get back to my town house, but I was keen to shake the dust of Makepeace from my boots.

My work here was done, my heart was full, and I had much to ponder.

"Julian, a moment." Lady Ophelia's voice rang out when I was three steps shy of the top of the staircase. Today was also, apparently, a day for ambushes. She stood in the foyer, the most public location in the entire dwelling.

I stayed right where I was. "My lady, I'm in something of a hurry."

So, of course, she swanned up the steps. "You don't want to rest on your laurels for a few days? Make the bachelors at least pretend to try where the young ladies are concerned? I vow I am disappointed in you."

Too rubbishing bad. "You are concerned for me, but you can't admit that, so you natter and carp and pluck at my last nerve. I love you too." Hyperia had discovered gold in my hair. I could be generous to the less fortunate.

"You young men," she said, coming level with me. "You think you're so dashing, when you're simply rude. My sentiments toward you have never been in doubt. You've had a note from Arthur. I'd tell you to take my coach over to Sussex, but my coach is transporting a criminal at present."

She passed me a folded missive sealed with the ducal crest. No franking, meaning Arthur had sent it by messenger.

"Did you read this?" I could find no sign of tampering, no indication she'd used a heated knife to ease the seal up without breaking it.

"I don't need to read it. Osgood Banter doubtless sent word to Caldicott Hall of your situation here, and Arthur's idea of helping is to invite you to go home."

I read the few words scrawled in Arthur's slashing hand. *A visit to the Hall at your earliest convenience would be appreciated. A.*

He'd signed his writ of summons as a brother, not as the duke, but the tone was pure peer. "You know him well, apparently."

"I know you better, and I'm coming with you."

Press-gang me once, shame on you. "I thought you were taking

Maria Cleary under your wing." More to the point, I wasn't about to loiter at Makepeace when Arthur wanted to see me. News that my memory problem had become public would be best broken to him in person—and when he had some other matter he wanted to bring up.

Oh, by the way, there'll be talk...

Arthur hated talk, but better to be a nine days' wonder than a traitor or a felon, I always say.

"I am taking Maria under my wing. Getting her weaned from those damned patent poisons will be a thankless job."

"Enlist Mrs. Waldrup's aid and go slowly. Maria does not want to be confused and helpless any more than you do." Any more than anybody did, ever.

"Oh, very well. Take yourself off to the Hall, and I will see to Maria, but warn Arthur and Her Grace to expect me once I get Maria situated."

"I will look forward to seeing you again soon." I wouldn't dread it, anyway. To my surprise, Ophelia let me go without bellowing any more warnings, instructions, admonitions, or exhortations at me.

I finally gained the sanctuary of my quarters and found Atticus attempting to properly fold one of my shirts.

"Canny said you're off to Town." He unfolded one sleeve and made another attempt. "Canny's staying here for the nonce. Says he can't sell his commission in time of war."

The house party had certainly been a battleground. "He's a good fellow, though I suspect his days at Makepeace are numbered."

"Ruddy shirt." Atticus made a third attempt at a precise crease, but the linen was fine, and he was too hasty.

Canning hadn't been my only ally here at Makepeace. Atticus had been loyal, brave, kind, and he'd followed orders.

"Do you fancy a job in London, Just Atticus?"

He left off trying to fold the shirt. "What sort o' job?" He spoke with the exquisite indifference of the often disappointed.

"General factotum, aide-de-camp, dogsbody, minion." His family was in London—his mother's family. Perhaps I could see him reunited with them, if they were suitable."

"Never been a minion before." He set about stripping the bed, yanking sheets from beneath the mattress, and heaping the pillows on the vanity stool. "I don't suppose you can get articles for being a minion."

The pillows toppled to the floor. I picked one up and tossed it at him. "A minion is simply a loyal retainer, a trusty henchman."

He tossed the pillow at me with some force. "Is it legal? I'm not leaving a warm bed and good food for no Town wickedness."

Lovely. A pint-sized Puritan would soon join my London payroll. "Your duties will be similar to the work you do here. Boot-boy, potboy, messenger, junior footman, occasional groom, assistant valet, substitute gardener, tiger. You will be bored witless, paid well, and educated enough to become a gentleman's gentleman."

Oddly enough, that last part wiped the diffidence from his face. "You'll teach me to read?"

"In as many languages as you like, and how to do sums, and stay on a horse." Dealing with new recruits simply took patience and humor, and I had modest supplies of both.

"I'll miss Cook."

A sentimental little Puritan. "You can write to her of your accomplishments in Town and work your wiles on my own cook."

"Is she nice?"

"Quite jolly." Mostly quite jolly, and she would delight in another mouth to feed. "If you want to discuss the offer with Canning, I won't be gone for another hour or so." I had packing to do, a formal leave to take of my host and hostess to endure, and arrangements to make for Atticus, who also could not be expected to leave Makepeace until the house party concluded.

"Nah," Atticus said. "I don't need to ask Canny. I'm nobody here. A dogsbody, like you said, and the housekeeper always says she'll start me on my letters, but she never does. Canny would tell me to go, so London it is. You're on your way back there?"

"By way of Sussex. His Grace My Brother needs to blame me for Mendel Cleary's mischief." I hoped that was what troubled Arthur.

"You aren't to blame."

"And the duke will not scold me, not truly. He frets in his way, and we indulge him in ours. Gather your belongings at the end of this house party and prepare for your next adventure."

As it happened, Atticus and I went on to further shared adventures, the next one at the Caldicott family seat. By the time I had that little contretemps sorted out, Arthur was scolding me in earnest, and I was not indulging him whatsoever.

Though that, as they say, is a tale for another time!

TO MY DEAR READERS

My father had transient global amnesia, a rare condition about which we still know little. People who have headaches seem more prone to these lapses, and there might be a family propensity. The problem is simply too rare—and fleeting—to have been studied much. You cannot, in fact, be officially diagnosed with this ailment unless a mental health professional examines you in the middle of an instance of memory loss.

Dad's first episode occurred during a public lecture. He was doing one of those, "make science accessible" presentations to a general audience, and between one notecard and the next, his whole mental canvas went blank. He had no idea who he was, what the notes on the cards were about, where he was, or what he was doing in front of all those people.

He was quite alert and articulate throughout.

He never gave another public lecture, but he did have more memory lapses. Like Lord Julian, when the bout of forgetting ended, he could recall his mental peregrinations, and no part of the memory loss was permanent or even long term. He'd be at sea for a few hours at most—completely at sea, did not recognize the home he'd dwelled in for decades or the woman he'd been married to for half a century—and then he'd be fine again.

In most other respects, Dad was cognitively with it until he peacefully expired in the 97th year of his age. His ailment has haunted me, because Dad relied almost exclusively on his mental powers to go forward in life. He was a bench scientist with a gift for experimental design. Asking "elegant questions" was his jam, and yet, later in life, along came this vexing conundrum of a mental illness.

So of course, I'm putting the condition in a book, where my readers can puzzle over it with me. Julian is quite young to have transient global amnesia, but he's also been through a war, so maybe he's just special, or specially cursed.

His next adventure, *A Gentleman of Dubious Reputation*, will introduce us to Julian's ducal brother, and to a few more secrets lurking in Julian's past. Excerpt below! Book Three—*A Gentleman in Challenging Circumstances*—is also available for **pre-order**.

If you'd like to stay up to date on new releases, discounts, and deals, please consider subscribing to my **newsletter**. If you aren't the newsletter type, then you might want to keep an eye on my **Deals** page. I try to do an early release or to discount a different title every month on the **web store**, and the **Deals** page is where I announce that information. Then too, I **blog** just about every Sunday, and that's where I collect volunteers for my advanced reader copy list or do giveaways of signed print copies.

However you like to keep in touch, I wish you always...

Happy reading!

Grace Burrowes

Read on for an excerpt from *A Gentleman of Dubious Reputation*!

EXCERPT—A GENTLEMAN OF DUBIOUS REPUTATION

Chapter One

On my lengthy list of reasons for avoiding the Caldicott family seat, Harry's ghost took top honors. My oldest sibling, Arthur (still extant), came third, and Lady Clarissa Valmond (lively indeed) occupied the spot between them.

Harry haunted me even when I wasn't at Caldicott Hall, appearing in my daydreams and nightmares. Like the good brother he'd been, he did not stand on ceremony in death any more than he had in life. I'd nonetheless been relieved to quit the Hall months ago to finish recuperating at my London town house, though I'd yet to achieve a full return to health.

After parting ways with the military following Waterloo, I'd come home from the Continent in poor health. My eyes still objected to prolonged bright light, my stamina wasn't what it had been on campaign, my hair was nearly white, and my memory...

My memory had been a problem before I'd bought my commission.

And yet, I knew every tree of the lime alley that led to the Hall, forty-eight in all, though two were relative saplings, having been planted in my great-grandfather's day. The other forty-six were nearly four hundred years old, but for a few new recruits necessitated by lightning strikes, Channel storms, and other random misfortunes.

Atlas, my horse, knew the path to the Hall as well as I did and picked up his pace as we turned through the ornate main gate.

"You would not be so eager to complete this journey if His Grace had summoned you," I muttered.

Arthur had signed his summons with an *A*, meaning as a brother, not as the Duke of Waltham and head of the family. He was six years my senior and possessed of worlds more consequence, not merely by virtue of his title. Arthur carried the dignity of his station as naturally as a gunnery sergeant carried a spare powder bag.

He had been born to be a duke, just as Harry had been a natural fit with the role of charming spare. Our father had assured me many times that my lot in life was to be the despair of his waning years.

Atlas marched on, his horsey imagination doubtless filled with visions of lush summer grass and long naps in sunny paddocks. Harry and I had raced up the lime alley more times than I could count, on foot and on horseback and, once when slightly inebriated, running backward.

In earliest boyhood, I'd routinely lost. Harry had had two years on me, and for much of my youth, that had meant size and reach. Then Harry attained his full height, and I kept growing. Had he lived to be an old, old man, I'd have delighted in reminding him that I was the tallest Caldicott son, having an inch on Harry and a half inch on Arthur.

What I would not give to gloat over that inch to him in person.

Harry had been taken captive by the French, and I had followed him into French hands, thinking the two of us could somehow win free where one could not. I am not the smartest of the Caldicotts, clearly. Harry had expired without yielding any information to his captors, while my experience as a prisoner was complicated by...

Many factors.

I'd survived and escaped, and I'd do the same again if need be, but now that I was back in Merry Olde, public opinion castigated me for having the effrontery to outlive my brother. At least one faction of the military gossip brigade concluded that I'd bought my life through dishonorable means—betraying my commission—though the military itself had cleared me of such allegations.

Arthur had welcomed me home with the reserve of a duke. Not until we had been private had he informed me that acts of self-harm on my part would reflect poorly on the family honor. I was not to indulge in foolish histrionics simply because I'd been labeled a traitor, much less because I could barely see, my memory was worse than ever, and I never slept more than two hours at a stretch.

Petty annoyances were no justification for imbecilic stunts, according to Arthur. He'd delivered that scold with characteristic sternness, though I'd never wanted so badly to hug him.

One did not presume on ducal dignity. My time among the French had also left me with a peculiar reluctance to be touched. With few exceptions, I kept my hands to myself and hoped others would do likewise concerning my person.

I emerged from the lime alley to behold the Hall, sitting uphill on the opposite bank of William's Creek. That placid stream was named for a multiple-great-grandfather, who'd no doubt played in its shallows as Harry and I had. Aided by juvenile imagination, that waterway had been the English Channel, where we'd defeated the great Spanish Armada; the Thames; the raging North Atlantic; and the South China Sea.

As Atlas clip-clopped over the arched stone bridge, a pang of longing assailed me, for Harry's voice, for his presence, for even his relentless teasing and boasting. Why did Harry have to die? Why had he left camp that night? Why hadn't the French taken my life as they'd taken his?

I'd asked those questions a thousand times, though I posed them now with more sadness than despair.

Caldicott Hall was sometimes referred to as Chatsworth in

miniature, meaning the Hall was merely huge as opposed to gargan-tuan. Like the Duke of Devonshire's seat up in Derbyshire, the Hall was built around a central open quadrangle. All four exterior approaches presented dignified, symmetric façades of golden lime-stone, with obligatory pilasters and entablatures adding an appear-ance of staid antiquity.

I drew Atlas to a halt, giving myself a moment to appreciate my family home and to gather my courage. My mother was off at some seaside gossip fest, thank the merciful powers, but Harry's ghost was doubtless in residence, as was my father's. And if that wasn't enough to give a fellow pause, my godmother, Lady Ophelia Oliphant, had threatened to follow me to the Hall once she'd tended to some social obligations.

Atlas rooted at the reins, suggesting a dutiful steed deserved his bucket of oats sooner rather than later. A slight movement from the window at the corner of the second floor caught my eye.

"We've been sighted," I muttered, letting the beast shuffle forward. "The advance guard should be out in less time than it takes Prinny to down a glass of port."

Half a minute later, a groom jogged up from the direction of the stable and stood at attention by the gents' mounting block. As Atlas plodded on, I nearly fell out of the saddle.

A footman coming forth to take charge of my saddlebags would not have been unusual.

The butler, Cheadle, might have welcomed me home in a fit of sentimentality, or one of my sisters might have bestirred herself to greet me if she were calling on Arthur.

Arthur *himself* sauntered out of the house, checked the time on his watch—which had been Papa's watch—and surveyed the clouds as if a perfectly benign summer sky required minute inspection. He was to all appearances the epitome of the reserved country gentle-man. Tall, athletic, his wavy dark hair neatly combed, his aquiline profile the envy of portraitists and sculptors.

To the educated fraternal eye, though, the duke was in the next thing to a panic. His Grace set very great store by decorum. When I had returned from France after escaping from captivity and before the Hundred Days, Arthur had received me in the library and offered me a brandy in Harry's memory.

All quite civilized, though at the time, I'd been barely able to remain upright, my hands had shaken like an old man's, and I'd managed a mere sip of libation. When I'd come home from Waterloo, Arthur had merely greeted me at supper as if I'd been up to Town for a few fittings.

Before my wondering eyes, he came down the terrace steps and joined the groom at the mounting block. I swung from the saddle, taking care to have my balance before I turned loose of Atlas's mane. I'd fallen on my arse a time or two after a hard ride, but I refused to give Arthur the satisfaction of witnessing my humiliation.

"You are a welcome sight, Demming," I said to the towheaded groom as I untied my saddlebags. "Don't bother too much brushing Atlas out. A stop at the water trough, a quick currying, and a shady paddock once he's finished cooling out will be the answer to his prayers. Then he will roll in the first dusty patch he can find."

"Aye, milord," Demming replied. "Does himself get oats for his trouble?"

"A mash tonight wouldn't go amiss, but no oats until tomorrow if there's grass to be had."

"We've plenty of that. Come along, beastie."

Arthur was an accomplished horseman and would not begrudge Atlas good care, but impatience rolled off the ducal person as Demming led Atlas away. Now would come an interrogation. Had my journey been uneventful? How was Lady Ophelia? Was there any particular news from Town, and what did the physicians say about my dodgy eyesight? What exactly had happened at the Makepeace house party, and where were my valet, footman, groom, and coach?

"She's driving me mad," Arthur said, striding off toward the terrace steps. "The damned Valmond woman leaves me no peace, and it's well past time you took a bride."

Order your copy of *A Gentleman of Dubious Reputation*!

Made in the USA
Middletown, DE
03 October 2023